COLD DEATH

DS Hunter Kerr Thrillers
Book Two

Michael Fowler

SAPERE
BOOKS

COLD DEATH

Published by Sapere Books.

20 Windermere Drive, Leeds, England, LS17 7UZ,
United Kingdom

saperebooks.com

ISBN: 978-1-913335-71-7

This is for Chris and Kyle.
'I've found in life you don't just teach your children, you learn from them too.'

ACKNOWLEDGEMENTS

My grateful thanks go out to my relatives up in bonnie Scotland — John, June, Iain and Sharon — the Watson clan — who between them over the years have introduced me to all the places which feature in this story. Especially to Iain, who spent one evening cruising Glasgow city centre finding and photographing an ideal murder scene for me: God knows what he would have said if he had been stopped by the police.

Also, to Inspector Dawn Watson, Strathclyde Police, who placed my characters in the right 'nicks' and who increased my policing knowledge as to the procedures back in her neck of the woods.

Finally, to Stuart Sosnowski, Crime Scene Investigator Supervisor, South Yorkshire Police, for his technical expertise after I had 'transported' him to all of my crime scenes.

PROLOGUE

November 1971
Glasgow's East End, Scotland

Iain Campbell wound down the window and switched off the headlights of the black Mercedes, swung the car into Fielden Street and straddled the middle of the road for several yards until his eyes adapted to the dimness. Then, following the pointing finger of his front seat passenger, he switched off its throaty engine and coasted quietly towards the nearside kerb where he slowed to a halt.

For a few seconds, the three occupants of the Mercedes sat motionless, watching and listening. Outside there was deathly silence.

As he stared out through the windscreen from the passenger seat, Billy Wallace's slate grey eyes darted from side to side, scanning the high tenement buildings each side of the street. Billy knew the area well. He'd lived here as a child, until his family went up in the world.

But the area had deteriorated over the past few years. Only recently, it had made headlines as one of the toughest, poorest places in Britain. Most of the people he'd grown up with here had moved out, leaving behind unfortunates who had fallen into the hands of the drug dealers and money lenders.

This was his turf.

He flung open the passenger door and used it as a springboard to launch himself upright onto the pavement, rocking for a second on the balls of his feet. Arching his back, pulling at the lapels of his signature black Crombie, he uncoiled his six-foot, four-inch, muscular frame and looked around. The old overhead street lights still hadn't been replaced, leaving most of the street cast in eerie shadow.

Some people had a fear of the dark, but Billy loved it — it was the perfect cover for what he had to do.

Raking fingers through his chestnut, collar-length hair, Billy surveyed the street again, searching for activity, narrowing his eyes to search within the shadows.

A light wind disturbed the dead leaves cluttering the gutter. Other than that, there was no other sound or movement along the road.

Good. He had a score to settle and he needed the element of surprise on his side.

He beckoned the back-seat passenger to join him. Rab Geddes was his most trusted henchman, chosen for his fearsome reputation, especially his penchant for violence.

Billy stuck his head back into the warmth of the car's interior. 'Just keep the engine running, Iain, we shouldn't be long,' he said quietly.

On Billy's nod, Rab nudged his door closed.

Somewhere nearby a dog started barking, its sudden bawl fracturing the stillness. Billy waited for the barking to stop, had a quick look around and, seeing only an empty street, set off at a jog across the footpath, dodging into the nearest passage that led to the rear of the tenement.

At the stairwell, Billy was greeted with the strong whiff of bleach and disinfectant, which was doing its best to disguise the stench of stale urine and animal faeces that stained the bare cement floor. He screwed up his nose as he mounted the concrete steps two at a time, Rab matching his pace, and, despite the rubber soles of their shoes, every footfall echoed in the enclosed stairwell.

At the first floor, they slackened their pace and slunk back against the wall. Their dark overcoats helped them melt like phantoms into the shadows. They slipped onto the walkway. For a few seconds Billy checked his bearings, then he nudged Rab and they moved on. At number 34, Billy paused, holding up a hand for them to stop. Satisfied that he had the correct address, he put an ear against the panelling and listened. He could hear a television playing inside and took another look along the walkway to check for witnesses. Not a movement. Then, stepping back two paces and flexing his muscles, he launched himself against the door. The flimsy lock was no match for Billy's fourteen stone and the door flew inwards, smashing against the interior wall.

The pair sprinted towards the well-lit room at the end of the corridor and were only a few feet from the doorway when a slim dark shape appeared as a silhouette in the opening.

The start of a scream was instantly silenced when Billy smacked the unknown individual square in the face. There was a sickening crunch of bone and gristle and the slender form flew backwards to the floor.

In the light from the lounge Billy recognised who he had thumped; for several seconds Morag McCredie lay motionless. Then she slowly opened her eyes, her face tightening as she strained to focus. A film of tears blurred her vision and she moaned as she squeezed her eyelids to force away the teardrops.

As she finally focused, Billy took pleasure in seeing the colour drain from her face, guessing from her reaction that she recognised him. He edged forward, leaning over her, pushing his face within inches of hers.

'Where's Davie, Morag?' Billy growled.

'He's —' She broke off, her voice trembling as she suppressed a sob.

'Nobody fucking rips me or my family off, Morag. Davie knows what's coming to him.' Billy pressed within an inch of her, giving her his hardest stare. 'Now — where — is — he?'

She pulled her head away. 'He's not here,' she spat out, cupping a hand over a nose that had already swollen to twice its size, then staring at the bright globules of blood dripping through her fingers. 'You've broken my fucking nose,' she groaned in her broad Glaswegian dialect.

'That's not all I'm going to break if you don't tell me where fucking Davie is,' Billy snapped back. He reached down and grabbed a handful of bottle-blonde hair and yanked hard, hoisting her upwards.

Morag swung up an arm to protect herself and a handful of hair ripped from her scalp. She yelped and bit her lip. Tears welled up again.

Billy fixed her with a hate-filled stare. 'I'm going to ask you one more time, Morag. Where's Davie?'

Quivering, she tried to move away but Billy grabbed hold, snaring his hands around her chin and jaw, seizing her in a vice-like grip. He dug his fingers into her skin until he was squeezing bone.

Morag gave a piercing scream and Billy raised a hand to silence her. At that moment the instinct to survive kicked in — she snatched up the kitchen knife from the nearby coffee table and with one swift movement lashed out. It slashed Billy's cheek, opening up his flesh.

He let go of her, stumbling backwards, slapping both hands over the gash. Blood was pouring from the wound, seeping through the gaps in his gloved hands and onto the front of his coat.

Rab Geddes had been too late to stop the damage to Billy's face, but he reacted to prevent a second attempt, smashing his fist into the side of Morag's head. She reeled back, flipping over the arm of an armchair.

Billy stared at the blood staining his gloves. His face contorted, taking on a demonic look. The pupils of his eyes became so dilated they were almost black.

'You fucking bitch,' he snarled, kicking aside the armchair. He towered above Morag, who was scrabbling around in a puddle of her own blood, a badly swelling face disguising once pretty features. She was groggy, trying to get up.

Billy reached into his Crombie, pulling the handgun from the waistband of his trousers. It became an extension of his arm as he aimed.

Morag tried to swallow. Her eyes pleaded and she swung up an arm to protect herself.

The bullet passed through her hand and into her right eye. She was dead before her head smashed against the tiled fireplace.

The reek from the cordite caught the back of Billy's throat and he swallowed hard and jerked back his head. Then he spotted movement to his left, a small shapeless form at the periphery of his vision. He spun around.

Rab followed suit.

In the doorway stood a dark-haired little girl, dressed in striped pink pyjamas, aged no more than four. She was rubbing the sleep from her eyes and under one arm she clutched a teddy bear. She stared at them through sleepy eyes. Then her gaze fell upon Morag lying prostrate, a puddle of blood spreading around her.

'Mummy,' she whimpered.

Billy raised the gun again and fired. The shot drilled a neat hole in the front of the child's head and smashed out of the back. Blood, brain and bone splattered the wallpaper behind her. She hit the ground at the same time as her teddy bear.

A halo of crimson began to form around the girl's head and Rab glared at his boss, stunned.

'Jesus Christ, Billy, she was just a kid.'

Billy stared back. 'She was a fucking witness,' he said brusquely. Then Billy looked down at the bloodstains on his overcoat. He tugged at the front of his Crombie, focusing on the wide lapels. 'Look what the bitch's done to my fucking coat.'

Billy raised the Smith and Wesson again, spun around and fired the remaining four rounds into Morag. Her body never moved; the first shot had taken her life. Billy continued clicking the trigger well after the gun had emptied and Rab had to grab hold of his arm. He fixed Billy's wild stare.

'We need to get out of here, Billy, before someone calls the cops.'

Slotting the handgun back into his waistband, Billy surveyed the carnage around him. Bending down, he grabbed the hem of Morag's dress and wiped the blood from his leather gloves.

'We need to set fire to the place Rab…' He paused for breath, getting back his composure. 'Get rid of any incriminating evidence. Know what I mean?'

Rab nodded and began scanning the room for suitable material to ignite.

Iain Campbell fidgeted in his seat. He had the driver's window down and was listening and looking nervously around — he had been doing so ever since Billy and Rab had disappeared. He looked at his watch and wondered how much longer they were going to be. They had already been gone twenty minutes.

This wasn't the job he'd been asked to do. 'Look after my son's back!' was what Billy's father had instructed and paid him for, but all he had done over the past three hours was chauffeur around the two thugs while they picked up drug debts. He had already seen them give one guy a good kicking, and from their conversation he knew they were chasing up another man who owed Billy the best part of two hundred pounds.

They could stuff the job after tonight.

He scoured the streets again. He felt cold and yet he was sweating. Fight or flight! It was a long time since he'd felt like this. He was sick to his stomach.

He was about to wind up the window when he heard a loud crack that sounded like gunfire.

No, it couldn't be!

He strained his ears. There was another! His heart leapt against his chest and he felt his stomach churn.

Four more shots followed in quick succession. He stiffened and gripped the steering wheel.

Less than a minute later, both nearside doors were yanked open, making Iain jump.

Billy threw himself into the front seat, his face covered in blood. Then Iain spotted the gun in Billy's hand.

'Billy, your face.' Iain could see Billy had lost a lot of blood. His shirt collar and the front of his coat were drenched and more was still oozing from a deep gash that snaked from the bridge of his nose and across his right cheek.

'Never mind that. Just get us the fuck out of here.' Billy threw the gun into the footwell. 'Come on, hurry the fuck up.'

Iain Campbell sharply engaged first gear and gunned the accelerator, spraying up loose road chippings beneath the spinning wheels, hurtling into the darkness as a second-floor window in the tenement exploded.

DAY ONE

24th August 2008
North Yorkshire

Tentatively, Hunter Kerr stepped to the cliff edge of the Cowbar and looked over. Only yards below, seagulls screeched and swooped, their fleeting shapes silhouetted white against the backdrop of Staithes, cloaked in early morning shadow. Opposite, above the harbour, the sun was beginning its ascent over the drab rock face of the Nab; an orange glow blurred the top of the hill giving the surroundings an almost mystical appearance.

Hunter raised his camera, clicked off a couple of frames and took a step back to where his painting easel had been set up some twenty minutes beforehand. He squeezed his blue eyes to slits and studied the vista, separating shape and tone in the landscape. Then, setting aside his camera, he picked up a brush and hurriedly mixed together some of the colours on the palette. From his previous painting ventures, he knew he had another thirty minutes to capture the first light bouncing across the haphazard rooftops of the white-washed cottages and punching its way through the narrow alleyways to the Beck, before the majestic effect disappeared and the blueness of the day took over.

As Hunter settled into his painting, switching his gaze between the tranquil scene of old fishermen's cottages perched above the Beck and the canvas board holding the start of his painting, he could feel the stress and tension of the past few weeks easing from his body.

Scrubbing in large blocks of colour, feeling the breeze brushing his unshaven face, he realised how glad he was that Beth had persuaded him to take this weekend off and spend time with her, their two sons and his mum and dad, in the cottage she had rented. When they had left home the day before yesterday, he had packed his painting gear because he rarely got the opportunity to paint these days, what with juggling his career as a murder detective and the needs of his family.

When he had seen the weather forecast last night, he realised this morning would be an ideal opportunity to complete a small oil sketch, and he had sneaked out of the cottage before daybreak without disturbing anyone. As he now built up his painting, he thought of them all still tucked up in their beds, and smiled.

Aspects of his last case had broken into his thoughts, too. Before leaving work on Friday he had given his team a list of instructions now that the investigation had finished, though he knew deep down they didn't need them; the squad was more than capable of closing down the enquiry they had been working on so intensely over the past five weeks.

He had handed his partner, DC Grace Marshall, supervisory responsibility and he could visualise her now, mothering the team in her own inimitable way, organising the clearing of the incident room, stacking the house-to-house documentation, categorising witness statement papers, sealing the hundreds of exhibits, and storing all the gory photographs into box files ready for the Coroner's Court inquest in a few months time.

This last case had been his most intense and testing to date — not just since his appointment as Detective Sergeant into Barnwell Major Investigation Team, but throughout his fourteen years as a detective.

When he had left to take this break, CSI had just removed the forensic tent from the back of the serial killer's home. One of his victims had been discovered in the house and the remains of another had been found buried in his garden. The week previous to that, the bodies of two more teenage girls had been unearthed from shallow graves at an old colliery site.

They had managed to identify all of the victims and matched them to missing persons reports, thanks to documents and photographs the killer had secreted behind a false wall in his loft.

The killing spree of the now infamous 'Dearne Valley Demon' — as the press had dubbed him — had shocked them all and would have lasting repercussions. So many revelations had come to light during the enquiry, some involving colleagues, some unwittingly involving him, and they had caused him much personal angst and soul-searching over the past few weeks.

The phrase 'tangled web' came to mind and a chill shot down Hunter's spine as he fought once again to push away any thoughts of the case.

Dismissing his thoughts, Hunter returned his gaze to the view across the Beck. The morning light had become less intense over the landscape. In another ten minutes, the artistic quality of the atmosphere would be gone.

A few more brush strokes and I'll head back for breakfast.

Ten minutes later, he set down his brushes, smoothed his hands into the base of his spine and teased the tension from his back, stretching himself up to his full six-foot-one. Before calling it a day, he took another couple of photographs that would enable him to finish the painting when he got back home, and was just lowering his camera when he spotted his dad on the opposite side of the harbour, leaning against railings that overlooked the beach.

Dad's up early as well.

He clicked off another frame and as the shutter snapped, he caught a fleeting movement to one side of the nearby Cod and Lobster pub. He was sure he'd seen someone dart into the shadows. His policeman's sixth-sense piqued, he zoomed in as far as the camera would allow, targeting the side entrance of the pub where he had last seen the figure.

He was right. There was someone, slinking against the wall, looking in the direction of his dad. Something wasn't right. He snapped another shot but the zoom was at its maximum and the image was blurred. All he could make out was a squat, stocky, white guy with a shaven head. His features were fuzzy.

Quickly lowering his camera, Hunter looked back at his dad, Jock, who was still leaning on the metal railings, one foot resting on the bottom bar, staring out to sea. From the relaxed posture, Hunter could tell his dad was unaware of the man ten yards away. Hunter dug his mobile from his pocket and flipped up the screen.

Damn. He'd forgotten he couldn't get a signal here.

He moved closer to the edge of the Cowbar, ready to shout, hoping his dad would hear. Then he saw his dad spin around — the shaven-headed man had emerged from the shadows and was striding towards him. The stranger halted just feet away and jabbed a finger inches from Jock Kerr's face. Although Hunter couldn't hear, their body language was telling him this was not friendly banter. He raised his camera again and shot off a succession of quick frames, not checking if the images were good or not. That was when he saw Jock slapping away the man's hand, slamming a punch into the stranger's chest, dumping him onto his backside. Towering above, Jock speared his own finger only a foot from the man's face. There was a frank exchange of words and then as quickly as it had started it was all over. Jock turned from the stranger and marched away.

The shaven-headed man picked himself up, dusted down his knees and took out his mobile. Seconds later, he pushed it away again in disgust.

'He can't get a signal either,' Hunter muttered to himself.

As the man turned, Hunter raised his camera again and rattled off several more frames before the stranger strode out of view.

At the edge of the cliff, Hunter scoured the cobbled High Street, straining his eyes into the narrow alleyways of the thrown-together houses but he couldn't see either his dad or the stranger. With a sense of urgency, he collapsed his easel and packed away his things.

Half-jogging, half-marching, and breathing heavily, Hunter trooped up the steep incline out of the old village and up towards the newer part of Staithes and their rented cottage.

He'd been keeping watch for the shaven-headed man but the only people he had come across were fishermen preparing their boats. As he neared the top of the hill, he saw his dad a hundred yards ahead, ambling along, hands thrust deep in pockets, as if nothing had happened.

Hunter took a deep breath and shouted after him. Jock stopped and waited. By the time Hunter had caught up he was gulping for air and beads of sweat were trickling from his hairline and down the sides of his face.

'I thought you were supposed to be fit, son,' Jock said in his strong Glaswegian accent, pointing to the glistening sweat on his son's brow.

Hunter set down the easel and wiped his forehead with the back of his hand, flicking the residue onto the footpath. 'I am.

It's that bloody hill, it's a killer.' He took in several deep breaths. 'I've been trying to catch you up to see what that was all about.'

'What was what all about?' said Jock, matter-of-factly.

'You know what I'm on about. Don't give me the all-innocent. That argument you've just had with that guy.'

'That wasn't an argument, just a case of mistaken identity. He thought I was someone else.'

'You don't dump someone on their arse because of a case of mistaken identity.'

Jock flushed. 'Leave it, son, it's nothing to do with you.'

'What do you mean it's nothing to do with me? My dad smacking someone is nothing to do with me? I don't think so.'

Jock held up a hand for silence. 'No, you don't think so at all. That was my business down there. I said leave it — and I mean it.' He spun on his heels and marched away.

It had been a mild day but the evening was giving way to a sheet of fine drizzle. It peppered the windscreen of Hunter's Audi, obscuring the view of the main road through Sleights village. Hunter flicked on the wipers to clear the screen. As he began the steep incline up towards Blue Bank, he saw his dad's car in front was almost at the top.

Hunter dropped down a gear, squeezed the accelerator and sped towards the summit.

Since they had set off from the cottage, Hunter had been at odds with himself. Beth had sensed it, asking what was wrong. He'd shrugged it off, telling her he was back to thinking about work. But he couldn't get the incident involving his dad and the shaven-headed man out of his mind. What made it worse was that his dad had lied and then dismissed him when he had tried to probe deeper. He'd tried to catch his dad's attention during the day but he had deliberately avoided eye contact.

Something wasn't right, but Hunter didn't know what — and it was frustrating the hell out of him. He'd thought he knew his dad, but a couple of things had altered his view recently. Throughout his childhood, teenage years and into manhood, he had never seen his dad lose his temper, and then three weeks ago that had changed. Hunter was getting a good hiding from three family members of someone he had just put into prison when his dad had come to his aid. Such was the viciousness of his dad's onslaught that Hunter had to drag him off before he caused a really serious injury to one of the guys. The man had ended up in hospital with a fractured jaw and a couple of busted ribs.

Today's incident had brought that flashing back and it was unsettling Hunter. He clutched the steering wheel tighter, willing his Audi faster up the hill. As they crested the brow of Blue Bank, he eased off the accelerator and began cruising along the moorland road that passed through *Heartbeat* country. Ten yards in front, it looked as though his parents were chatting. He wondered if his mum, like Beth, sensed something wasn't right.

Hunter didn't see the silver BMW until it shot past. It was so close that it rocked his car, almost catching the wing mirror, and for a split-second he lost control, veering towards the grass verge. He braked sharply, corrected the steering and swung back into lane.

'The bloody idiot!' Hunter shouted, then halted his tirade, remembering that Jonathan and Daniel, his young sons, were in the back.

Up ahead, the speeding BMW was getting dangerously close to his parents' car and he dropped into third gear, squeezing the accelerator, so that he could make up ground and take note of the car's registration number.

Just when it looked as though the BMW was about to hit the rear of his parents' car, it swung out into the opposite carriageway and began overtaking. Hunter heaved a sigh of relief. Then, without warning, the BMW swung hard left, smashing against the driver's side. His parents' car snaked and blue smoke emerged from beneath the wheels as the vehicle began to crab. Chippings flew up from the surface as the car lurched sideways and began to bounce out of control. It hit the damp moorland grasses at the road edge, throwing up huge tufts, then bucked into a ditch, bounced back out, flipped over onto its roof, before returning back on its chassis, rebounding into the heather and finally coming to a standstill when it thumped into a peat bog.

Hunter stamped on the brake, bringing his Audi to a screeching halt as he flung open his door. It felt as if everything had gone into slow motion.

He was conscious of Beth fishing around in her handbag trying to find her mobile, while on the back seat he caught a quick glimpse of the boys, straining against their seatbelts, both pale-faced and frightened. Fifty yards ahead, he saw the BMW's brake lights flash on as it skewed to a halt.

About to sprint to his parents' rescue, he stopped mid-pace as the BMW driver's door flew open.

Hunter heaved another sigh of relief. He had initially thought this was going to be a hit-and-run. Now the car had stopped he guessed it was just bad driving and the driver was coming to help.

That was until he recognised the man who emerged. It was the shaven-headed guy he had seen arguing with his dad earlier.

The man took a long hard stare at Hunter, and with outstretched hand he reached across the roof of the car and pointed towards his parents' upturned car. He fashioned two fingers and a cocked thumb into a makeshift pistol, and jolting his hand, mimicked a firing action. He never took his eyes off Hunter, fixing him with a malicious grin before mouthing the word 'pow!'

Then the shaven-headed man jumped back into his car and the BMW squealed away, throwing up a film of spray in its wake.

Hunter clocked the registration before it disappeared over the brow.

He shouted to Beth to dial 999 and then bounded across the moor to where a plume of steam was masking the predicament of his parents.

I just know this is going to be cold, Katie Williamson thought to herself as she stepped into the murky waters of Barnwell Lake, disturbing the stillness of its surface with her fins. Once she was fully submerged beneath the water, it would be even colder; from a previous dive here, she knew in a few minutes the pain inside her head would be as intense and sharp as if she had eaten ice cream.

'I'll be only a couple of feet behind you. Remember the signals?' her dive instructor, Craig Palmer, said.

Katie formed an 'O' shape with her thumb and forefinger, feeling the resistance in her neoprene gloves as she forced them together.

'Good. And if you need to come up quickly?'

She stuck a thumb in the air and jabbed it skywards several times.

'Okay. Final checks.'

Katie watched her dive-buddy's eyes roaming over her body — not eyeing her up, just double-checking all her diving equipment was in place.

'This is your last dive and then we can sign your logbook up for your first qualification. Looking forward to it?'

'In these freezing waters? You're joking!'

A smile creased her instructor's face. 'You are such a wimp. Twenty minutes and the ordeal will all be over and this time next year you'll be able to take a novice out yourself. Now check your air pressure and make sure your hoses are not tangled.'

Katie slotted the mouthpiece of her breathing regulator into her mouth, adjusting it so that it fitted snugly between teeth and lips. She purged the demand valve and a blast of concentrated air shot into her mouth, plumping out her cheeks. She swallowed, tasting the freshness and purity of the compressed air and formed another 'O' with her fingers.

'Okay, mask on and let's make our way to the centre of the lake.'

Katie fitted her facemask, waited a few seconds for the glass to clear and began walking penguin-fashion over the loose stones and moss, edging slowly into the waters.

As she reached chest height, she felt her buoyancy jacket taking up her weight, keeping her afloat, enabling her to flip her fins and push towards the middle of the lake. She could hear Craig splashing closely behind. After five minutes of gentle kicking, Katie felt a tap on her shoulder.

'Okay, this is it. Let the air out of your jacket and let's drop to the bottom. We're going to swing left and circle the lake, okay?'

She formed another 'O', and then slowly released the air out of her buoyancy jacket, feeling herself sink below the surface.

It wouldn't be long before she hit the bottom, the depth was only five metres.

Katie felt the slippery fronds of the reeds brush against her as she gradually dropped. Four metres down, the water was so murky that her visibility was just a couple of feet and she had to sweep her hands before her, feeling her way through the gloomy depths. Turning left as instructed, she was surprised that the water wasn't as cold as she had expected.

This is not going to be too bad after all, she said to herself, kicking hard and dragging one hand along the silt bottom.

Katie felt a sudden tap on her calf and guessed Craig wanted her to take in another turn. She pulled her wrist close to her mask and checked her watch. They had been diving for just over ten minutes.

Halfway there already, time has flown.

With a series of quick kicks, she propelled herself left again and adjusted her movement with a graceful flip.

Then her knee hit something solid, taking her by surprise and she stumbled across the object. She spun around, seeking out her dive-buddy. He was only a couple of yards behind and she began waving frantically for him. Seeing him stop kicking and using his hands to slow she jabbed her thumb downwards.

Katie dropped to her knees, sitting almost astride the entity and began rubbing her hand over it. She could make out what appeared to be a rolled-up carpet, enmeshed in the weeds. Curious about the bundle she felt for an edge to unfurl and, finding a corner, she tugged hard. Something appeared from one end. For a split-second her mind wouldn't take in what was peeking out. Then it hit her. The bloated green-grey distorted blob had a face — a human face. Katie was looking at a dead body. Gasping, she almost released her mouth-piece. In that instant the water rushed into her mouth, hitting the back of her throat and causing her to gag. There was no time to signal to her dive-buddy. Blind panic took over and Katie kicked frantically for the surface.

With increasing pace, Detectives Grace Marshall and Mike Sampson quick-marched along the path that led from the car park to the entrance of Barnwell Country Park.

In the two-hundred yards from where they had left their car, the blazing heat had got to them. Mike was gasping for breath, having difficulty keeping up with Grace, and she was hot and sweaty and her shirt and jacket were starting to stick. Grace slackened her pace to let Mike catch up, unbuttoned her jacket and gathered her mane of tight black curls into a tidy bunch and fastened it with an elastic band.

Picking up her pace once more, she threaded between two lines of tall laurel bushes that marked the route towards the lake. For a moment her thoughts drifted. Being here brought back happy memories of strolling around the lakeside path watching the world go by with her two daughters and husband. They were times she still treasured in her bank of memories, especially now that the girls were teenagers and no longer wanted to do such things.

Coming across a young-looking PC, who had been given the job of preventing the uninvited from getting to the crime scene, Grace and Mike flashed their IDs, announced their names and waited as he scribbled down their arrival on his log.

They ducked below the blue and white police tape, passed another line of laurel bushes and entered the inner cordon.

Grace paused by the second line of police tape and surveyed the scene. Three CSI Officers were already in situ, dressed in their white forensic suits. Two were in the process of cordoning off a small wooden jetty which led out into the lake, while another was taking photographs. Grace recognised the cameraman as Duncan Wroe, the Force's experienced Scene Manager.

At the lake's edge, a uniform sergeant was briefing her team before they began a search of the area.

On the water, a couple of yards from the edge of the quay, two wet-suited police frogmen steadied their motorised dinghy. A third was in the water, placing his breathing regulator into his mouth. Grace assumed that beneath the dinghy was where the body had been discovered and the Underwater Search Unit was now going to haul it up.

By picnic benches, next to the country park reception centre, Grace spotted two other divers. The female was seated on one of the benches, doubled-up, her head in her hands. A male with a tanned complexion and short crew-cut hair stood over her, resting a hand on her shoulder. She guessed these were the two who had found the corpse. She took out her warrant card again and popped it into her breast pocket with the police crest on display. Hunter had handed her the mantle of Acting Sergeant while he was away and she was going to show she could handle it.

'What do you want me to do, Grace?'

Mike's question broke into her thoughts. 'I'm guessing those two are the ones who've found the body,' she said, pointing in the divers' direction. 'You go speak to them and I'll go and have a word with uniform and also see what SOCO have got for us.'

Mike set off, tugging the sleeves of his oversized jacket away from his pudgy fingers. Mike had to buy jackets several sizes larger so that they would fasten over his beer-belly, which meant the sleeves were always too long.

'Oh, and Mike,' Grace shouted after him. 'Be professional. Don't start playing pocket billiards while you're interviewing her.'

'I shall ensure my afflictions are kept under control at all times, Acting Sergeant Marshall.'

Grace smiled to herself. Despite Mike being the joker in the pack, when he was given a task, he always approached it as the consummate professional.

By the time Grace reached Duncan Wroe, the SOCO manager was aiming his camera at the Police Frogmen. There was still no sign of the body being brought to the surface.

'What have you got for me, Duncan?'

The SOCO manager turned, lowering his camera. 'Oh, hi Grace, I saw you arrive but I was busy.'

With his sharp features, unruly hair and unshaven face, Duncan looked nothing like the sharp-minded and experienced forensic specialist that he was. Fortunately for Grace, any prejudices she had about his appearance had been blown away early in her career. He had attended her first rape case as a detective, a teenage girl attacked while out walking her dog. A good quarter of a mile from the scene, Duncan had found trainer marks and several discarded cigarette butts in some bushes and, acting on a hunch, he had recovered them. Within a week they had DNA of the perpetrator, and while carrying out a search of the young man's home, Duncan had found his trainers secreted amid the rubbish in a wheelie bin. It transpired the man had carried out two other similar crimes and at court he was given a life sentence. Since then, Grace had worked with Duncan on many cases and knew his technical craft and knowledge of forensics were second to none. He was one of the very few civilian scenes of crimes officers in the country to be promoted to the position of manager — most supervisors were police officers of rank.

Grace nodded towards the lake. She watched air bubbles bursting on the surface. 'No sign of the body being brought up yet?'

'I'm told it's in a bit of a mess. I think they're trying to secure it tightly so it doesn't lose any of its limbs when they bring it up.'

'What do we know then, Duncan?'

'Well, we don't know anything about the body yet. I've been told it's bound inside a carpet or rug of some kind so I don't think we'll know anything straight away. When we do get it to the surface, I'll give it a once-over, but we don't know how long it's been in the water, so we'll need to get it to the mortuary as soon as possible because once its exposed to the air there will be a rapid acceleration to the decomposition.'

'Have you got anything in the forensics line yet?'

He shook his head. 'Too early, Grace. What I can say is that I'm pretty confident the body was thrown off the edge of the jetty there.' He pointed to the wooden platform leading from the banking out into the lake. 'You see where the Search Unit's dinghy is? Well, that's roughly above where the body is. That's about six feet from the edge of the jetty and that's why I say thrown. Because of how far away it is from the jetty I would say at least two people were involved in dumping it.'

'Two?'

'Yep, two — at least. If one person had carried that body they would only have been able to drop it or roll it off. It's virtually impossible for one person to sling a dead body any distance. With two people, they would have been able to get enough swing to heave it that far into the water.'

'Couldn't they have used a boat?'

'And only gone out a few feet?' He dismissed her suggestion with a curt shake of the head. 'No, it was thrown, trust me.' He tapped his nose and a smile crept across his wizened features. 'Simple when you've dealt with as many bodies as I have,' he added. 'Because the body's wrapped up I'm running on the assumption that the person was more than likely killed elsewhere and bought here and dumped. Nevertheless, we're taping off the jetty and checking it for bloodstains, hairs and fibres. It's a hands and knees job, but we'll be searching for footwear marks as well. I'm also setting up a search grid and looking for tyre tracks. The underwater search unit will be bringing the body up to another landing stage and then I'll secure the body to be transported to the morgue. I understand Miss Marple is already making her way there and will be performing the post mortem later this afternoon.'

He was referring to the forensic pathologist Professor Lizzie McCormack, who had acquired her nickname not only because of her ability to catch killers through her forensic skills but also because of her uncanny likeness to the actress Geraldine McEwan.

Grace thanked Duncan with a smile and headed to where Mike Sampson was still talking to the two divers who had found the corpse. As she was running through everything again inside her head, marrying what the homicide investigation manual recommended together with her experience of attending murder scenes, her mobile rang. She delved into her jacket pocket and pulled it out. The screen displayed the name of her work partner — Hunter. He was somewhere up in the Whitby area in a rented cottage with his family.

I bet someone back in the office has rung him and told him about this and now he's phoning to check up that I can cope.

Even though she knew he would be enquiring in that nice, caring and unobtrusive way of his, he was still checking on her. She needed to do this without someone holding her hand — to prove to herself more than anything that she was capable.

'Well, Sergeant Kerr, I am coping very well, thank you,' Grace muttered beneath her breath. 'And I don't need you checking up on me.'

As she waited for the call to go through to voicemail, she heard a shout from the lake and turned to see the police frogman's head break the surface. His hand was raised. It looked as though they were about to bring the body up.

Her phone stopped mid-ring. She would listen to the message later. She placed it back into her pocket, telling herself she'd ring him this evening — once she had got everything up and running.

Screeching to a halt in the rear car park of the Medico Legal Centre, Grace checked her watch for the umpteenth time. She cursed; she was running late and regretted not having followed the body carrier from the Country Park as she should have done. Instead she'd sat in her car, on her mobile, updating her Detective Inspector, Gerald Scaife, who was setting up the incident room back in the MIT department.

She had given him as much information as she could, but because the post mortem was yet to be done she couldn't answer the majority of his questions. It only reinforced the fact that she should have followed the body.

To cap it all and cause further delay, the DI had then passed her across to DC Isobel Stevens, the HOLMES (Home Office Large Major Enquiry System) supervisor, who had begun logging the information onto the National network, and she had found herself listening to another round of questions which she was unable to answer. Fortunately, because she was the same rank as Isobel, she was able to politely fend her off, promising to get back to her the minute the post mortem had concluded.

Grace entered the Medico Legal Centre through the rear doors and hurried along the corridor to the post mortem suite, pulling off her elastic hair fastener and shaking out her thick mane of curls. In the locker room, she slipped quickly into a protective body suit, and in her haste, as she slotted the shoe coverings over her ballet pumps, she stumbled forward, shouldering the wall. She cursed again under her breath, rubbing the top of her arm as she barged through the double set of doors which gave access to the autopsy room, causing the occupants to snap their heads in her direction.

'Quite a dramatic entrance — Miss?' Professor Lizzie McCormack said, glancing over the rims of her spectacles.

The way the pathologist had paused and then added 'Miss' made Grace feel like a schoolgirl. She smiled apologetically. 'DC Marshall,' she responded, feeling herself blush. 'Grace,' she finished and scanned the faces of Detective Superintendent Michael Robshaw and Scenes of Crime Manager Duncan Wroe, who not surprisingly, had beaten her there. Disconcertingly, the Superintendent was frowning.

'Ah yes, of course — Grace. You have to forgive me, I'm terrible with names these days. We met several weeks ago at the old farm near Harlington, a fourteen-year-old girl mutilated by our infamous serial killer, if my memory serves me right.'

Grace nodded. 'Terrible business that. You finally got him, though.' Grace felt her chest tighten as a flashback of the images of the murders burst inside her head. Although twelve days had gone by since that fateful evening, the memory was still as sharp as if it had happened yesterday. That last investigation had caused her mental pain and left her physically exhausted. She had only just got back to work after taking a week off sick to get her head right. The mental pictures from that night were going to live inside her for quite some time to come; the Force's counsellor had told her so.

She took in a deep breath, held it, and let it out slowly — just like she'd been advised at the onset of a panic attack.

'Anyway, that's all in the past now. Back to the present, eh!' Lizzie McCormack's voice snapped Grace out of her reverie. 'Well, Grace, you're not a moment too soon — we are just about to start.'

The petite grey-haired woman peeled on her latex gloves and pulled a metal trolley closer. Upon it, laid out in pristine condition, glinting beneath the bright artificial lighting was every surgical tool and evidence collection container imaginable.

The body, still wrapped up in its bundle, was laid out on one of the steel mortuary tables. Despite being covered by a substantial amount of silt and broken reeds, Grace could now see the body was shrouded inside a rug of Asian design.

Professor McCormack reached up and switched on a microphone above her. In her soft Scottish accent, she began her PM preamble, beginning with the time and date. Instructing her technician to cut away the bindings, she took a step back and slid the green scrub mask up over her mouth and nose.

He began to snip at the cord securing the rug. The binding was white plastic-coated washing line.

'Careful as you unwrap it,' said Duncan Wroe to the technician, moving in closer with his camera. 'In the past I've known the murder weapon to be included when the killer has wrapped up the body.' He looked from Detective

Superintendent Robshaw to Grace. 'By dumping the body in the lake, the murderer was obviously hoping it would never be found and therefore they might just have thrown in the weapon.'

The second the technician carefully peeled the sides of the rug away from the cadaver, the stench hit Grace and she quickly pulled on her facemask. The air conditioning that was supposed to deal with the smell of rotting and decaying flesh did not dissipate it completely.

The body was grotesque; bluish-purple and swollen beyond recognition, though there was no mistaking it was female. Long, black, matted hair covered most of her face and neck, and she was naked.

The technician moved aside and Professor McCormack took over, exploring the cadaver inch by inch, pausing from time to time to scrutinise certain marks before moving on. She cleared her throat and continued with her commentary.

'The covering has been removed to reveal the body of a woman of Asian appearance in a state of advanced decomposition. This is manifested by skin slippage, discolouration, bloating and the presence of a foul odour.' With thumb and forefinger, she began sliding the long strands of black hair away from the deceased's face. 'Well, well,' she said. 'I think I've more than likely found this young lady's cause of death.'

Angling a slender forefinger over the corpse's neck, she stepped back to allow the SOCO manager to take more photographs. Grace and the detective superintendent took a step forward, leaning in to see what the pathologist had discovered. The gash stretched almost ear to ear across her throat.

Photographs taken, Professor McCormack continued with her examination. 'On the left-hand side of the neck, approximately two and a half centimetres below the jawline, is an incision which is approximately fifteen centimetres in length. The large vessels either side of the neck have been severed. The larynx has been severed below the vocal cord through to the intervertebral cartilages. The arteries and other vessels contained in the sheath have all been cut through. The cut is very clean, very precise.' She raised her eyes and caught Grace's gaze. 'Her death would have been immediate.'

Professor McCormack returned to the corpse, picking up limbs, examining the hands and fingers. Then she began to turn the body. As she rolled the cadaver onto one hip, she gave off a surprised, 'Mmm,' and beckoned to the SOCO Manager. 'Mr Wroe, I take my hat off to you.' She supported the bloated body as he shot off a series of frames. After he had finished, she pulled out an object which had been hidden beneath.

Duncan was doing his best to suppress a triumphant grin.

'In all my years as a pathologist I have never seen anything like this,' she said, holding up something which closely resembled a knife.

Grace stared at the object and exchanged glances with her colleagues. None of them had seen anything quite like it.

Professor McCormack dropped it into an exhibit bag and handed it to Grace, who eyed it again through the plastic, turning it over repeatedly.

'A real vicious looking thing,' said Detective Superintendent Robshaw from over Grace's shoulder.

The weapon was twenty centimetres long and had a curved blade. Half of it consisted of a black metal handle or grip with two small metal hoops at either end.

'These loops look like where your fingers should go — you know, like a knuckle-duster,' Grace said. She searched for agreement from her boss but he merely shrugged. She scrutinised it one further time before handing it over to the SOCO manager as the pathologist began her internal examination of the body. Picking up a scalpel, Professor McCormack began the Y-shaped incision at the front of the torso, cutting from the breastbone down to the pubis.

A rancid gas erupted from the body and Grace gagged. She pressed her head down into her chest and tried to breathe in the perfume she had sprayed herself with in the car before entering the centre but that didn't help much.

An hour later, after careful removal and examination of the corpse's internal organs, Professor McCormack rounded off her head-to-toe examination, reported on her findings and wrapped things up. She reached up, switched off the microphone, snapped off her latex gloves and turned to face everyone.

'The girl has taken a severe beating prior to her death. I've found at least thirty blunt trauma wounds to her head, upper torso, buttocks and legs, caused by clenched fist and boot. Three of her ribs are broken — she would have been in a great deal of pain before she died.' She shook her head in disgust. 'Duncan should be able to get at least one good sample of a shoe print from the girl's left thigh. She also has defence wounds to her hands and arms. Several of her nails have been broken and I have managed to swab them for perpetrator DNA. There is also bruising to the inside of her thighs and genitalia. In other words, she was raped prior to death.

'I have examined the girl's trachea and lungs and there is no airway froth or sediment indicative of drowning. And there is no fluid in the paranasal sinuses or stomach. Therefore, she was already dead before she went into the water. In conclusion, death was the result of the severe haemorrhaging of the carotid artery in the neck caused by a sharp-edged instrument. Forensics will no doubt match the wound to that weapon we've found.' She dropped her latex gloves into a biohazard bin. 'The incision across the throat is left to right and the penetration angle of the cut suggests that the killer was above or on top of her to carry out this action. That leaves me to believe your killer is left-handed.'

'What about identification of the girl?' enquired Grace.

'Other than what I have already said, height, weight, of Asian appearance etc., that's all I am able to give. The bloating and decomposition has put paid to physical identification. She has also lost a number of teeth from the blows she received but dental records might be still of use, and of course I have taken a blood sample for DNA purposes, but that only helps if she or her family are on the database.'

'I will sort out the dental impressions and fingerprints,' interjected Duncan Wroe. 'I've had a look at the ridges and they are in a bit of a mess. There is a lot of skin slippage because of the length of time the body has been submerged. What I can do, however, is cut around the top section of each finger and peel off the flesh and then put them over my gloved fingers and roll an impression. I've done that once before and it worked.'

Grace felt her skin go goosey.

'I can show you how to do it and then let you have a go if you want,' he added with a mischievous grin

'Duncan, that is gross.'

'Needs must, Grace, needs must!'

It was well after 9 p.m. before Grace eventually got home, and she was mentally and physically drained.

She had spent the past two hours apprising DC Isobel Stevens so the HOLMES system could be updated ready for the following day's briefing. She had also begun the timeline sequence on the incident boards, finishing the task by Blu Tacking photo images of the crime scene, including a sequence of mortuary shots — rug-wrapped body, unwrapped body and the unusual looking weapon used to kill the unknown woman. She'd then sat down with DI Scaife to fill in the gaps in his journal ready for the 8 a.m. briefing. It was only when she had finished all that it hit home to her what the responsibility of acting Detective Sergeant meant. She'd never given any thought before to how much additional work Hunter put in after they had headed off home or down to the pub. She made a mental note — from now on she would always ask him at the end of a busy day if he needed any help.

She unlocked her front door and called out. There was no reply. She headed for the kitchen, where she found a note on the table, picked it up, headed back into the hallway and climbed the stairs slowly, reading as she went. It was a mixture of scribbles made by David, her husband, and Robyn and Jade, her daughters. They had gone out for food and then onto the cinema to see the *Twilight* movie. The note ended with 'love u lots', and kisses, three times in different handwriting. She mouthed the words silently and smiled to herself.

Grace stripped off her things on the landing and dumped her clothes in a pile without going into the bedroom. The stench of rotting flesh still clung to them and she decided to wash them straight away and not put them in the dirty clothes basket for fear of contaminating the rest of the washing.

She turned on the shower, cranking the temperature gauge up a couple of notches before climbing in, then lingered longer than usual under the powerful jet of hot water and scrubbed herself until her skin tingled.

Ten minutes later, feeling cleansed, she towelled herself off in front of the bathroom mirror. As she dabbed the moisture away from her tawny coloured skin she lingered over her reflected image. She turned sideways and clenched her stomach muscles and liked what she saw. Although she maintained her fitness through regular swimming sessions, Grace owed her lithe well-toned figure and height to her Yorkshire-born mum, while her hair, skin colour and burnt umber eyes were the product of her Jamaican father's genes.

Half an hour later, dressed in a T-shirt and joggers and clutching a glass of chilled Chardonnay, Grace flopped onto the sofa. She tucked her legs beneath her and began to run through the day's events. Graphic images kaleidoscoped around and she reflected on the post mortem, especially how indifferently Professor Lizzie McCormack had treated the corpse. She had seemed so brutal, slicing open the young Asian woman, almost defiling her — but then Grace recalled how gently she had washed and combed the hair and washed out the nasal passages for evidence. She recalled what the forensic pathologist had said as she had gone about her work: 'The body gives up so much of where it has been before it has had its life ended. Pollen or fibre samples can be matched to the place where it met its death,' and Grace had resolved to store those words for the future.

She jumped out of her reverie, remembering the early phone call which she had left to voicemail. She had forgotten to return Hunter's call. She scooped up her mobile from the coffee table. She couldn't wait to tell him how she had coped being in charge of her first murder.

Jock Kerr stirred and gave a low moan as he shuffled uneasily in the bed. The groaning snapped Hunter out of his doze and he drew himself up in the bedside chair in time to see his dad's face twisting in pain. He'd been in and out of a restless sleep since his admittance to the hospital ward that afternoon, despite being heavily dosed with a strong painkiller and sedative.

'Okay, Dad?' Hunter asked. 'Do you need me to call a nurse?'

Jock eased opened his eyes. 'I'd rather have a dram, son.' He started to laugh, then winced. 'Jeez, son, I feel like I've gone ten rounds with Muhammad Ali.' He licked his dry lips. 'What's the doc's verdict? What's the damage?' Jock's voice was brittle and more laboured than normal.

Hunter leaned forward, resting an elbow on the edge of the bed, and cupping his chin. He was in need of a shave. 'Bruised ribs, a few cuts and bruises and a couple of stitches above your right eye. You'll live.'

'How's your ma?'

'She's on Ward Two.' Hunter saw his dad's anguish and concern. 'Don't worry, she's only there for observation. She's had a nasty bang to her head — she actually *looks* like she's done ten rounds with Muhammad Ali.' He cracked a wry smile. 'Beth and the boys are with her, keeping her company.'

'I'm glad she's okay, son. I wouldn't know what I'd do if anything happened to your ma.' An attempt to clear his throat sent Jock into a paroxysm of coughing. His chest shook fitfully and he groaned.

Hunter felt helpless as tears welled up in his dad's eyes.

'Bloody hell, that hurt,' Jock moaned, clutching his chest. 'What happened, son?'

Hunter recounted the incident, the silver BMW ramming the car and how they somersaulted across the moorland. 'You're lucky to be alive.'

'Some accident, eh?'

'That was no accident, Dad. The BMW deliberately rammed you.' Hunter sat upright. 'And I recognised the driver. It was the guy you were arguing with this morning.'

Jock tensed. 'I've already told you what that was about. Leave it,' he snapped.

'Look, you and Mum were nearly killed today. You need to tell me what's happening.'

'And I said just leave it. I'll sort this once I get out of here.'

'Dad, you're in no state to sort anything out. Leave me to deal with it. That's what I get paid to do. That's my job. You need to tell me what that was all about this morning. It's too much of a coincidence that what happened with the car was only a couple of hours after you've dumped a guy on his backside. What are you hiding, Dad?'

'Nothing,' Jock snapped again. 'Just leave it, I said.' He suddenly paled and dropped back against his pillow, his face glistening with sweat.

Hunter got up. 'Do you need me to get a nurse?'

'I could do with a couple of painkillers. I hurt all over.' Jock closed his eyes.

Hunter thought his dad looked tired and drawn, almost frail. He made for the nurse's station and was asking a staff nurse for extra painkillers when he felt his mobile vibrate in his pocket. He quickly fished it out and viewed the screen — Grace. He'd been trying on and off for most of the afternoon to get hold of her. He answered the phone, indicating to the nurse that he needed to take the call and jogged away from the nurse station and along the corridor.

'Hi Grace,' he answered, exiting the ward and stopping in the corridor. 'I've been ringing you most of the day and all I've been getting is your voicemail.' He didn't wait for her to reply. 'Listen, I need a favour.'

Hunter rattled off what had happened that morning — how he had seen his dad arguing with the shaven-headed man, following up with details of the incident involving his parents' car — barely pausing for breath. 'I've only managed to get a part index, and I've given that to North Yorks police but I could do with someone following it up.' He paused for breath. 'Grace, do you remember a few weeks ago when we dealt with Steve Paynton?'

He was trying to visualise her reaction. It was Grace who had found the photographs behind a bath panel during the search of Paynton's home; undraped images of pre-pubescent children. He had seen how it had disgusted her.

'Do you recall I had a run in with his two brothers and a cousin shortly after we got him remanded? I think they might have something to do with this. I think the Payntons could be trying to get back at me and Dad, and they may have sent a heavy to deal with us, but my dad won't tell me anything. Could you do me a favour and find out where the Payntons were today and see if they have access to a silver BMW? It'll have some nearside damage to it.'

'Hunter, I can't.'

Hunter stopped and listened as Grace explained about the body at Barnwell Lake. In the glass panel of the door he was facing, he caught his ghost-like image. He looked disappointed and he was glad she couldn't see him. As she finished, he composed himself.

'A real baptism of fire, eh? Good for you. Okay, Grace, don't worry. I can see you're going to have your hands full and it sounds as though you've got it all well under control. Listen, I'm going to be up here for another couple of days until they release my parents. You crack on and I'll ring you daily so you can update me.'

Hunter ended the call brightly but deep down he was agitated. He needed someone to do some discreet and maybe underhand digging for him. Someone he knew he could trust — and Grace had been his best hope. Then someone else sprang to mind; someone who he knew always got a result. Hunter scrolled down his contacts, selected the name he wanted and made the call.

DAY TWO

Warm sunlight streaming in through the windows and the scent of fresh furniture polish greeted Grace as she breezed into the MIT office. She must have missed Angie the cleaner by minutes, she thought to herself. A pity, because she loved having girlie chats with Angie, who knew all the building's gossip, especially the real juicy stuff — like who was having an affair with whom.

She shrugged off her jacket and draped it over the back of her seat before sitting down, then pulled a bunch of papers from the top of her tray, sifted them out over her desk and fired up her computer.

Grace had got into work early. In Hunter's absence she was responsible for pulling together the inquest file for 'The Dearne Valley Demon' case, and she wanted to make inroads into it before things got manic.

As she waited for the program to load, her mind wandered — mulling once more over the events of August 12th — and she felt her chest tighten. The blood pounded inside her head, causing a rushing sensation in her ears and she took several deep breaths in an attempt to regain control. She felt sick to her stomach. She hated the sensation these attacks brought and wondered if they would ever go away.

This isn't fair. I want my life back.

After a couple of deep breaths, she felt the tight band across her chest slacken. Regaining control, she returned to the job in hand, opening up the inquest document folder. She'd already drafted a large part of the summary prior to being called away to the lake yesterday and she speed-read back over it. Closing her eyes, she thought about the final points she needed to add. Moments later, her next steps decided upon, she snapped open her eyelids, scanned the screen, scrolled to the point where she needed to pick up and began typing.

Footfalls along the corridor outside the office broke into Grace's deep concentration. She glanced at her watch; the past hour had flown. The first detectives were beginning to filter into the office and as the doors opened a new aroma assaulted her nostrils — the greasy smell of bacon sandwiches from the canteen. Her stomach rumbled and she realised how hungry she was. She had given breakfast a miss.

Mike Sampson and Tony Bullars, her team members, were among the first in. She acknowledged them with a smile and a nod. Mike headed for the office kettle. He stopped mid-stride, caught Grace's attention and mimed the act of bringing a cup into his mouth, silently mouthing the words, 'Want one?'. She nodded gratefully and began bundling up her papers. Less than a minute later, Mike was clonking down a mug of freshly brewed coffee in front of her as she was saving her report. She glanced up at his cheery, well-rounded face. 'Right, let's get ready for briefing,' she said, closing down the computer.

Detective Superintendent Michael Robshaw took up position next to the incident board, giving it the once-over and flicking through his notes. He had been appointed the Senior Investigating Officer for the Barnwell Lake murder.

He peered over the top of his spectacles, taking a deep breath that swelled his muscular chest, straining his crisp white shirt. 'Good morning, ladies and gents. In the words of the old adage it never rains but it pours — we have just cleared up one set of nasty murders and now we have another particularly grisly one turn up.' He paused, then added, 'This is playing havoc with my budget.'

A ripple of laughter filled the room.

He tapped the mortuary photograph of the bloated grotesque face. 'Okay, on a serious note, our job is to find out who murdered this young woman. As you can see from the decomposition she is unrecognisable. She was found stripped naked and with no identification marks. We have her DNA and her fingerprints but we do not know who she is or anything about her life.' He moved to the next photo. It was a full body shot of the victim prior to the autopsy. 'But what we do know is that three to four weeks ago she was badly beaten, raped, had her throat cut, was bundled inside a rug and then dumped in the bottom of Barnwell Lake, where she lay until yesterday afternoon when two divers on a training session found her.

'Our main priority is to find out who this young lady was. We also have quite a wide time frame between the murder and the body being found and as yet we don't know where she was killed, only where she was dumped. We are up against it, but we have all been here before and I know you lot will fill in the gaps.'

He tapped the incident board again, glancing behind him before focusing on the faces of the detectives.

'What we do have is the rug she was found wrapped up in and the weapon that was used to slit her throat. These appear to be foreign and these are our leads at the moment. If no one has any questions, you can now all report to DI Scaife who will give you your tasks so you can get out there and clear this up.'

There were no questions. The briefing broke up and the MIT detectives picked up their assignments for the day.

Grace was still acting DS. The DI told her Hunter had been in touch and wouldn't be back for at least another three days. She collared Mike and Tony.

'Right you two, we've got the job of checking missing persons because of our experience with the last set of murders, and also finding out about the murder weapon, especially to see if there are any local outlets who sell anything like it.' She snatched her jacket off the back of her chair, picked up the car keys and slung them towards Tony. 'Bully, you're driving,' she said and led the way out of the office.

Hunter paced the hospital corridors, frustrated and tired. He had slept very little the previous night. They had managed to book a family room in a motel not too far from the hospital but he had spent a restless night going over the events in his head. The more he mulled over the incident, the more frustrated he became.

Now he had another long day before him at the hospital, unable to make any inroads into finding out the identity of the shaven-headed man responsible for doing this to his parents.

Beth and the boys were flitting between Ward Two, where his mum was 'comfortable and stable', and the ward where his dad was resting. He was having trouble being in the same room as his dad, who refused to say anything. Hunter had tried to be patient but he knew his dad was holding back on some secret and was refusing to give it up. It had got to the stage where his dad lay with eyes shut, refusing to respond to his questions.

Hunter had tried several times to call the number he had rung last night but it was switched off and on divert. His head was swimming.

Even though he hated drinking out of plastic cups, Hunter strolled down to the drinks machine on the floor below and dropped some change into the slot. They were out of tea. He kicked the bottom panel and growled. Then his mobile rang. He viewed the screen. 'Withheld' flashed up.

'Hello?' Hunter answered.

'Hunter, it's me.'

He recognised the voice. It was the Major Investigations Team's civilian investigator, Barry Newstead. Barry was one of the few workmates whom Hunter also counted as a good friend. They'd met twenty years ago, shortly after Hunter's first serious girlfriend — Polly Hayes — had been found murdered.

Barry had been one of the investigating detectives on the case and early on in the enquiry he had interviewed Hunter as a suspect. Barry's questions had been so probing that Hunter had been glad he'd had a solid alibi. Polly's killer had never been found and it was Barry who had broken the news to him that the enquiry was being wound down because all leads had been investigated. That was twelve months after her murder — Hunter had been almost eighteen years old. And it was when he decided to join the police.

He bumped into Barry four years later, as a nineteen-year-old uniform cop. Barry had been at the peak of his career and had taken Hunter under his wing, showing him all the tricks of the trade. That learning had gained Hunter an early entry into CID and they had formed a formidable team until Hunter was promoted to Detective Sergeant eight years ago and transferred to District CID. Since then Barry had retired, but following the 'Demon' case, Hunter had persuaded him to come back as a Civilian Investigator.

Barry was the only person, other than Grace, that Hunter trusted enough to help investigate his dad's secretive behaviour.

'Have you got anything for me?' Hunter asked.

'Sorry mucker, afraid not. I've made quite a few phone calls but there's not a whisper down here. I also went round to all of the Payntons' houses, and the lock-ups they have access to, but there's no sign of a silver BM. And everyone I spoke with yesterday had never seen any of the family driving one, or in one. I've checked with Intelligence and nothing with that part registration features on our system. It's a blank at the moment but I've put a few feelers out, so if I turn up anything, I'll bell you. Okay?'

Despondently, Hunter thanked him and rang off, though he knew he shouldn't feel down. If villains from his back yard had carried this out, then his source would get to hear. He would have to rely on that for the moment — until he could get back to base and shake some trees himself.

DAY FOUR

Keeping to the shadows of the dilapidated buildings on Sauchiehall Lane in Glasgow, Fraser Cullen slowly made his way to the entrance of the derelict car park, constantly checking behind him. There he stopped, leant against the crumbling brickwork and lit up another cigarette. He'd only just finished the last one — but he was nervous.

He pulled up the collar of his jacket. Was it his imagination or had the temperature dropped in the past half hour? It must be the damp, he told himself.

Every time he heard a car's engine, he stuck his head out from behind the wall and scoured the partly cobbled street. Fraser glanced at his stolen Rolex; he'd give them another ten minutes, then he was off.

He almost missed the silver BMW. It coasted past, hardly making a sound. He took a final drag on his cigarette, dropped the burning remnant and scrunched it underfoot before he stepped out into the lane.

The car pulled up sharply, then reversed and halted alongside Fraser, its nearside tyres squealing as they scraped the kerb. Fraser bent down, blowing the smoke from his mouth as the passenger window slid down.

The front passenger wafted a hand in front of his face. 'Fucking hell, do you have to do that?' he said.

The deep gravelly tones had not changed, even after all this time, thought Fraser, though the man's appearance had. The hair was ravaged by grey and he couldn't miss the scar that ran from the bridge of his nose down towards his jaw. The occupant of the front seat had been a hard bastard thirty odd years ago, now he looked even harder.

'What have you got for me, then, Fraser?'

Fraser bent forward, resting a hand on the car door and meeting the stern gaze of the front passenger. 'I found him, Billy. It wasn't easy, mind,' he said in his harsh Glaswegian dialect. 'You'll find him drinking regularly in Lauders on Sauchiehall Street. He's there most days. Goes in about four in the afternoon and usually leaves about half-seven. He comes down this way to get to the subway. I've followed him three times now without him knowing. And there's nae CCTV,' he said, his eyes roaming around the high buildings lining the narrow lane.

Billy smiled, reached inside his coat pocket and brought out a handful of notes. He peeled off five 20s. 'There's a ton, Fraser. Now piss off and keep your mouth shut.'

Before Fraser could reply, the dark-tinted window powered shut and the rear wheels burned rubber as the BMW lurched towards the main road.

Alistair McPherson stood at the front of Lauders bar, tapping the cigarette on its packet before popping it into his mouth. He lit it in cupped hands, an old habit from his army days. His first drag was a long one, which triggered a spluttering cough. It lasted several seconds before he banged his chest and brought it under control.

Jesus, these things are going to kill me one day.

He stood for a good minute, taking in the sights and sounds of Sauchiehall Street. How it had changed over the years! It had gone upmarket since his time working here. It was now a busy thoroughfare full of high-class shops, and many of the gracious houses had been converted into offices.

He stepped onto the pavement and began his steady meander home. He'd pick up a fish supper on the way back, he told himself. He turned into Sauchiehall Lane, heading for the subway on Bath Street. As he rounded the corner, he heard a car slowing behind him and guessed it would be someone wanting directions — lots of tourists got confused by the Glaswegian traffic system.

He stepped to one side, waiting as it drew level and, removing the cigarette from his mouth, he held it in his cupped hand. The window coasted down and Alistair turned to talk to the driver but could only see his chest and shoulders. He bent to get a better view and was met by a piercing stare from the scar-faced passenger leaning across the shaven-headed driver. There was something about that face that registered.

'Remember me, Mr McPherson?' said the passenger. The voice was deep and menacing and a wave of panic shot through Alistair.

The DOA — 'dead on arrival' — call was logged at 7.50 p.m., discovered by a young waiter who had slipped out through the rear emergency doors of the restaurant into the derelict car park for a smoke-break. He'd got the shock of his life when he tripped over the crumpled mess. At first, he'd thought it was a pile of rags — people were always dumping their rubbish here — but then he'd spotted the thick congealed blood beneath his feet. The sight of the mush, which had once been a head, had almost made him throw up.

He had dialled 999 on his mobile, requesting an ambulance — because the body was close to the fire-escape he had assumed the dead guy had accidentally fallen from the top. Then he'd fled back inside the restaurant and dragged out his boss to bear witness to what he had found.

The ambulance crew who turned up could see the horrific injuries were not the result of an accident and they requested immediate police attendance.

The first officers were on scene in a matter of minutes; Pitt Street police station was only three-hundred yards away. The uniform sergeant studied the dead man but the victim's face had taken such a severe hammering that he was barely recognisable.

'Looks like somebody's tap-danced on his heed,' he said to his colleague, slipping on a pair of latex gloves.

He began to search through the dead man's pockets for some ID, found the man's wallet in an inside jacket pocket and began rummaging through the cards. In the back section, he found a laminated National Association of Retired Police Officers membership card which grabbed his attention. He stared at the name and then at the photograph. He glanced at his junior colleague in disbelief.

'Bloody hell, I know this guy,' said the sergeant. 'He was in CID at Shettlestone nick.'

By 8.15 p.m., the full length of Sauchiehall Lane had been cordoned off. A murder enquiry was underway.

DAY SIX

Grace took a final look over her notes to gather her thoughts and then turned her attention to the colleagues seated around the room. She had centre stage this morning because Detective Superintendent Robshaw had been called into headquarters to liaise with the press office. He had a meeting booked with the local press and TV news teams to give an overview of the murder investigation and to make an appeal for witnesses.

Grace's stomach turned. Pangs of nervousness drifted from her gut up into her throat. This was her first up-in-front briefing and she was outside her comfort zone. She sought out Mike and Tony, who were giving her the thumbs up. It made her realise how much support her two team-mates had given her during her spell as acting Sergeant. She gave them a grateful smile.

The three of them had not stopped over the past two days in their attempts to identify the murder weapon. She'd split the jobs between them. They had searched the internet, made dozens of phone calls, and finally had teamed up to trawl the many and varied Asian artefact and martial arts shops in South and West Yorkshire.

Their efforts had paid off. Late the previous morning they had found their answer in Bradford, in a small warehouse that sold Asian ceremonial weapons — items more for show than for use. Along with a brief history of the weapon, she had watched in amazement as one of the young male storekeepers had given a demonstration in its application.

Grace had requested a list of people who had purchased such a weapon, but they only dealt in cash and kept no till receipts.

Even Mike's veiled threats of letting the tax man know of their accounting methods hadn't taken them any further forward, other than to provide the store's distribution outlet over in Pakistan. Grace and her team settled on a free replica of the murder knife, and left.

Grace perched herself on the corner of her desk ready to feed her information into the morning's briefing. She cleared her throat, picked up the replica murder weapon and began. 'A bagh nakh.'

She held up the knife with its curved angled blade and brass knuckles fixed into the hilt. Behind her, pinned to the incident board, was the SOCO photo of the weapon found with the girl's body. The weapon from Bradford was identical to the killing instrument on the photograph.

'An Indian hand-to-hand weapon designed to fit over the knuckles or be concealed against the palm. This is a variant of a traditional weapon that consisted of four or five curved blades and is designed to slash through skin and muscle, mimicking wounds inflicted by a wild animal. The bagh nakh features in many of the video games the kids play these days. It was originally developed primarily for self-defence, but in this case, as we know, it was used to attack and slit the throat of our victim.'

She explained how they had got hold of the replica.

'Unfortunately, even though this is a strange knife to our eyes, among the Asian population it is not. There are a number of outlets for this weapon both in this country and abroad and at this moment we are unable to find out who purchased it. Detective Superintendent Robshaw will be showing this as part of his appeal so we're hoping it will jog someone's memory.'

Grace put the knife down on the desk and went on to explain that they still had no positive identification of the body.

She had gone back into the National Missing Persons database but such was the putrefied state of their victim that it was hampering the search parameters, and despite the DNA database having some six million indexes and the National Fingerprint Database having eight million individuals they still had no trace.

'We can only hope that the Super's TV broadcast will give us a lead,' she finished, and dropped down off the edge of the desk and returned to her seat so that DS Gamble from the other Syndicate could finish off the morning's briefing.

Mark Gamble took Grace's place in front of the incident board, picking up where she had left off, running through yesterday's day long footslog around the traditional Asian carpet stores in Bradford.

Two of his team had eventually tracked down rugs of a similar make and design in a warehouse on an industrial unit on the outskirts of the city. Shipping receipts held by the owner identified they were part of a large consignment from the Punjab province of Pakistan. They had pressed the owner to narrow down the location but he had been unable to help — many of the rugs were crafted in small factories and family homes to a specific design, picked up weekly and delivered to a warehouse by the docks. Dozens of villages would be involved in one single design; it was impossible to pinpoint where the rug had been made.

DS Gamble cleared his throat. 'We also had the task of gathering any CCTV evidence at the country park. There is some, and it does have night vision software, but unfortunately it only covers the Lakeside Café, reception area and storeroom and is a good hundred metres from the jetty where we believe the body was thrown from. Having said that, there is some coverage to the outside of the building for security and so anyone passing close by would be picked up by the system. They store discs for a month before they are reused so we have got our civilian investigators currently going through days and weeks of footage. If whoever killed this girl carried the body past the main building before dumping it off the jetty, they will have been picked up by the cameras.' Mark paused again, massaging and stretching the back of his neck. 'It's a long shot but fingers crossed.'

The briefing broke up with the DI handing out fresh enquiries for the day. Grace scanned the half-dozen sheets generated by the HOLMES team. She had been given the task of tracing and interviewing the Countryside Rangers at the park. She handed them over to Mike and Tony to complete; she still had the Coroner's Inquest file from the last case to finish.

Hunter drove the two hours back from Scarborough District Hospital hardly uttering a word. His head was thumping. His dad, beside him, had sat throughout the journey with his head back and eyes shut. Only Beth and his mum had struck up any conversation, and that had been idle chit-chat between themselves. Even the boys were unusually quiet. It was a very strained journey and one he was glad to bring to a close as he pulled up outside his parents' home.

He followed his dad in through the front door, carrying their overnight bag which he set down in the hallway. He checked Beth and the boys were helping his mum, then strode after his dad who had made for the kitchen.

His dad had filled the kettle and was reaching into the cupboard for crockery. 'Tea, son?' he asked rhetorically, setting out four cups. He grimaced, gritting his teeth and biting down, doing his best to disguise the pain.

Hunter edged forward. 'Let me do that, Dad.'

'Nae, I'm fine, son, it's only a twinge.' Jock spooned in sugar for himself and Hunter.

'Look, Dad, I don't want us to fall out over this,' Hunter said quietly. He could hear Beth fussing over his mother in the next room.

'And neither do I, son.'

'I know something's not right, maybe it's the policeman in me, I don't know. You haven't wanted to talk about it, but just think about what happened up on those moors. If I hadn't been following, you could have been there for hours. You and Mum could have been killed. I don't know what you're covering up but it seems to me to be too dangerous not to share it.'

Jock turned and touched Hunter's arm, looking at him squarely. A film of tears flooded his intense blue eyes; eyes so like Hunter's. 'Give me some space, son. I won't promise you anything but I need some time to think it through.'

Grace ducked beneath the police crime scene tape and stepped towards the edge of the lake next to the jetty, focusing on the spot where six days earlier she had watched the Underwater Search Unit haul up their so-far-unnamed body.

She listened to the sounds around her; the lapping of the water and the regular thunk of the moored rowing boats against the damp wooden pilings of the quay. Behind her she could hear instructions being shouted to the line of officers who were on hands and knees carrying out a fingertip search in one of the areas marked out by the forensics team. Most of Barnwell Country Park was still off limits, cordoned off as the search for evidence continued. She scanned the park, a place she had visited so many times and which she normally associated with peace and tranquillity.

She had come for some fresh air after finishing the Coroner's Inquest file half an hour ago. It had taken longer than she had anticipated. All that was needed now was for Hunter to read it through before it was submitted. She wondered when he would be back.

DAY SEVEN

Hunter sat at his desk at Barnwell police station, running fingers through hair still damp from his shower twenty minutes earlier. After a restless night he had awoken just after 6 a.m. and decided to run into work to clear the past week's cobwebs from his head.

He booted up his computer, preparing to tackle an abundance of emails waiting for him and leaned back in his chair. As he waited for the system to go through its firewall security checks, he gazed at his desk calendar, then picked up his pen and crossed off several past dates. He'd been away from the office for eight days.

Tomorrow would be the first of September — the date pricked his conscience. It was on that date twenty years ago that he received news which tore his world apart. Polly had been walking her dog in woodland close to her home when she was attacked. The dog returned home without her, sparking off a search. Police found her body three hours later. She was the reason why he had joined the Force seventeen years ago.

Polly's killer had never been caught and he always hoped that one day he would get justice — not just for himself, but for her parents too. They were still around, and he called on them from time to time — though those times were becoming less frequent with the passing of years. He made a mental note to visit in the next couple of days, especially with it being the anniversary of her death.

He broke out of his reverie, looked away from the calendar, lifted the handset of his phone and dialled the Force's voicemail system. Upon hearing the mechanical voice, he switched to speaker phone and punched in a six-digit password to retrieve his personal messages.

'Hi, its Zita,' the first communication greeted him. 'It's three-thirty on Friday afternoon. Just wanting a quick chat about the country park murder. I think I might have something for you. I'm in the office tomorrow from eight. Can you give me a call? You've got my number.'

Hunter gave a wry smile — a quick chat was definitely not what she meant. Zita wanted the heads up on the investigation but he wasn't in a position to help her. He had met her six months ago at an awards ceremony at Barnwell Museum and Art Gallery, where he had won the Open Art Exhibition. She'd introduced herself as the reporter for the *Barnwell Chronicle* and wanted to do a piece on him. Once she had discovered he was a DS with MIT she had rung him almost weekly. Deep down, he didn't mind. He never gave anything away which would compromise an enquiry, though he had called her first after the 'Demon' case.

Hunter made a note to get back to her once he was up to speed and then hit the next message button, got up and made for the office kettle. He was in need of a strong, sweet, cup of tea. He switched on the kettle and listened to the next recorded call as he dropped a teabag into his mug. It was an ex-colleague who was now the safety officer at his beloved football club, Sheffield United. He had a couple of tickets in the directors' box for next Saturday's home game and asked Hunter to give him a call. That was too good an offer to miss. Hunter checked the time on his watch — he would make that his priority call straight after the morning briefing.

He took his hot drink back to his desk and returned to his emails. Most of them were in-force spam — good news, because he had come into work early to clear up as much of the accumulation of paperwork as he could before the start of the day's play. Grace's Coroner's inquest file was at the top of his pile. He picked it off and opened it.

Twenty-five minutes of reading, chewing on his pen top, saw him making headway and as he finished the last paragraph of Grace's report, he became aware of the clamour of voices further along the corridor. He checked his watch and cursed. The team were already beginning to filter in for briefing and he'd not made a dent in his 'to do' tray. He was in for a long day.

Hunter picked up the bundle of papers, jostled them together into a semblance of neatness and added a post-it note reminding Grace to have all the exhibits ready for the inquest proceedings, including photographs and video evidence.

He signed it off with 'good job' and 'thanks' before dropping it onto her desk, and finished by fixing the well-chewed plastic pen top back onto his biro. He glanced at the damaged pen and shook his head. Terrible habit, but better than biting his nails like he used to.

Scraping back his chair, he pressed the stiffness out of his back and made for the office kettle again; he'd let the last cuppa go cold before he had finished it. As he listened to the water boil, he updated himself with the timeline sequence on the incident board and studied the mortuary shots for the first time. They were horrific; such appalling violence had been meted out by someone before they had snuffed out her life. And she still had no name, despite the detective superintendent's TV appeal. He had caught it twice last night, first at the end of the early evening news and then after the ten o'clock news.

Hunter double-checked the log to ensure nothing significant had happened overnight. The HOLMES team would have been covering a late shift yesterday evening to take any calls prompted by the news plea.

Grace entered the office at bang-on 7.30 a.m. and followed a similar ritual to his, slipping off her jacket and making a beeline for the kettle.

A few minutes later, hugging a steaming cup of coffee, she sunk gently into her chair. He saw her react as she spotted the post-it on the front of the inquest file. After a few seconds, she looked up with a smile and responded with a thumbs-up and 'thank you' before placing the file into her tray.

The morning's briefing was a low-key affair. The HOLMES team were still checking through all last night's calls but there appeared to be nothing new to add to what had already been uncovered. DI Scaife issued some fresh priorities but Hunter's team still had a couple of the park's rangers to interview. Hunter asked Grace if she, Mike and Tony could finish off the actions without him. He made the excuse that he wanted to clear his tray, but in reality, he had more personally pressing things to sort out.

'Fine, Hunter, no problem. We should be able to clear them all by late this afternoon, but do you fancy working a bit over tonight?' said Grace.

'Not really,' he hesitated. 'Why, is there something urgent to follow up?'

'Not urgent as such. One of the park rangers we tracked down yesterday said something which could lead somewhere.'

'What's that then?' Hunter asked, leaning across his desk, resting his elbows and interweaving his fingers.

'Apparently, after the park closes, the back of the car park is occasionally used by courting couples in cars. The rangers have been told by their boss that whoever covers a late shift should try to discourage it, because there had been a few complaints from dog walkers. One girl in particular turns up quite regularly in different cars and with different guys. They know her as Tanya and it seems she has spun them some yarn about being a Russian dancer who has fled her brutal husband and is trying to make ends meet.' Grace rolled her eyes and clucked her tongue against the roof of her mouth dismissively. 'It's obvious she's a street worker who's using the car park as a regular spot. I just thought that if she is a regular visitor, she'll know the comings and goings of other regulars and there's the off chance she will have seen something suspicious but is afraid to come forward because of what she's doing there. I thought we could stakeout the lake for a couple of evenings, and see if she turns up.'

Hunter unlocked his fingers and pushed himself back into his seat. 'I'd love to say yes, Grace, but I've got something else planned tonight.'

'Oh, okay, sorting out your parents — I understand.'

'In a way — just something I need to follow up, that's all.'

Grace's gave him an inquisitive look. 'That all sounds rather mysterious, Hunter.'

'That's because it is,' he said, rising from his seat. 'It's top secret and if I tell you I might have to kill you.' He smiled, tapped his nose and headed towards the door.

Hunter tracked MIT's civilian investigator, Barry Newstead, to the CCTV room, where he found him going through footage from the country park's security system. Barry was sitting at one of the viewing consoles concentrating on speeded-up images floating across the screen. Pausing the footage, Barry acknowledged Hunter with a quick nod and then returned to the TV monitor.

Hunter fondly ruffled a hand through Barry's rumple of dark dyed hair. 'How's it going, big man? Found anything?'

The thickset investigator grunted, shaking his head away from Hunter's rifling fingers.

Hunter pulled up a chair next to his old friend and colleague.

'Not a damn thing so far,' said Barry, not taking his eyes off the screen. 'I've been here looking at this lot for the best part of a day and a half and I'm getting square eyes. The most exciting moment was watching a female mallard and her seven chicks waddle across the front of reception. This is almost as boring as going through all the missing-from-home files from the last job.'

Despite Barry bemoaning the task, Hunter knew it would be done thoroughly. He edged his seat closer. 'Glad I've caught up with you. Sorry to have put you on the spot with those enquiries, but I was stuck up in North Yorks and there was only Grace and you I could trust with something so sensitive, and Grace had just taken on this job.'

'No problem, that's what buddies are for.'

'Anything new cropped up?'

Barry pressed pause again and faced Hunter. He smoothed a thumb and forefinger across his dark, bushy moustache. 'I followed up a few calls late yesterday but there's nothing on the grapevine at all about what happened. I've only given my snouts half a story, they've no idea it's your parents, just told them it's a hit-and-run near the east coast. That way if someone does come back with something I'll know if they're telling me the truth.'

Hunter patted Barry's shoulder. 'Cheers for this — I owe you one.'

'No problem, Hunter. You getting me this job has more than paid a debt. I was bored stiff at home. It's great to be back in the thick of it, especially after being thrown on the scrapheap.'

Six years ago, Barry had been forced into retirement. A newly promoted Chief Inspector, wanting to make his mark, had targeted him because of his unorthodox methods. It had happened while Hunter was at District, and word had got back to him that the new man had threatened to discipline Barry for bringing the force into disrepute, before finally side-lining him to a desk job which he knew he would hate.

Hunter had caught up with Barry at his retirement do and ended up laughing with the rest of those attending when Barry had ended his retirement speech with 'I'm going to call it a day before I smack that bastard.' Word had got back to the Chief Inspector but it was too late for him to do anything about it.

Since then there had been regular phone calls and the occasional beer together, getting fewer over the years. Then six weeks ago his ex-buddy had come back into his life again. Barry had rung him out of the blue with vital information on the serial killer case which they had just put to bed, and Hunter had managed to persuade the boss to take him on as a civilian investigator at a time when their backs were against the wall and the team needed more experienced staff.

'Fancy doing some night-fishing?' Hunter asked. He caught Barry's smile. They had used the term so many times over the years, their coded phrase whenever one of them had decided to engage in underhand activities and needed backup.

'I've nothing much else on. What do you have in mind?' Barry said, interest piqued.

The Masons Arms on Barnwell High Street was a drab Victorian pub that had not changed much in decades. It had a reputation and decent local folk and anyone with an ounce of sense gave it a wide berth. Such was the clientele who frequented it that a simple brawl always turned into a wild-west saloon fight.

It was the first time Hunter had been there for a drink — under normal circumstances he would have avoided the place — but tonight he was on a mission.

Hunter and Barry entered the lounge, or at least that's what it said on the door. They stepped into an interior that belonged somewhere in the past — dingy, low-lit, and with the smell of stale tobacco hanging heavily in the air. Because of the smoking ban, Hunter guessed it was emanating from the pores and clothing of the dozen or so customers who hugged the bar. But then he took a closer look, recognising some of the faces, and wasn't so sure. Some of the people in here didn't give tuppence for society's rules and regulations.

The room fell silent as the regulars clocked them, but as Hunter and Barry strode past, they returned to their drinks and continued their conversations in low voices. Although they appeared to be minding their own business Hunter knew eyes would be covertly watching them until they left.

He scanned the room and spotted his quarry, sporting a Mohican style haircut, tucked into a corner, nursing what looked like a half-finished pint of lager.

He and Barry had snuck over and pulled up chairs before David Paynton realised they were there.

'Mind if we join you?' Hunter said, squatting down on his seat, slotting his legs under the small round table that separated him from his foe. Barry took up a position at the side, leaving David Paynton boxed in.

Paynton's eyes burned with hatred. 'What the fuck do you two want?'

'Now that's not a very nice greeting for two old friends of yours, David, is it?' Hunter surveyed Paynton's disfigured nose with satisfaction. It gave him the look of a boxer who had lost more fights than he had won. It was Hunter's handiwork and had been well deserved. A month ago, David, his brother Terry and his cousin Lee had ambushed Hunter coming out of his dad's gym. Thankfully, Barry and Jock had come to his aid and between them they had hospitalised all three of the Paynton clan. It was at the forefront of Hunter's thoughts as he said, 'How's your Steven? Heard from him?'

David looked menacing. 'You fucking know how he is. You and that bitch are the ones who got him banged up. He's on the nonce's wing for his own protection, thanks to you.'

'Now, now David, don't get yourself worked up,' said Barry. 'Steve has only himself to thank for that. He was the one who raped those women and abused those children. He admitted it, remember?'

'So you say, so you say.' Paynton pushed his wiry six-foot frame back into the faux-leather seat. 'Anyway, what do you two fuckers want?'

'A little chat, that's all,' said Hunter.

'A little chat, my arse.' Paynton took a sip from his pint, never taking his eyes off them. As he set it down, he said, 'Just piss off and leave me alone.'

'Look, David, we can do this the easy way or the hard way.' Barry snapped one of his shovel-like hands across P aynton's knee, then squeezed, digging his fingers into the joint. The man twitched. 'The easy way is we ask you some questions to which you give some honest answers. The hard way is I walk over to that bar, buy a fresh pint of lager, set it down in front of you, drop you a tenner on the table and we walk out of here. I'm sure those at the bar will not be too impressed, especially if they think you're a grass.' Barry released his grip. 'Now, which is it to be?'

Paynton pushed Barry's hand away. 'What do you want?' he growled.

'That's better,' said Hunter. He leaned in towards Paynton. 'First question — what car do you own?'

Puzzled, Paynton raised his eyebrows and seemed to think about the question for a good ten seconds, then said, 'Astra, blue, O five plate, you know that. It's on your computer.'

'Second question; which one of you or your mates owns a silver BMW?'

The puzzled look deepened. Paynton shook his head. 'None of us.'

'Sure about that?'

Paynton swelled his chest and stroked at uneven tufts of bristle peppering his jawline. 'Sure, I'm sure. We've never owned a BMW — German crap.'

'Who do you know that owns a silver BMW?' Hunter persisted.

'No one. BMs are for flashy-gits and pimps.' Paynton looked back and forth between Hunter and Barry. 'Look, where is this going? All these questions about a silver BMW. Was it used in a robbery or something?'

'A hit and run,' Hunter said, watching for a reaction. There was none.

'Look, I'll say this once more and only once more. None of us have ever owned a BMW. It's not our style. British every time. We're patriots. And as far as being involved in a hit and run, I have absolutely no idea what you are on about. When was this? Was it in Barnwell?'

'On the North Yorkshire moors six days ago,' Hunter told him. 'Ring any bells?'

'I can't even remember the last time I was anywhere near the moors.' Paynton stroked his chin, then blurted out, 'Six days ago! Ha! It can't have been me! I was with our Terry. We had to go to the Job Centre for an interview — they were going to stop our benefits. A bloody waste of time that was as well.' His face creased into a smile. 'Check it if you want.'

'Don't worry, we will,' said Hunter, scraping back his chair. He tried to hide his disappointment.

Paynton looked more confident. 'Now, wind your neck in and get off my case.'

Barry leaned to within an inch of Paynton's face. 'Watch your mouth. We can still do the dirty on you.'

Paynton stared back defiantly, picked up his pint and took a long swallow.

Hunter and Barry kicked back their chairs and left the way they had come.

Outside, Hunter paused on the footpath and studied the quiet High Street. It was just turning dusk, an orange glow low on the horizon poked between a band of grey cloud.

'Think he's telling the truth?' he asked.

'It wouldn't be hard to check out, would it?' Barry replied. 'I hate to say this, Hunter — because he's a Paynton — but I think he is.'

DAY EIGHT

The sky had been filled with dark leaden clouds all day but the rain had held off and all that was left of the northerly weather front was a gentle breeze. At Barnwell Country Park, Grace and Hunter stood at the lake edge, listening to the water lapping against the shale. The surface undulated as a cool evening wind whipped across the murky lake.

Hunter looked skywards to watch tufts of pink cloud scoot across a blue-green sky. The sun was beginning to drop low. He glanced at his watch. 9.10 p.m. The summer was drawing to a close. Another month and autumn would be here.

It had been a day of mixed fortunes so far. Hunter had listened to the briefing earlier that day with a degree of enthusiasm. It was a mixture of bad and good news. Although the team had been working flat out for over a week, the enquiry was stalling. None of the detectives were bringing anything new. They were still no nearer to identifying the victim; there had been no luck with dental records, fingerprints or DNA, and they hadn't been able to match the rug the victim had been found in to a crime scene.

But the Detective Superintendent ended the session on a high as he told them about a phone call from Professor Lizzie McCormack. The pathologist's niece was a forensic medical artist whose skills lay in facial reconstruction and she had agreed to rebuild the victim's face so a fresh appeal could be made on TV. Work to build up the victim's facial features was to begin in the next few days and should be finished in a week.

After the briefing, Hunter had got to grips with his overdue paperwork. Then he'd caught up with Grace and fixed up the stake-out at the country park to see if Tanya would turn up. An hour earlier, they had left their unmarked car near the reception centre and begun their reconnaissance of the car park where the street worker had been frequently spotted.

Dressed in fleeces, they looked like any other couple on an evening stroll around the lakeside. And thanks to a ranger's advice they were in a hidden spot with a clear view of where Tanya parked up with her clients. It was now a waiting game.

From the corner of his eye, Hunter studied Grace, watching the gentle breeze lift the curls from her face, revealing dark summer freckles. He'd often commented on how they made her look like a cute little schoolgirl and she'd responded by slapping his arm.

He grinned — she always blushed at his comments but sometimes used her naive schoolgirl look to good advantage. On several occasions, he had watched on in amusement as villain after villain, as well as the odd Alpha male colleague, had been thrown off guard by Grace's innocent childlike-look and demeanour. It was like watching a python hypnotise its prey.

She turned and he averted his gaze; he didn't want her to know he'd been watching her. After a couple of seconds, he said, 'By the way, Grace, I've been waiting for the right moment to say that you've made a cracking job of leading your first murder case. You've made it so easy for me to pick up. I've been conscious about taking it back from you, especially as you've put in so much hard work. And you've managed to fit in the inquest file as well, that's no mean feat.'

'To be honest, Hunter, I'm glad you came back when you did. Don't get me wrong — I loved it and the team have been stars but I was feeling the pressure. In fact, I've not being able to switch off when I've got home and just now, I need to.' She looked out over the lake. 'Anyway, did you get done what needed to be done last night? You don't have to tell me if you don't want.'

'No, I don't mind. I just didn't want to say anything yesterday. Not that I don't trust you but I needed to check things out.' He outlined the previous night's events with David Paynton, constantly switching his gaze between Grace and the car park — he didn't want to miss their target.

'So, you're no nearer to finding out who ran your mum and dad off the road?'

'No, and it's doing my head in. I know my dad's hiding something but he's refusing to talk about it. I thought it might have been that bother we had with the Payntons after you and I locked up Steve. But after last night I think I need to be looking elsewhere.'

'What about the photos you got of the shaven-headed guy? Have they thrown up anything?'

Hunter shook his head. 'Unfortunately, they're not that good. I've tried messing about with them on the computer but the light wasn't that brilliant and he was too far away to identify.' He gazed down to the water's edge as a line of ripples broke across its surface. 'Anyway, enough about my family's problems, how are you coping?'

'Oh, so, so. It's Dave I feel sorry for. It can't be easy being married to a copper, especially as this cop's burdened him with so much just lately. I've promised to make it up to him. I'm going to take him away for a long weekend. Paris or something — once this job's wrapped up.'

'We're worse than teenage kids, aren't we?'

Their attention was diverted by the sound of crunching gravel across the lake. After a few seconds, a dark blue Rover saloon appeared in a gap in the laurel bushes and headed towards the rear of the parking area. It was in view for a moment and then disappeared behind another line of bushes. Hunter and Grace waited for it to reappear but when it didn't, they swung into action, bursting into a jog. An earlier test run had shown they could be at the location in just under three minutes — more than enough time to catch the mysterious Tanya if she was with a punter.

Two-hundred yards from the car park, they slowed to a fast walk. They could make out a front grille and headlights of a car through a gap in the bushes. Crouching low, Hunter and Grace moved off the path and onto a stretch of grass which would bring them up behind the vehicle. It gave them a chance to get their breath back.

The blue Rover was rocking from side to side on its suspension as they approached. Hunter and Grace smiled at one another as they moved to either side from the rear.

Hunter banged on the roof and yanked open the driver's door. 'Police,' he shouted.

Simultaneously, Grace had the front passenger door open.

Inside were two very surprised faces, a man in his early forties, and a much younger woman, both in the early stages of undressing — the man had his trousers around his knees and she was dropping her leggings. They grabbed at their clothing in a state of panic.

'Okay,' Hunter said loudly, 'put it away, sir, and get out of the car.'

'And you rearrange yourself, young lady, and do the same,' said Grace.

The two detectives turned their heads away but kept a firm grip of the door handles as the pair got themselves sorted.

Minutes later, the driver was standing before Hunter, trying to fasten the belt of his trousers, finding it difficult because of his shaking hands. He looked a nervous wreck, avoiding any eye contact and was most apologetic. As Hunter checked out his details, the man kept repeating that he was sorry and asking if his wife would find out about this.

Hunter glanced at Grace. She was enjoying watching the guy squirm.

The driver checked out; no convictions for anything. Hunter berated him for his actions and told him this was a warning and to sling his hook. He couldn't get away fast enough, slamming the car into reverse and throwing the girl's red high-heeled shoes and matching handbag out from the passenger seat, while Grace held onto her as the car moved backwards.

In less than a minute, the blue Rover was heading towards the park exit, a cloud of dust spinning up from its rear wheels.

Hunter and Grace got their first good look of Tanya. She was skinny, with pale skin and couldn't have been more than nineteen.

She bent to slip her shoes on and then hoisted up her leggings over a black thong that left nothing to the imagination. 'Bastard,' she mumbled with not a hint of embarrassment.

'Now, young lady,' began Grace, 'you and I are going to have a long chat.'

'I didn't do anything wrong. You can't prove it.'

'Oh, believe me, we can.' Grace grabbed the girl's handbag, unclipped the fastener and turned it upside down. Lipstick, a compact case, half a dozen twenty-pound notes and at least ten condoms spilt out onto the grass. 'That should be enough evidence for a police caution — unless you've been cautioned before and then it's a court appearance.'

'Bitch,' Tanya snarled and snatched her handbag. She dropped to her knees and began picking up the scattered contents, mumbling under her breath.

Grace bent down and aligned her face with Tanya's. 'I need to ask you some questions. If I get the right answers, then you and I will part the best of friends. If I don't, it's back to the station, and you make no more money tonight. Have I made myself clear?'

Grace's opening gambit reminded Hunter of his and Barry's interview technique with David Paynton the previous night. He turned away to hide a smile.

The girl stuffed the spilled contents back into her handbag, checked the ground to make sure she hadn't left anything and hoisted herself up.

Hunter looked her up and down, studying her face. Her dark eyes were sunken. Foundation and blusher had been heavily applied to cover blemishes and soften her prominent cheekbones. He realised she wasn't slim and petite because of her build, but because of her habit. He had seen the tell-tale signs many times during the three years he had served in the Drug Squad. This girl was a druggie, heroin by the looks of her.

'First what's your name?' asked Grace.

'Tanya. I'm Russian.'

Hunter tried to place the accent. It had a foreign twang to it but somehow it didn't sound Russian.

'Not what people call you. What's your real name?'

'Tanya.'

'Didn't I make myself clear?' said Grace, pushing her face nearer. 'This is not a good start. It looks like you and I are going back to the station to do a few checks. We'll take your fingerprints and photograph and bring in immigration if you persist with this.'

With a pissed-off look on her face, Tanya switched her gaze between Grace and Hunter for the best part of ten seconds, then slamming her hands onto her hips she responded, 'Okay, it's not Tanya.'

The foreign accent had gone, replaced by a broad South Yorkshire dialect. It sounded to Hunter as if she was from the Barnsley area.

'It's Kerri — Kerri-Ann Bairstow,' she continued, looking down at the ground. 'I found I could make more money with a foreign name and fancy background.'

'Right. Now we've got that sorted, let's stop mucking about because I've got some really important questions to ask, and I don't want any more of your bullshit.' Grace placed a hand under Kerri-Ann's chin. 'Look at me now. I want to see your face when I ask you these questions.'

Kerri-Ann lifted her head and Grace drew back her hand. The girl looked sorrowful and lost.

'I believe you use this place quite a lot. Bring your punters here on a regular basis?'

Kerri-Ann nodded. She began fiddling with her fingers, picking skin at the side of her cuticles.

'How many times a week, would you say?'

'A couple of times in mid-week, but quite a lot at the weekend, that's when there's not so many people about the place.'

'And how long have you been using this park for your sessions?'

'Six — seven months.'

'And do you always get the guys to park up where we found you?'

Kerri-Ann nodded again. 'It's out of the way if people are walking round the lake.'

'Have you heard about the body recovered from here just over a week ago?'

Kerri-Ann gulped and coloured up, turning away.

Grace grabbed Kerri-Ann's chin again and looked at her squarely. 'You have, haven't you?'

Kerri-Ann shook herself free. 'Course I frigging have. You can't miss it. It's all over the news.'

'Look, Kerri-Ann, this is very important. A young woman's body was dumped in that lake just over a month ago, and where you park up with your punters is in clear view of the jetty over there.' Grace pointed towards the mooring dock. 'I need to know if you saw anyone on there during any of your visits here. Especially if you saw anyone carrying anything.'

Kerri-Ann looked away again. That told Hunter she was hiding something.

'This is very serious, Kerri-Ann,' he said. 'A young woman has been murdered and her body dumped over there. If you've seen anything we need to know.'

'I don't want to get involved. I'm only talking to you now because I want you off my bleeding back. What if whoever did it comes looking for me?'

'You don't need to think about that. There is no way we are going to give out a witness's name. Anyway, what are you worrying about? You've been using a false name for ages — just change it again and do your trade somewhere else,' said Grace.

'I don't know. I feel scared about this.'

'Kerri-Ann, listen to me, so far you're our only lead. You really might be able to help us catch this girl's killer.'

'I didn't see that much.'

From that comment, Hunter knew Grace had managed it. This could be the breakthrough. A tingle of excitement ran through him. He wanted to jump in but this was Grace's call.

Grace touched Kerri-Ann's arm and looked into her sunken eyes. 'That's the hard part over. Now just tell us, slowly, what you saw.'

'Look, if I tell you will you stop hassling me and let me earn some money? I've got a two-year-old at home and I didn't see the dad for dust once I told him I was pregnant. I can't manage on the benefits they give me.' Her eyes darted between Grace and Hunter.

There was silence for a good thirty seconds and Grace was about to prompt her again when Kerri-Ann blurted out, 'All right, if it'll keep you off my back and you promise I won't go to court.' She began to pick at her fingers again. 'It was either a Friday or Saturday evening. I know that much because those two nights are my busiest time and I was with my fourth punter. Probably be about half past ten.'

'Can you remember how long ago?'

'You're joking. As you said could have been four to five weeks ago. I don't keep a diary.'

'Okay, Kerri-Ann, that's a start. You said it was about half ten at night?'

'Yeah, that's roughly the time because the guy I was with said he needed to get back into town for eleven. Anyway, we'd finished business and I needed a piss so I got out of the car to go behind the bushes. I was just about to get back in the car 'cos he'd promised me a lift, when I heard voices near that jetty thing you've pointed out and it made me jump. I sneaked a look through a gap and saw these two guys struggling with a bundle half way along it. I thought they were just dumping rubbish.

'Anyway, I went back to the car and the guy starts having a go at me. He'd had second thoughts about giving me a lift and we ended up having a row. Finally, he agreed to drop me off in a pub car park near town. I jumped in his car before he had chance to change his mind and we'd just set off when this white van came from nowhere. Almost cut us up. It had no lights on and really freaked us both out.

'At first, I thought it was cops, especially 'cos the guy said he didn't want to get caught by them. He stopped for a good couple of minutes. He was really freaked out by it. In fact, he wanted to leave me there and then and piss off back home. I told him there was no way I was leaving the car. Anyway, after about five minutes he decided to leave, but he drove really slowly and I could tell he was nervous all the way to where he dropped me off.'

Hunter said, 'Kerri-Ann, you've just said the guy you were with said he didn't want to be caught by them — as if he knew who they were. Am I right in thinking that?'

'That's what I thought when he said it.'

Hunter exchanged a look with Grace. This interview had just thrown up something he hadn't expected.

'Kerri-Ann, this punter you were with — do you know him?'

'No, it was a first time and I haven't seen him since.'

'Can you remember what he looked like?'

'Vaguely. He was in his early twenties and quite good looking — most of them are fat or ugly.'

Hunter and Grace both grinned.

Hunter asked, 'Anything else you remember about him?'

'He was about your height and build, and he had brown curly hair, which was about shoulder length if I remember rightly. Oh, and he was wearing a suit, like a businessman or something.'

'Where did he pick you up?'

'Down by the industrial estate where I normally hang out.'

'Can you remember the car he was driving?'

'Now cars I'm good at — have to be — you know, in case something happens? I text it into my phone.' Kerri-Ann unclasped her handbag and fished out her mobile, flicked it open and began tapping the keys. Thirty seconds later she looked back at them before glancing back at the screen. 'A silver Volkswagen Golf. I've entered the first few letters and numbers.' She turned the screen to let Grace see the registration.

'YP02,' Grace read out loud.

'I'm sorry, that's all I had time to put in.'

'Don't apologise, Kerri-Ann, that's brilliant. Did you manage to get his name?'

Kerri-Ann started to laugh. 'You are kidding, aren't you?'

Grace blushed. 'Sorry, stupid question. Anything else you can remember about him — distinguishing marks, scars, etc.?'

Kerri-Ann shook her head.

'Did your punter drop you back off?'

'Yeah, eventually. In the end, I got him to drop me off near the bus station. He wouldn't drop me near the pub. As I say, he was a nervous wreck.'

'Can you remember roughly what that time would be?'

'Elevenish, or something like that.'

'Okay, that's good. Now I just want to take you back a bit. We'll not keep you much longer. Did you manage to get a make or number of the white van?'

'No. As I say it just came out of nowhere. It scared us to death. It wasn't a big van like a Transit or anything, just a small one. I didn't get a number, it happened so fast.'

'Did you notice anything special about the van? Anything written on the sides?'

Kerri-Ann seemed to think about it a few seconds, then shook her head. 'Sorry, it was dark and as I say it hadn't got its lights on.'

'What about the two guys you saw with the bundle on the jetty?'

Kerri-Ann shook her head again. 'Sorry, it was so dark. They were just shapes. I never got close enough to even see what they were wearing. As I say, at the time I just thought they were dumping rubbish.' She paused and studied Grace and Hunter's faces. 'I'm not lying, I really didn't see their faces or anything — they were too far away and it was dark.'

'Okay, Kerri-Ann, I believe you,' Grace replied. 'Well done. Now let's get back to our car and get a statement from you.'

As they set off towards the car park Hunter knew that this was the kick-start the investigation needed.

Rab Geddes flung open the car door and flopped into the driver's seat. 'Still no sign of anyone — could be he's on his hols.' He examined his shoes in the footwell. 'Jeez, just look at the state of these. The fields are full of mud. Your turn next time.' He wiped his loafers on the car mat and checked them again.

'Will you shut the fuck up moaning,' said Billy Wallace, leaning forward. With the back of his gloved hand he rubbed the condensation from his side of the windscreen. Though bushes prevented them seeing their destination, he continued staring out along the uneven track. From an earlier reconnoitre, Billy knew the secluded bungalow they had been searching for lay less than a hundred metres away.

This was the third parking spot they had chosen that afternoon, spending the time in between going for a drive around, so that they didn't attract attention from the locals.

Billy powered down the window. Outside, a strong wind whistled through the trees nearby, making an unpleasant sound as resisting branches squeaked and creaked. In the past hour the weather had turned; the wind had picked up fiercely and was whipping across the fields. He thumbed the window back up. Splodges of rain were beginning to scar the windscreen, distorting his view ahead. He wasn't complaining, though. It meant people wouldn't be straying far from their homes. The last thing he needed was witnesses.

They had driven the hour or so to Killin early that morning. At first, he wasn't sure he had heard the name right when he'd eventually beaten it out of Alistair McPherson four days ago, and he'd had to search for the place in the road atlas. But when he had found the small village and confirmed the name it made him smile.

What an appropriate name. Especially for what he had in mind for his next quarry.

He and Rab had entered the picturesque village mid-morning, by the stone bridge which spanned the Falls of Dochart. As they crossed, Billy got a sense of déjà vu and for a few seconds it had puzzled him. Then he realised why as he stared across at the foaming water pounding between the huge grey rocks and boulders below. He had seen this location so many times. It featured in the 1950s film, *The 39 Steps* — one of his all-time favourites. How ironic that the film was about a fugitive on the run and he should be here, though in his case he wasn't an innocent man. It had prompted another twisted smile.

They had checked out the place, driving up and down the main street. Rab had made a few enquiries about the man they were looking for, explaining he was an ex-colleague, they were on a fishing trip and wanted to catch up with him. It had not taken long to find out he was a regular in the bar of the Clachaig Hotel located beside the falls. A quick visit there and the pair had left armed with the man's address. That was seven hours ago.

Now they lay in wait, watching for the occupant to return to the white-washed bungalow in the middle of nowhere.

Billy climbed out of the car, stretched and then relieved himself by the bushes that were keeping them hidden. He fastened his zip and glanced at his watch. 'We'll give it another hour,' he called back over his shoulder, 'and then call it a day if he doesn't return.' He stood, peering over the top of the brambles, feeling the breeze brush his face, looking towards the property. He was still there as dusk settled and seemed unmoved by the sudden biting north easterly and slanting rain.

Then his heart jolted. A light appeared through the bushes — the bungalow's windows were lit up. In the warm, yellowing glow he saw a human shadow passing across the right-hand window. He stood transfixed for several moments, watching for more activity, but there was none. He stretched his gloves tighter over his hands, so tight he could see the outline of his knuckles against the black soft leather. He turned sharply. 'Come on, Rab, get your arse in gear. He's back.'

They crossed the field, hugging the bushes, Billy leading, his Crombie flapping in the wind. Rab had to put in a jog every couple of paces to keep up. Twenty metres from the rear of the bungalow Billy halted and pushed against the hedgerow. He stared about him, listening. There was only the sound of the wind and the rain lashing against the tops of the trees.

'Right, remember what we rehearsed?' Billy whispered.

'Sure.'

'Okay, let's do the business.'

Rab brushed droplets of rain from the front of his jacket and tiptoed towards the door. Billy never took his eyes off him. Rab knocked and a few seconds later the door opened. The man who answered had put on some weight since Billy had last seen him and the hair was thinner and greyer, but this was definitely the guy they were after.

Billy caught up as the man was asking for Rab's ID. He jammed a foot in the gap before he had time to close the door. 'Mr McNab — long time no see.' He grinned menacingly.

Ross McNab's face was a picture.

Billy slammed a clenched fist into his pudgy belly. It dropped him to the floor and as Billy was about to deliver a kick, he caught movement through the open door which led into the lounge to his right. A woman, who he guessed was Mrs McNab, stood open-mouthed only a few yards away. There was terror in her eyes. He strode into the room and had a hand clenched around her jaw before she had time to scream.

'Rab, get the fat bastard up and get him in here!'

Mrs McNab jerked her head and pushed out with her hands, trying to get free of Billy's grip. He responded by digging his fingers deeper into her mandible and then smacked her across the ear. He felt her jaw pop and she wailed as she fell from his grasp, to the floor.

Rab forced Ross McNab's arm up his back, hoisting him forward, hustling him into the lounge.

'Put him there, Rab,' Billy said, pointing to an oval dining table with a seating arrangement of six chairs.

Rab manhandled McNab towards the table, kicked out the nearest chair and slammed him into the seat.

McNab was fighting for breath, his face covered in sweat.

Billy checked on Mrs McNab — she was out of it. In two strides, he was beside McNab, delivering a vicious blow to the man's head. McNab jolted sideways, almost taking the chair he was seated on with him. Rab pulled him back upright.

'Right, you fucking bastard, do you remember me?' Billy hissed.

The man groaned and brought his hand up to his reddened cheek. 'Course I do, how can I forget you? Billy Wallace — the bastard who murdered Morag McCredie and her wee bairn.' He paused. 'For nothing.'

Billy had a flashback. They were becoming far more frequent of late. His mind transported him back to that night, re-living the horror when that junkie slag had ruined his looks. And, as if it was happening there and then, he felt a sharp sting across his nose and cheek and reached up and stroked the outline of the ugly, irregular, leathery scar, snaking across half of his face.

'And you're one of the fuckers who helped put me away,' he growled.

'And you're going away again for this, you bastard. If I was ten years younger…'

Before he had time to finish the sentence Billy smashed his fist into McNab's face, breaking his nose.

'Grab his hand,' ordered Billy.

Rab Geddes snatched hold of McNab's wrist and forced his hand flat, palm downwards, onto the table. He tried to resist but Rab was too strong.

Billy pulled out a knife from his Crombie. 'Now, you bastard, me and Rab here have spent thirty-six years in prison because of you and that Campbell who grassed us up. It's payback time.' He sprang the switch-blade and held it over McNab's hand.

Ross tried to pull away again but Rab's grip held him firm.

'I want to know where Iain Campbell is. I know you know where he is.'

McNab's face turned white and a stain-patch of sweat began spreading across the front of his shirt. 'I don't know what you're on about. Stop this now, Billy. This is your final chance or you'll be back to Barlinnie and you'll nae see the light of day again.'

Billy started to laugh. Then a look of malevolence crept over his face. 'You are in no position to threaten me, Mr McNab. One more chance. Where does that bastard Campbell live?'

'Don't be so fucking stupid.'

Billy slammed the blade down onto Ross McNab's little finger, using his other hand as a lever. The knife sliced through the digit easily, cutting through into the dark wood of the table in the process. The finger shot across the surface and a gush of blood sprayed out across the polished veneer.

A guttural scream exploded from McNab.

Billy started jumping up and down, patting his hands together like an excited child. 'Oh, I bet that hurt,' he said laughingly. 'Did — it — hurt?'

McNab was drenched in sweat now. It was running in rivulets down the sides of his waxen face, and his chest was heaving, breathing as fast as if he had been jogging.

Billy heard loud moaning noises behind him and realised Mrs McNab was coming to. He slipped the knife back into his pocket, took the few steps to where she was laid out and grabbed a handful of her hair, hoisting up her head. Her eyelids snapped open from the pain. A gurgling sound broke from her and she tried to shout, but her jaw was hanging at an awkward angle and all that came out was an incoherent mumble.

Reaching into another pocket of his coat, Billy took out a washing-up bottle. He popped the plastic top and squeezed the contents over her head, then dropped the empty bottle and let go of her hair. She dropped back onto the carpet into a crumpled heap, then forced open her eyes and blinked as the liquid trickled over her eyelids and onto her cheeks. Her face took on a look of unimaginable horror.

The vapours had invaded her nasal passages.

The smell of petrol filled the room.

Billy took out a disposable lighter from his trouser pocket and held it above her.

'Now, this is your last chance, McNab. Tell me where that bastard Iain Campbell is.'

Billy and Rab returned to familiar territory in Glasgow and dumped the car in the labyrinth of roads around one of the notorious sink estates of Easterhouse.

The pair wiped much of the interior clean with petrol-soaked rags and Rab dropped the keys onto the driver's seat before closing the door and striding away with Billy.

Billy had thought it all through. He had spent enough time in prison to make his plans and consider all eventualities. This was all going to plan and he liked the feeling of being in control. He took another look back at the silver BMW. Sooner or later, one of the gangs around here would realise it wasn't a police trap and nick it. Hopefully the crew would get involved in a chase with the cops and get arrested.

If by chance anyone had clocked the car near the scene back in Killin, that would throw them off his scent for quite some time: enough time for him to do what he needed to do.

I've come too far now to get caught.

Billy checked he still had the package in his coat pocket, nudged Rab and pointed to a gap between the high-rise buildings. They increased their pace, slipping between the tenements, melting into the dark.

The salt in his sweat stung Jock Kerr's eyes and he closed them. He took a step back from the punch-bag and wiped away the perspiration from his brow. Opening his eyes, shaking away the residue from the back of his training glove, he resumed his session, bobbing and weaving around the sand-filled bag hanging from one of the gym's roof beams.

He dashed off a series of quick-fire blows to the bag. It hardly moved; it was momentum he was aiming for rather than impact. Catching his reflection in one of the mirrors that ran along the length of a wall, he smiled to himself. If he saw one of his boxing trainees performing like this, he would have bawled them out.

Stop tickling it, he would have barked. *Give it a good thumping.*

Thankfully, Jock was alone and wouldn't be embarrassed by his performance. His chest still hurt — the heavy breathing was causing a strain. It was his first time back in his gym since the accident and he'd decided to go in after everyone had finished, to give things a try out.

The session had not gone too badly. Another week, he told himself, and he should be back to tip-top condition. He gave the bag a final punch, wincing as sharpness gripped his rib cage, forcing him to clasp the sides of his stomach.

He caught another glimpse of his image in the mirror. In spite of his injury, he still looked in pretty good shape for his fifty-six years, though, he had to admit, his face looked tired and drawn. He put the hangdog look down to the lack of sleep over the past week and things being strained at home. Fiona, his wife, was pressing him to talk to someone, and on a couple of occasions he had reacted towards her like he had with Hunter. Unlike Hunter, however, there was a reason behind her pushing him — she knew what lay behind the attack.

Two nights ago, they had sat down and discussed at length how his past had finally caught up with them, and they gone over, time and time again, the 'what ifs', were they to tell Hunter. He felt guilty that Fiona had got dragged into this and cursed himself for being so naïve as to believe he could bury everything that had gone before. The crux of all their deliberations was not if, but when, they should tell Hunter. Fiona felt it was time, he wasn't so sure. Having made his decision an hour ago, Jock had pulled on his training top and jogged down to his gym.

The past half hour on the bag had reinforced his thinking. It was time to make that call.

Jock pulled off his training gloves, slung a towel around his neck, and began to steady his breathing, gazing around his gym. For a split second, a wave of satisfaction washed over him. He could remember the sight that had greeted him the first time he walked into this place thirty-five years ago. Then, it had been a derelict drill hall once used by army cadets. It had swallowed up all of their savings and taken lots of physical work to lick it into shape before he could open it up as a gym. But it had been worth it. Now it was one of the best boxing academies in the Yorkshire region.

Jock had gained a reputation as a boxing coach; he had a good stable of future young champions-in-the-making, and as an added bonus it was a profitable business. As he dabbed the last remnants of sweat from his face, he hoped against hope that what he had achieved over the years wasn't going to come crashing down around him because of one night from his past.

Jock wandered into his office and dropped into his Grandfather's old captain's chair behind his desk, leaned back on its springs and surveyed the cluttered room. For a few seconds as he pondered putting off the inevitable, his gaze skimmed the walls, checking out the boxing promotion posters hung all around. Every one of his achievements was recorded on them, all of the fights he had won in his heyday as a professional.

He shivered, mulled over in his head what he needed to say and then yanked open the desk's top drawer. After ferreting around in the loose paperwork, he found the card that had been buried at the back for years. He took up the handset and punched in the number and listened to the ringing tone. It took what seemed an eternity before anyone answered. He had almost given up hope and was ready for hanging up, then a voice came on he didn't recognise — a woman's voice. It sounded younger than he expected. The voice just said a simple 'Hello,' to which Jock repeated the same greeting.

'Who is this?' said the woman.

'Jock — Jock Kerr, who is this?'

'Detective Chief Inspector Dawn Leggate,' she answered. The voice was slow and distinctive with an air of confidence. 'Who is it you are after?'

'Sorry, I must have the wrong number. It was Ross McNab I was after.'

'Oh, you have the right number, all right.'

DCI Dawn Leggate closed her driver's door and pulled on her windbreaker. As she zipped it up, she stood for a few seconds taking in the surroundings, preparing for what lay ahead. She'd deliberately parked twenty metres away from the scene, where the lane turned into the driveway and gave her a clear view of the setting.

Ahead, parked on the gravel hard-standing were two marked police vehicles, a fire engine and an ambulance, crowded together, blocking the entrance to the McNabs' bungalow.

Spinning blue and white strobe-lights picked out the shapes of surrounding trees and hedges and skirted across the fields, lighting up the waving fronds of wild grasses before washing over the white walls of the secluded dwelling.

For a split-second there was darkness as the blue lights spun away and then everything lit up once more as they continued their sweeping sequence. The image felt staged, like the opening sequence to a TV drama, yet Dawn knew this was for real. Thirty-five minutes ago Communications had rung her work mobile while she was in the middle of her evening meal and she'd had to leave it and break the speed limit to get here. Thank goodness the roads had been relatively clear.

She'd driven like a mad woman — a mixture of frustration and resolve — but it was her turn as the on-call SIO and as she'd tore up the A84, she'd told herself this was what her job was about. Though having just finished yet another long day at the office, and with her personal life in chaos, she didn't need this pressure right now.

Another gust of wind rose over the hedges, whipping Dawn's ginger hair across her face. Coaxing the shoulder length strands into a loose ponytail, she tucked it into her jacket collar and walked up to the McNabs' home, slipping on a pair of latex gloves as she avoided the puddles in the divots along the track.

Passing between the emergency vehicles, the only light she could pick out inside the smoke-ridden place appeared to be coming from torches, dancing back and forth through the soot-stained windows. She guessed the fire had taken out the electrics. A couple of the windows were open and wisps of white smoke drifted through the gaps before being whisked away by the north easterly and up into the leaden night sky.

She let herself into the darkened hallway. No one was on the door, the crime scene had not been sealed off yet. She mentally ticked it off as one of her priorities.

The air was heavy with soot and smoke and it clogged the back of her throat, making her gag. She clasped a hand over her mouth and loosely pinched her nose.

'Hello — anyone there?' she called, despite the activity in the bungalow.

A bright beam appeared from the doorway to her right and flashed across her eyes, temporarily blinding her.

'Sorry, ma'am, didn't hear you arrive,' she heard a man's voice say. The light had blanked her vision for a few seconds, she couldn't see a thing.

'The bodies are this way.'

She blinked frantically, desperate to see. Gradually, through a haze of orange flashes, a silhouette appeared. She picked out the shape; a uniform cop barred the door. She recognised his face from back at the station but couldn't remember his name.

'They're in a bit of a mess,' he said, stepping back.

She took out her own powerful Maglite and switched it on. An intense beam of light pierced the drifting fire smoke, hitting the opposite wall of the hallway. She swept it through the open doorway into the room, along the floor, up onto the walls, picking out bits of furniture.

She deduced this was the lounge area of the bungalow. The smell in here was different, soot and smoke, but in the pungent mix was something sweeter. It reminded her of a barbecue. Then her beam fell onto a body and she realised why.

Mrs McNab — from the remnants of a charred dress which was still smouldering. Her upper body was chargrilled black, except where the skin had split from the intense heat and gashes of raw pink flesh gaped through. Eyes stared back at her and white teeth glistened because the soft tissue of the eyelids and lips had shrivelled away. It was a surreal sight.

'The fire officer says she's been set alight with an ignitable solvent of some type — probably petrol,' said the uniform cop who had followed her into the room. 'When I got here, they were just dousing her out. She was the seat of the main fire.'

Dawn shuddered. She felt her skin prickle.

'It's even worse back here ma'am.'

She followed the light from the officer's torch as it settled on a human form seated and slumped over a dining table.

Striding around the charred remains of Mrs McNab, she stepped warily towards the table arrangement. Moving to the left and right of the humped figure, she said, 'And this must be Mr McNab?' His head was face-down on the table, a halo of thick cloying blood surrounding it. A chunk of flesh was missing from his frontal lobe; it looked as though attempts had been made to scalp him. His skin and clothing were in the main charred and blackened, though parts of his bare forearms displayed heat blisters.

'It looks as though he's been tortured,' said the officer. The beam from his torch flooded the grimy mahogany surface and settled on an outstretched hand. 'Three of his fingers have been chopped off,' he continued, 'and look at this, here.' He flicked the torch light over to a packet of fish fingers resting in the centre of the table. 'There's a note underneath them. I've already read it but not touched.'

Dawn crossed the officer's ray with her own Maglite beam, fixing onto an A4 sheet of paper. Despite the film of soot, she could make out the black capital letters scrawled across it, which read — THESE ARE TO REPLACE THE MISSING ONES.

She tried to make eye contact with the uniform cop but he was in semi-darkness. Her gaze flickered between the disfigured hand of Mr McNab and the fish finger box.

'What sick bastard would do this?' she said, then shook herself back from her thoughts, quickly turning to crime scene investigation mode. She went through a check-list in her head.

Earlier, while speeding towards the scene she had been told over the radio that SPSA were on their way; getting the Scottish Police Services Authority forensics team here was one job she could tick off.

'I want you to start the visitor log please.' She threw the cop her car keys. 'There's a clipboard and paperwork in my boot. And seal the area off with tape before you come back to the house. Oh, and before you go, point me in the direction of the senior fire officer.'

Her instructions were interrupted by the ringing of a telephone. It was coming from somewhere back in the entrance hall. She paused in mid-flow, waiting for voicemail or an answer machine to kick-in but that didn't happen and the phone continued to ring.

She stepped around Mrs McNab's body and strode into the hallway where she found the ringing phone on a small table close to the front door. Lifting the handset, she could feel a slimy, greasy film covering it as a result of the fire and she raised it towards her ear; close enough to hear, yet not mark her face.

'Hello,' she answered. There was no response but she could make out someone breathing heavily at the other end. 'Hello, can I help you?' No response. 'Who is this?'

'Jock — Jock Kerr.' She thought she heard the man say. She made a mental note of the name for later, tried to determine the region of the Scottish accent but somehow it had lost its twang. 'Who is it you are after?'

She listened carefully to the answer, making another careful record in her head.

When he had finished, she answered, 'Oh, you have the correct number all right. This is Detective Chief Inspector Dawn Leggate. Can you give me your details and telephone number? I'm investigating Mr McNab's murder.'

The caller hung up. She was left listening to a long, purring noise. She checked her watch and noted the time; she would make a request for caller ID when she got back to the incident room.

Returning the handset, she stepped to the front door and took in a couple of deep breaths of fresh air. At the entranceway she took a long look around to see if any neighbours overlooked the bungalow. There were none. This was going to be a difficult case.

While she was thinking about the phone call, a flitting movement up to her right surprised her. A couple of black shapes flashed in front of a pale moonlit sky — bats taking to the night.

Dawn stood and watched, fascinated by their swift movement, zipping and swooping and zooming so close to the trees and at the last moment diving and swinging away. Living in the city she didn't usually see such a stage-show. It made her night.

For several minutes she stood there, mesmerised. Then she shook herself out of her reverie and fished her mobile out of her pocket. It was time to bring in the Procurator Fiscal and call out the troops.

DAY TEN

Hunter stepped through the French doors from his kitchen and onto the patio, nursing a steaming mug of tea. He took a long and measured look over the garden. Most of the flowers were beginning to fade and needed deadheading, he thought. With the exception of the potted plants, most of them were looking tired. What with the events at work over the past few months he had hardly had time for any gardening. In fact, it seemed like he'd missed summer altogether this year. He'd never experienced a year like this before.

He settled down onto one of the four chairs arranged around the mosaic tiled patio table and put down his drink. He loved the view from here. This was where he and Beth sat on warm summer evenings, sharing a bottle of wine, grateful for a little peace and quiet after they had tucked Jonathan and Daniel up in bed.

Hunter felt relaxed. Last night, he had finally put an end to all those restless nights. It had been his best sleep in ages. It also helped that he didn't have to go in early to work. He had arranged to have a coffee and chat with Zita, the reporter with the *Barnwell Chronicle*, and then he was off to the Forensics Lab to see how Professor McCormack's niece was shaping up with the facial reconstruction.

He'd spoken on the phone with the forensic medical artist yesterday and she'd invited him up to see the work in progress. He was looking forward to the trip. From an artistic point of view, he couldn't wait to see the result of the application and flair employed by another artist, and as a cop, he was eager to see the likeness that could possibly lead to the identification of their victim.

It had been arranged for him and Grace to visit the lab, but last night those plans had changed; Detective Superintendent Robshaw had requested that Grace join him at Barnwell Country Park that morning, where he was making a televised plea for witnesses. When Grace had told Hunter about appearing in front of camera, he had seen how nervous she was and had reassured her, saying she would be fine — it was all good experience for a future promotion board. But as they parted, he could tell his words hadn't allayed her fears.

Before leaving work, he'd asked Mike and Tony to make a start on the vehicle owner checks; the information from Kerri-Ann Bairstow had given the enquiry fresh impetus. Not only had she provided them with a partial index number of a Volkswagen Golf, but from further questioning, they had gleaned the white van was a Renault Kangoo, and Kerri-Ann felt confident it was a 53 plate — registered in 2003.

It was a real boost and the investigative machinery had cranked up as a result. The HOLMES team had submitted the Golf's partial registration number to the DVLA for a search. At the same time they had extracted the names of all the local owners of Renault vans and tracking them down was the fresh focus of the MIT teams.

Barry Newstead had been given new CCTV work — to scrutinise town centre footage, especially around the bus station, and also identify and flag up any white vans seen around the country park, including searching through stills obtained from speed site cameras.

The enquiry was slowly, but surely, gathering pace.

Hunter was meeting Zita in a coffee shop tucked away inside a ladies' high-end fashion shop on the High Street. When Zita had invited him, he'd had to double-check the address. He'd passed the shop many times over the years — in fact, it was one of Grace's frequent shopping haunts — but never realised it had a cafe. He was even more surprised as he ambled past the racks of ladies' clothes to the back of the shop and found a bright and airy bistro-style cafe, furnished in a contemporary style. The original artwork adorning the walls brought him to a standstill for a moment as he browsed.

Zita was waiting for him at a table in a corner of the room. She was wearing a white cotton shirt tucked into a pair of jeans and her shoulder-length flaxen hair was tied back, accentuating her high cheekbones.

Hunter pulled back a chair, slipped off his jacket, hung it over the back and seated himself opposite.

'I've ordered a pot of tea for us. It is tea you drink, isn't it?' Zita flashed him a welcoming smile. 'I told them I was waiting for someone and to serve it when you come in. Is that okay? You said on the phone you could only spare an hour.'

'Yeah, thanks, Zita, that's fine.' As Hunter made himself comfortable, he told her about his visit to the forensic lab and his reason for going.

'Oh, wow, that's cool. You will let me have an early look at the results, won't you?'

'I'll be getting some photos done of it so I'll get one of those across to you as soon as they land on my desk.'

'I appreciate that. Anyway, how are things with you?'

Hunter was just about to reply when a shadow fell across the table. A young girl dressed in black was sidling towards them, carrying a tray of cups and the pot of tea Zita had ordered. He waited as she set it down, acknowledging her with a smile before she returned to the kitchen. He picked up a cup and locked on to Zita's hazel eyes. A hint of peacock blue mascara lined them, highlighting their colour.

'When you say, how are things with you? I'm guessing you don't really mean in my personal life. You really want to know how the investigation is going, don't you?'

Zita held up her hands in mock surrender. 'There's no flies on you, Hunter Kerr. I guess that's why you're a detective.' She flashed another bright smile. 'Are there any new leads?'

'We have one lead, Zita, but it's in the very early stages. In fact, the team are following it up this morning. If it comes to anything, you know I'll give you a call.'

Zita turned her attention to the teapot, lifted the lid, glanced inside and then picked up a spoon and began stirring the contents.

'Will it lead to the killer?'

'I honestly don't know. We only came across the information two days ago and as I say the team are out there following it up.'

'Is there nothing you can give me for our next edition?'

Hunter pursed his lips. 'We still have no idea who the victim is. We don't even know where or when she was killed. All we know is that whoever killed her wrapped her up in a rug and dumped her in the lake. We're obviously going through the routine stuff to try to identify her, but locally there's no report of anyone missing who matches her description, so we don't even know if she's a local or not.'

'Nothing to identify her then?'

Hunter shook his head. 'Nothing. I'm hoping the facial reconstruction will do that. And as I've said, once I get some photos done you are first on my list to get a copy.'

Zita replaced the lid on the teapot and poured some tea into Hunter's cup. 'Well, I might be able to help you out in return.' She filled her own cup.

'You mean identify her?'

'Maybe. When I got the info regarding the murder, especially that the victim was Asian, I made a few phone calls to some of my contacts. One of those contacts is a woman who runs an Asian women's refuge across in Sheffield. I've done a few stories in the past about domestic violence and this lady provided me a couple of horror stories which affected Asian women. Anyway, she told me that recently a couple of young girls had approached the refuge for support and one in particular had made arrangements to stay there but failed to turn up and had not contacted her since. She told me she had tried the girl's mobile several times but it was always switched off.'

Zita took a sip of her tea and Hunter fixed her gaze.

'It may be nothing, Hunter, but it's obviously concerned the woman who runs the refuge enough for her to mention it to me.'

'And it's certainly enough for me to raise an enquiry and check it out. Can you give me her details?'

'I need to hold on that, Hunter. I haven't told the woman I was going to have this conversation and I don't want to betray her trust. I'll need to get back to her and fix up something for you. I'm sure she'll be all right because she does deal a lot with the police, but just to make sure, if you know what I mean.'

'No problem, Zita. It's good of you to tell me. And anyway, if it comes up trumps you can splash across the headlines how the *Chronicle* helped with the murder enquiry.'

Zita gave him another smile.

It took Hunter slightly over an hour to drive to the Forensic Lab at Wetherby. As he slowed for the gate, he pondered upon how long it was since his last visit. *It must be at least 10 years*, he thought, as he approached the main gate. He had been a young detective, given the task of safely delivering evidence — now civilian drivers delivered the exhibits.

He flashed his warrant card to the uniformed gate guard and answered a few security questions before being pointed towards the visitors' car park. Strolling towards the laboratory, he could see that with the exception of the increased protection since his last visit, very little of the physical structure had changed. The building was a 1960s design — flat-fronted concrete and glass — though up-to-date colourful signage did its best to break up the grey drabness.

The reception area was remarkably light and airy and he checked in with the receptionist, telling her that he was expected.

Hunter had only just taken a seat when Frankie Oliver — he saw her name badge — breezed into reception. She thrust out a hand and greeted him with a beaming smile, displaying a set of perfect white teeth — so white in fact that Hunter wondered if they had been cosmetically bleached.

Frankie was slim and petite just like her aunt, Professor Lizzie McCormack. Hunter guessed she was in her late twenties and he could see that she had been blessed with a faultless complexion and pretty features. A hint of mascara framed soft blue/grey eyes. What made her stand out though was her hair — short and chopped and dyed jet black with hints of burnt copper.

As she led him to her lab, Hunter explained the dual purpose of his visit — his fascination to learn the process, but more importantly, to see the artistic representation.

'A detective with a soft side, eh?' Frankie commented as she swiped her security card. 'That's unusual, and refreshing. At least for once I'll know my work will be appreciated.' She opened the door and held it for him to pass through. He caught a whiff of her perfume, a hint of flowers, subtle, expensive.

As she led the way to her work-station, Hunter saw half a dozen other white-coated technicians beavering away in the lab. From her station, Frankie pointed at a tall white plinth a few metres away. On it was a grey half-executed bust, with all the appearance of a head but without fully formed features. Plastic teeth and prosthetic glassy eyes were set but not covered, giving it a surreal effect.

'I'm afraid I haven't finished it yet, but I can take you through what I've done so far,' Frankie said, slapping a hand over the lumpy cranium.

Hunter was studying the craftsmanship that had gone into the project. 'Give me the full works. I'll let you know if you're boring me.'

She laughed, displaying those perfect white teeth again. 'Don't beat about the bush, will you! Okay, pin back your lugholes and if there's anything you don't understand, stop me. I must warn you that once I'm in full-flow I take some holding back.' She moved closer to her sculpture. 'Firstly, I did a cast of the girl's skull. My aunt helped me with that. In the past, I have worked with clean skulls from skeletons dug up, but in your case the body was intact, despite its state. Anyway, I digress.'

She pinched some of the clay away from the head and worked it into a lump. 'We use an oil-based clay.' She thumbed it back onto the bust. 'Sticks easily to the cast and can be manipulated for longer. First, plastic pegs are inserted at specific anatomical sites around the skull to indicate the level of tissue required. Those enable me to begin the muscular build up with the clay — like I have done here.'

She stroked an index finger around contour lines of the face. 'Big muscles which form the sides of the face onto the jaw, around the eyes,' she continued, stroking the clay form to make her point. 'Once the muscle structure is in place, I can think about the thin fatty layer which lies on the surface — the connective tissue as it is called. A lot of formation was already there on your body, even though it was bloated and disfigured. For instance, creases and folds from the underlying muscle structure, especially the mouth and shape of the nose, were in place. The nose is generally one of the most difficult facial features to reconstruct because the underlying bone is limited. However, because the girl's face is almost intact this model should be exact.'

As she was talking Hunter through her handiwork, Frankie was smoothing dainty, slim fingers around the clay head. She picked up a cloth from a tabletop and wiped some oily deposit from her hands. 'Another couple of days and I'll have the face finished. Then it'll undergo a paint job. I can match the skin tone exactly from the body colour. Finally, I'll add a similar style and colour hairpiece and you should have a vision of your victim. It won't be an exact portrait but the main features will all be there to enable you to have as near a match as possible for identification purposes.'

Hunter thanked her. This is what he had been waiting for. Having a name for the victim always gave an enquiry an extra dimension — family, friends, associates and a background — which provided a wealth of additional information to point them in the direction of the suspect or suspects. He couldn't wait to see Frankie's completed work.

DAY TWELVE

'Okay, what have we got?' DCI Dawn Leggate asked, pushing open the door to the CID office, fighting with her waterproof jacket as she wrestled to free an arm from its sleeve. Every member of her team was hard at work at their desks. They looked up as she entered.

'I wouldn't take your coat off yet, boss,' said Detective Sergeant John Reed, rising from his seat. He snatched his coat from the back of his chair and picked up a file from a mountain of paperwork strewn across his desk. 'We've got a meeting with Glasgow A Division CID,' he continued. 'I said we'd join them —' he glanced at his wristwatch — 'ten minutes ago.' He skipped past her and held the door while pointing down the corridor, urging her to hurry up.

Dawn fought to slot her arm back into her waterproof as she dodged past the DS.

He handed over the folder he was holding. 'That's the file for the job. I'll fill you in on the way.'

In the rear yard of the station John Reed started the engine of the CID car and waited for the screen to de-mist. Dawn shot him a sideways glance as he combed his fingers through his dark, wavy, collar length hair.

'You're going to love this job, Dawn,' he said as he drove out of the yard, leaning across and tapping the paperwork spread open on her lap. 'Traffic spotted a silver BMW in the early hours of this morning cruising around one of the Easterhouse estates. The car's registration number pinged up on their ANPR.'

John was referring to the Traffic car's on-board computerised Automatic Number Plate Recognition system linked to the National Vehicle Centre.

'There were three recorded hits for various parts of the registered number. Firstly, a hit-and-run in North Yorkshire, secondly, it was clocked driving away from the scene of a murder on Sauchiehall Street, and finally, as you know from our enquiry in Killin, a silver BMW was spotted by a local walking her dog, who was suspicious about its activities around the village. Anyway, traffic had a hell of a blues-and-twos chase last night, but they finally caught it when it crashed into a lamp post.' He tapped the paperwork again. 'It was two-up. Unfortunately, the little bastards didn't get hurt — not even a scratch, would you believe?' John gave a wry smile before returning his gaze to the road in front. 'And look at the intel sheet of the two they arrested.'

Dawn licked a forefinger and turned several pages until she found the section she was looking for. She started to read the typed sheet following the route of her shaking finger because of the erratic motion of the car. John was trying to make up for lost time, but she wished he would just slow down a fraction; she was being bounced around uncomfortably in her seat.

'Driver was Sandie Aitkinson and front seat passenger was Bruce McColl. Both are well known and have form for burglary and car crime and a bit of anti-social behaviour, but none for violence. It turns out the car is on cloned plates. We visited the address of the registered keeper according to the number plates on it and they still have their own silver BMW on the drive. Anyway, after Traffic checked out the chassis and engine number, they discovered that it belongs to someone living at an address in Bellshill. We asked uniform to do a visit there for us early this morning and they've found the house broken into and the guy who lived there battered to death.'

Dawn gave a low whistle.

'Told you you'd love it.'

'Are the two prisoners saying anything?'

'No one's interviewed them yet. We're letting them stew in their cells.'

'Do we know any of the victims of the other two jobs — any links to our case at Killin?'

'The names are somewhere in the file, I can't remember them off-hand. North Yorkshire faxed us a copy of the statements from the man and woman who were rammed off the road. They're from Yorkshire.'

Dawn began to search the folder.

'The murder on Sauchiehall Street happened just over a week ago. And get this, it's another retired cop — worked out of Shettlestone nick many years ago.'

'Just like Ross McNab?'

'Exactly.'

Dawn pursed her lips and gave a low whistle. 'Did they work together?'

'Don't know much about the Sauchiehall Street murder at all, other than he was found dumped near a subway and had been given a real good hiding. His face apparently was barely recognisable — IDed from his NARPO card. That's why I've fixed up our meet with CID from Stuart Street nick. They are dealing with the job and they're now at the scene of this latest killing in Bellshill. It's a DI McBride we're liaising with there.'

Dawn knew that name and was trying to put a face to it. She continued picking through the file and found faxed copies of the witness statements of the hit and run in North Yorkshire.

One of the witnesses was a DS in South Yorkshire — Hunter Kerr.

A Yorkshire man with a Scottish surname.

Then the alarm bells started ringing in her head. Kerr — she had heard that name recently.

Now, where was it? Then the light switched on. It was the guy on the phone at the McNabs' bungalow. He was a Kerr — Jock Kerr. She recalled him telling her that before he hung up.

She flicked through the faxed statements. And there it was, the driver injured when his car was rammed off the road by the silver BMW. He was also called Jock Kerr. 'This is just too much of a coincidence,' she muttered.

Through the windscreen she saw the sign for Bellshill and closed the file.

They entered the old part of the town, driving past row upon row of high-rise old pink sandstone tenements, now refurbished. Within five minutes they were turning into a newer estate. The road was cordoned off and they had to leave the car at the junction because of abandoned police vehicles blocking their way. After locking up, they headed for the blue and white tape strewn across the street.

The first people they came across were press photographers, but they pushed their way through to the PC guarding the scene. Dawn and John flashed their warrant badges and she asked for DI McBride. They were pointed towards a tall, slim man, with thinning wavy hair, who had his back to them watching the forensic team erect a blue tarpaulin around the front door of a pair of modern semis.

Dawn called his name as she got closer. The detective spun around. She recognised him; they had been on the same hostage negotiator's course.

He flashed a smile and held out a hand for her to shake.

She took it and introduced her DS.

'You know the reason why we're here, don't you, Alex?' She recollected his first name.

'Aye, your DS told me over the phone. You've trapped up two who were caught in this victim's car. It was on false plates, I'm told.'

'Aye,' replied Dawn. 'And we've linked the car to a murder we're dealing with in Killin five days ago. A retired cop and his wife tortured and then set on fire. A local saw the BMW driving around the village several times on the day of the murders, thought it was suspicious so she noted down its number.'

'So I heard. And the same car could be linked to a murder just off Sauchiehall Street. We've got CCTV evidence of a silver BMW driving away, close to the scene around the time. We're currently enhancing the images to see if we can identify the driver. My team are dealing with that. I suppose you've heard that the victim was also a retired cop?'

'Aye.'

'Well, this latest killing is going to grab you as well. I've just been told he's a retired DS who also used to work out of Shettlestone CID. He retired back in 1994. Whoever killed him has left him in a right old mess. I've not been inside yet. Forensics are setting up things so we can walk around the scene.'

Three retired detectives murdered, and all from the same station.

DAY THIRTEEN

In the busy lounge of the George and Dragon, Hunter nursed the last of his beer and stared into space. His mind was elsewhere — revisiting the images he had seen several times that morning.

The bound book of colour photographs had been waiting on his desk for him and he had viewed them the minute he had got in. He was impressed with Frankie Oliver's work, especially the life-like features she had managed to form on the reconstructed skull of their victim.

The photos had been revealed to the team during the Detective Superintendent's morning's briefing and were going out on the local news broadcast later that evening.

The announcement had caught Hunter by surprise and he had shot out straight after the briefing to get a set over to Zita at the *Chronicle*. The last thing he wanted was for her to see them on the TV when she hadn't got her own copies as he had promised.

Hunter wondered if Grace would be on tonight's local news. He remembered their conversation three days previously, how nervous she had been about being with the boss for the press conference. He hadn't spoken with her since. He'd been so wrapped up in things that he had forgotten to ask her how it had gone.

'Penny for them, Hunter.' Grace sidled up next to him.

'Crikey, you made me jump! I was just thinking about you and your fifteen minutes of fame.' He pointed to a wall-mounted TV playing without sound. The national news was

112

on. 'Are we going to see your bright, cherubic features this evening?'

She dug his arm. 'Hey! Less of the cherubic. That means fat, doesn't it?' She took a drink of her wine. 'After spending all morning tramping round the country park the other day, I didn't even get a look-in with any of the TV crews. All they wanted was Mister Robshaw. It was a waste of bloody time. And I'd got myself all done up for it as well.'

Hunter smiled. He knew what Grace was like for her make-up and fashion, even on a normal working day. She would have spent hours the night before sorting out a suitable wardrobe for her TV debut, and here she was telling him she didn't get a look-in.

'That's because to the press you're a lowly detective, while he's an interesting, high ranking Detective Superintendent who's running a murder enquiry.'

'Are you saying I'm uninteresting?' Grace dug Hunter again. 'It's us who does the leg work and solves the crime.'

'Ha, but that's not what the public think.' Hunter drained his beer and thrust out the empty glass. 'Fancy another?'

Grace swilled the remnants of the Chardonnay around the bottom of her glass before swallowing the last mouthful. 'Just get me a Coke. I'll have that then make tracks home, I daren't be late this evening. I promised the girls I'd take them out for a bite to eat. And I need to catch up with Dave. Things have not been easy over the past couple of weeks.'

'Know that feeling. The job just gets a hold of you, doesn't it? I sometimes wonder why Beth puts up with me.'

'Must be those rugged good looks!'

'Flattery will get you everywhere,' Hunter said, taking her empty wine glass. 'One more won't do you any harm.'

'Oh, go on then, you've twisted my arm. Then I definitely must go.'

Hunter yawed his way to the bar. The MIT team had taken over half of the lounge. They had left work early to have a couple of swift drinks and to watch their SIO's appeal on the local news broadcast before they all headed home.

Hunter squeezed between a small group of regulars congregated at the bar and caught the eye of one of the staff. He ordered a pint of Timothy Taylor and a glass of Chardonnay. As he ferreted around in his pocket for money, a loud cheer and several wolf-whistles went up behind him. He spun round to see a sea of detectives' faces all fixed on the television.

Someone shouted to turn it up and Hunter began to decipher the sound. The shot was zooming in on their Senior Investigating Officer, Detective Superintendent Michael Robshaw, and the announcer said they were speaking from the lakeside at Barnwell Country Park. The newscaster was dubbing the storyline 'The Lady in the Lake'.

Michael Robshaw was commenting on the status of the enquiry, and as he began to make his plea for witnesses the scene panned out and was replaced by the stills of the reconstructed face of their victim. Blown up and backlit, the result looked spectacular.

Someone just has to recognise this woman, Hunter thought.

DAY FOURTEEN

Hunter didn't hear Grace approaching, his thoughts were elsewhere and he jumped as she slapped a fresh sheet of paper on top of the small pile of vehicle enquiry forms he was scrutinising. The paperwork had been left on his desk from the previous day's tasks and he was checking if all the outstanding enquiries had been completed before he handed them over.

'Come on. Get your lazy butt in gear, we've got a prime witness to interview.' Grace stabbed at the pink form she had deposited across his papers. As Hunter started to read, she snatched it up. 'Isobel from the HOLMES team has just handed this to me. She said it's the breakthrough we've been after.'

Hunter tried to grab back the paper Grace was waving but she spun quickly away, snatching her jacket from the back of her seat. She fixed him a look. 'What are you waiting for?'

Hunter picked up his coat and wrestled the car keys out from a pocket before following Grace out of the office.

'Are you going to tell me what we've got then?' Hunter asked as he swung the CID car out through the gates of the station's rear yard. 'All you've said so far is drive to the hospital.'

Grace pulled down the passenger visor and checked her make-up. She smoothed a hand across her nose and cheek before turning to Hunter. 'We're off to see a junior doctor, name of —' she took a quick glance at the paperwork — 'Chris Chambers. He works on Medical Ward Three at the General. Isobel says he rang in last night after the news and he's certain he knows who our victim is.'

Taking the back roads through the woods, Hunter was able to push the car faster than the speed limit because there was no traffic, so he made the hospital in just over quarter of an hour. He parked the car in one of the mortuary visiting bays, took the POLICE VISITING card from out of the glove box, slid it on top of the dash and then he and Grace took a rear entrance to the lifts. They knew the hospital layout like the backs of their hands.

'Ward Three you say?' said Hunter, pressing the lift button.

Grace double-checked the document and nodded.

They rode the lift in silence. It squealed and juddered up the two floors before opening up to a directional sign for the ward they wanted. They followed colour-coded tramlines along the corridor, taking a sharp left when the yellow line peeled off from the red.

Medical Ward Three lay behind a set of closed doors, behind which Hunter could hear a commotion and he wondered what was happening. After dispensing a large dollop of antiseptic handwash, he opened the doors with his shoulder as he cleansed his hands. He entered a world of chaos, bustle and raised voices and it stopped him in his tracks. Everything seemed to be happening behind a screen around one of the beds.

He exchanged looks with Grace and shrugged, before branching away to the nurse's station. That was busy too.

After a few seconds, Hunter caught the attention of an auburn haired, plump woman, dressed in dark blue. Her name badge identified her as the ward sister. He flashed his warrant card. 'I bet the last people you want to see right now is us?' he said, nodding towards the commotion.

The sister sighed. 'They brought in a twenty-two-year-old girl in the middle of the night, suffered a stroke just after she'd had a baby. Looks like we've just lost her.'

Hunter gave a sympathetic look as he returned his ID to his wallet. 'We contacted the hospital this morning. We were told a Dr Chambers would be on duty.'

'That's right. He's behind the screen.'

Hunter and Grace took another look down the ward.

'We need to speak with him, I'm afraid,' said Grace, returning her attention to the ward sister. 'We can disappear for half an hour for a coffee and then come back.'

'Is it urgent?'

'Could be. He contacted us last night.'

'Okay, just give him twenty minutes. It looks as though we can't do anything else for her anyway. They've been working on her for over ten minutes now, he'll be calling time soon and should be out in a bit.' Her response to the young girl's death seemed matter-of-fact, devoid of any feeling. Hunter guessed her job was very much like his — in times of crisis you remove the emotion in order to cope.

They had just taken a seat in the sister's vacant office when Dr Chambers tracked them down. Dressed in a light blue, open necked shirt tucked into a pair of jeans, he looked very young. In fact, if it hadn't been for his nametag and the stethoscope draped around his neck Hunter would never have guessed he was a doctor. He remembered Grace mentioning he was a junior but this guy didn't even look like he'd started shaving yet.

The doctor shook their hands and dropped into a seat, beckoning them to two seats next to a filing cabinet.

'We'll try not to take up too much of your time, we can see how busy you are,' opened Grace.

'A bit like your job, eh? No rest for the wicked.' The doctor ruffled his fingers through his light brown hair, leaned back in his seat and crossed his legs. 'Is this about my phone call last night?'

'You left a message that you think you know who the victim is?' Grace passed across one of the colour photographs of the facial reconstruction.

The doctor accepted it and took a long, lingering look, then nodded. 'The guy on TV said this is the girl found at the bottom of Barnwell lake, right?' He sounded nervous.

'Yes, a couple of weeks ago. She was murdered and dumped there.'

'Shocking. Truly shocking.' He shook his head.

'Do you recognise her?'

'Well, it certainly resembles a girl I used to go out with. Samia. But I can't believe it, she's such a lovely girl — or was, if it's her.'

'Samia?'

'Yes, Samia Hassan. She lives, or rather she used to live, with her parents in Hoyland before we went out together.'

'Are you certain? That photo is just a facial reconstruction. She was in a bit of a mess because of how long she'd been in the water,' said Hunter.

'It definitely looks like Samia. Has anyone else phoned in — her family, or maybe her friends?'

'You're the first.' Hunter paused, gathering his thoughts. 'You said you used to go out with her?'

'We were at Sheffield Uni together. I was doing my last year when she came. A group of us hooked up with her and her mates on rag week. That's how we met.'

'When was this?'

'Year before I started my doctor's training — 2006.'

'Do you know how old she was then?'

The doctor thought for a moment. 'I'm 23 now so I would have been 21 back then,' he appeared to be talking to himself. 'She would have been 18 or 19.' He paused and then said. 'We went out for a short time. Well, until we had all that bother.'

Hunter glanced at Grace.

'Bother?' said Hunter.

'Yeah from her cousins. As I say, we met on rag week. We got chatting. She was doing her first-year medicine and she wanted to know what to expect. We just hit it off, you know. After that she'd come round to my place from time to time to borrow some notes and chat through stuff. After a couple of months, I asked her to go out for a meal and she agreed. I was in student accommodation and she was in halls of residence and she started staying at mine on a regular basis. Sometimes even at weekends when she should have gone home. That's when the trouble started.'

'What trouble?'

'Let me just give you some background. Samia's parents are Pakistani but she was English. She told me they owned a shop in Hoyland and lived in the flat upstairs. She had her heart set on being a doctor but they continually badgered her to go to Pakistan for an arranged marriage to her cousin. Apparently, the only way they allowed her to come to university was because she promised she would go to Pakistan to meet the cousin during the summer break. She was dreading it because she had never been to Pakistan in her life and didn't want to marry any cousin. She'd seen a photograph of him and he was a lot older than her — in his thirties, I think she said — and she didn't know him or fancy him. I heard her a few times on her mobile having a row with her father about wanting the freedom to choose who she wanted to marry.'

'What about the trouble?'

'That was about a year ago. I had just finished uni and started my medical training. I got a newer flat and she moved in with me. She didn't tell her parents because she knew it would cause problems, though she had told them she was seeing me. They had another blazing row. They were threatening to disown her and said she was bringing shame on the family and should marry the cousin in Pakistan. I know it upset her a great deal. She tried to speak with her mother a few times but her mother would hang up.

'Then one night we had just come out of this bar and this car pulls up. Two Asian guys get out and just set about me, gave me a right hiding. They tried to drag Samia into the car, but there were quite a few people about that we knew, thank God, and they intervened and phoned the police. The two guys took off before the cops arrived. Samia told me they were relatives, she'd seen them before at her house. She didn't like them. She said one of them had been in trouble with the police. I was going to make a complaint but she persuaded me not and said she'd sort it. She guessed it was because her parents had found out about us sharing a flat.'

'So, you never made a complaint?'

'I wanted to. My face was in a right mess. I couldn't work for a couple of days and I got a rollicking from my consultant for turning up to work all bruised. Said I didn't set the right image for a doctor.'

'Was that the end of it?'

'Christ, no. There was a couple more. One night we came home and the flat was trashed, and I mean trashed. Everything was in pieces and they had cut up all of Samia's clothes.'

'Did you report that?'

'I did that time. I had to, for the insurance. We told the police about Samia's relatives, but there were no witnesses, and they didn't find any evidence to connect them, so that was that. The final straw came when I was on lates one day. I finished my shift just before midnight and I was walking across the hospital car park when the same two guys grabbed me. They'd wrecked my car. One of them got me by the throat and told me in no uncertain terms I had to finish with Samia or I'd end up at the bottom of a lake. Those were his exact words.'

DCI Dawn Leggate's alarm woke her at 6.30 a.m. and despite having only had five and a half hours sleep, it had been undisturbed and she felt remarkably refreshed. As she brushed her teeth, she could already feel a buzz as she thought about her day. She always felt like this when a big investigation was running.

She made herself coffee, put bread from the freezer into the toaster and dialled Alex McBride's mobile.

From his voice she could tell she'd woken him and she apologised when he said it had been 2 a.m. before he'd finally got to bed. She offered to ring him later, but he responded by telling her he needed to be up to brief his team.

'I've got an early briefing as well, and I just wondered if you had any update from things your end?'

He brought her up to date on the Bellshill murder and told her he was sending over two detectives from his team to join her briefing.

Entering the office, Dawn saw several new boards had been set up. The Glasgow city centre and Bellshill murders had a board each, abutted onto the Killin enquiry. Already, the important components of the investigation were on there. Looking them over, she rubbed her hands. The compilation, which included the three victims' names, addresses, witnesses, timelines and photographs, now took over the entire frontage of the room.

She checked the three timelines — the handwriting was wonderfully neat, a rarity among police officers. Also attached were copies of the gruesome Scenes of Crime shots, plus crime scene locations and maps of each of the surrounding areas. Her eyes moved from log to log. Everything was here. Thorough updates on those charts kept them all in touch with the case. The information they contained invariably pointed them in the direction of the perpetrator. Dawn made a mental note to find out who'd made the effort and congratulate them.

She double-checked the contents and recollected the notes she had made during her phone call with DI McBride, the morning's briefing was going to be intense.

She opened her journal, picked up a dry-erase pen and added a couple more notes to the boards, doing her best to replicate the script. Stepping back for one final look, she saw that the link to each case was the stolen silver BMW, presently with forensics.

Ten minutes later, standing in front of the incident boards, Dawn waited for her team to finally settle down. She could tell they were fired up. It had been a long time since they had been involved in a major joint investigation and the fact that each of the victims had been one of their own would make them even more determined to catch the culprit.

She banged a hand on the nearest board. 'Guys, we've got a busy day ahead of us, lots of work to do, so give me your eyes and ears for the next half hour.' Then, pointing to the furthermost panel, she continued, 'Firstly, our own Killin enquiry. Ross McNab, aged sixty-four, and his wife, sixty-three, were murdered on the afternoon of the thirty-first of August, at their isolated bungalow. As you know they were both beaten and Ross was tortured prior to his death. Everything about that scene indicates that more than one person was involved in their deaths.

'A sharp instrument, most probably a knife, was used to remove three fingers from Ross's right hand and those have not been found. It looks as though the killers took them from the scene and then left behind a box of fish fingers with a handwritten note which stated —' she paused and glanced at a photograph of the message recovered next to Ross McNab's body — '"These are to replace the missing ones." Before the killers left, they set fire to Mrs McNab using an accelerant. The PM indicates that she was still alive when they lit her.'

Dawn paused for maximum effect. She scanned the detectives' faces again. 'A woman walking her dog in nearby fields spotted smoke coming from the bungalow and called the fire brigade. The same woman also spotted a silver BMW driving along a track close to the scene. She had seen this car earlier driving around the village and thankfully had noted its number because she thought it was acting suspiciously. The resulting fire has damaged forensics but we might be lucky with the note and box of fish fingers. As you all know Ross was a retired detective. He retired thirteen years ago in 1995.'

Dawn took a side-step. 'Okay, moving on.' She stabbed a finger below one of the scenes of crime photos depicting a battered face, barely recognisable as a man's. 'Alistair McPherson, sixty-one years, another retired cop, was found beaten to death near a subway close to Sauchiehall Street, at 7.50 p.m., on the 27th of August. We have him on CCTV coming out of Lauders bar on that street ten minutes prior to his body being discovered. A very small time-frame.

'CCTV also picked up several sightings of our silver BMW driving in and around Sauchiehall Street before and after the attack. The images have been enhanced but both the driver and passenger had their visors down and so there are no clear images of their faces. What we can distinguish, however, is that it is not the two young men we have trapped in the cells.'

Dawn moved back from the second board. 'Finally —' she slapped her hand over several photographs taken from different angles, of an elderly man slumped in a carver type chair — 'Donald Wilson, a retired DS, 69 years old. His body was discovered two days ago in the lounge of his home at Bellshill. His hands had been nail-gunned to the arms of his chair and there was an iron burn mark in the centre of his chest. His throat had also been cut. The pathologist has indicated he was killed approximately two weeks ago. The body had early stages of decomposition. The silver BMW on false plates, which we have recovered, belonged to him.'

Dawn studied the faces of her team — they were focused. 'There are two links to all these three killings, firstly the BMW owned by Donald Wilson, which was stolen from outside his house and which has been sighted around the locations of the other two murders. The two young men, Sandie Aitkinson and Bruce McColl, who were caught driving it, have form but it's petty stuff and one of them has a cast-iron alibi for the Killin murder. They are sticking to their story, that they found it parked up with the keys on the front passenger seat and we can't knock that. By the end of play this afternoon the Procurator Fiscal has indicated we should bail them.'

Dawn was in full flow now. 'There is another incident involving the BMW but I don't know if that is linked yet or not. On the 24th of August, three days before the murder of Alistair McPherson, it was involved in a hit and run in North

Yorkshire. The driver and his wife were injured in that accident and we have discovered from statements that they have Scottish surnames.'

Dawn hadn't told the team about her telephone conversation with the man who had called himself Jock Kerr. That was one enquiry she and her sergeant were going to follow up personally. 'Coincidence or not, we will be looking into that as one of the actions. The other link, as you all now realise, is that they are all retired detectives who at one time worked out of Shettlestone CID. The key tasks which are being pushed out from this briefing are related to that. I want to know the relationship, working or otherwise, that these three had and what jobs they worked on together. There are checks to be done with Personnel and the Retired Police Officers' Association. I want everyone traced who knew these three. I am convinced our answer lies in their past associations. I want the evil bastards who did this trapped up as soon as possible.'

DAY FIFTEEN

Hunter left the station locker room after a shower and change of clothing. He rolled his neck and flexed his trapezius. He felt tight but sharp after an intense training session and three-mile run into work.

He'd risen a good hour earlier than normal, promising Beth before he left that he'd get a flyer and take the boys to their football coaching session that evening. Then he headed to his dad's boxing gym where he'd let himself in and trained alone. He'd spent twenty minutes working the punch-bag, twenty minutes pushing weights, and ten minutes doing sit-ups before locking up and running into work.

As he passed the Detective Superintendent's open door, he saw his boss at his desk.

'Morning, boss,' Hunter greeted him as he passed.

He had only gone a few yards when Michael Robshaw called out, 'Hunter, have you got five minutes?'

'Sure.' He stepped into the tidy office and stood by the desk. The Detective Superintendent was writing a memo on the front of a CPS file. Behind him, warm light cascaded through a huge window, backlighting the SIO. His reflection bounced off the surface of his polished desk. Hunter glanced around the room. It was plush and organised — just what he'd like to aspire to, he thought.

Robshaw signed off his paperwork with a flourish, clicked the top onto his fountain pen and laid it square across his jotter. He slipped off his spectacles and lined them straight, alongside his pen. Raising his head, he regarded Hunter seriously. 'I've had a complaint about you.'

Hunter looked puzzled. 'A complaint about me! What am I supposed to have done now?'

'David Paynton ring any bells?'

Hunter took a long, hard look at his boss. The last thing he wanted was to give him any bullshit. He'd known the Superintendent far too long, and trusted and respected him too much to pass off an answer which would be an insult to his intelligence. When Hunter was a fledgling detective constable, Michael Robshaw had been his DI. Robshaw had achieved his current status because of his ability to juggle the management of many successful teams as well as handle the politics which came with his rank. Hunter also knew him personally — they had trained together at his dad's gym and they had run together many times during lunch-breaks.

He settled for, 'What's he said I've done?'

The Detective Superintendent interlinked his fingers. 'Apparently, you and one other, and I'm guessing from the description that the one other was Barry, waylaid him in the pub a few nights ago and gave him the third degree about your father's hit and run. Says you were trying to fit him up with it.'

'Just a minute, boss, I never…'

Unlocking his fingers, Robshaw held up a hand. 'I'm not going to quiz you on what you did or didn't say to David Paynton. I'm here to tell you to lay off him. He's flagged as part of an ongoing drug squad operation. He's giving them a couple of major players knocking out cocaine, so they want him around. Besides, I can tell you he definitely wasn't involved. I got a call from North Yorks police late yesterday afternoon. It would appear the silver BMW involved in your parents' road accident has been found in Scotland on false plates and two young thieves are locked up for aggravated vehicle taking. I suggest you give them a call.'

Robshaw handed over a post-it with a telephone number. 'That's the officer in North Yorkshire who's dealing with the incident.' He leaned back in his chair. 'Hunter, you're a great cop, don't put your career in jeopardy for that little shit, and besides you've still got an unsolved murder here to focus on.'

The morning briefing focused on Hunter and Grace's meeting with junior doctor, Chris Chambers.

Perched on the corner of his desk, nursing his second cup of tea, Hunter repeated, almost word for word, what Dr Chambers had said. In addition, the doctor had given them the names of some of Samia's close friends from university who would need chasing up. And the doctor had also made time to do a composite e-fit of the two Asian men who had beaten and threatened him.

Printed copies of the computer-generated images, together with a note stapled to them — stating that the doctor had confirmed they were good likenesses — had been waiting on his desk that morning. Hunter handed them around as he briefed, but he could tell that no one recognised the pair.

Overnight, the HOLMES team had done background checks on the address of Samia's parents. There were three incidents logged — all 999 calls requesting police attendance for detained shoplifters. A voter's check listed Samia Hassan at that address, along with her father, Mohammed, and mother, Jilani. There was no record of her being reported missing.

'We don't know what we are walking into today,' Hunter concluded. 'The doc is convinced our body from the lake is his ex, Samia Hassan, but no one else has called us about her being missing, including her parents, so we don't know what kind of reception we're going to get when we visit. Grace and I will do a softly-softly approach and check out if she is still living there, or if not, if they have heard from her recently. We'll meet back after lunch for a scrum-down once we've done the visit.'

Hassan's convenience store was nestled between a hairdresser's and a small post office on one of the arterial roads leading into the small town of Hoyland. It had only taken Hunter and Grace ten minutes to drive there.

As they entered the brightly-lit store, the first thing that hit Hunter was the pleasant aroma of spicy food.

To their immediate left, a long counter spanned the frontage. An Asian man, who appeared to be in his early fifties, was working behind it. Hunter looked him over. The man was slightly smaller than he was and overweight, a well-rounded stomach strained the bottom buttons of his blue and white striped shirt and sagged over his trousers. Thick black hair skirted the sides of his head, but he was bald on top. His most striking feature was his hooked nose.

Hunter thought of the image of Samia — if this was her father, then she didn't get her looks from him. He surveyed the shop. Most of the brightness came from overhead fluorescent lighting. It was set out like a miniature version of a supermarket, with well-packed shelves of fresh produce, tinned and packet foods. The back shelves were stacked floor to ceiling with wines, beers and spirits, and close to the door newspapers and magazines took up the remainder of the space. There was a large flat-screen TV suspended behind the counter, its screen split into six sections, each showing a different part of the store. The CCTV images were of good clarity for a change, Hunter thought. He made a mental note; they might need that to back-check footage.

'Mr Hassan — Mohammed Hassan?' Grace said.

The man greeted them with a cheery smile, suspicion in his eyes.

'Don't worry, we're not selling anything.' Grace showed her warrant card.

He looked surprised and nodded.

'Mr Hassan, we're just making some enquiries regarding an investigation we have running. We're trying to track down people who we think might be of help and a witness has given us your daughter's name, Samia. Is she around?'

Good start, Grace, thought Hunter, focusing on the man's face. Watching and listening was just as important as talking when it came to interviews, and having a partner who was on the same wavelength was a big advantage.

The man looked down for a second or two, enough for Hunter to realise Grace had hit a nerve.

'Samia? Er no, she's not here.' He stumbled over his words.

'Do you happen to know where she is?'

Hunter became conscious of someone moving at the back of the store. Into view appeared a slim, petite Asian woman, dressed in a peacock blue sari. She ambled towards them and despite being older she bore a remarkable likeness to the photograph of the facial reconstruction. There was no doubt this was Samia's mother. She was talking rapidly in her mother tongue as she approached.

Mr Hassan responded in the same language. The conversation lasted for a good thirty seconds.

Hunter could only pick out the words 'police' and 'Samia'.

Grace said, 'Mr Hassan, could you speak in English please?'

He turned to Grace. 'Sorry about that. My wife doesn't speak any English. I told her you were making enquiries about Samia. She wants to know what type of enquiries you are making?'

'There is no easy way to say this, Mr Hassan, but we are concerned as to her whereabouts.'

Mr Hassan's eyes shifted again and he shared a glance with his wife. Her eyes were wide and searching. There was a slight delay in his response. 'Why are you concerned?'

'Well, we're trying to track her down but we don't know where she is.'

Mrs Hassan started chattering unintelligibly again. Her husband replied, his hands animated.

'Mr Hassan, if you wouldn't mind?' checked Grace.

'Sorry,' he apologised, 'my wife is asking what is going on — why are the police here?'

'Do you know where your daughter is?'

'Of course I do, she is in Pakistan.'

'In Pakistan,' said Hunter. 'Are you sure about that, Mr Hassan?'

'Of course I am. Why are you asking me these questions about my daughter?'

'As my colleague has already said, we have concerns about her whereabouts.'

'Who has said these things? Who is causing us this trouble?'

'No one is causing you any trouble, Mr Hassan. All we are here for is to check on your daughter's whereabouts,' continued Hunter.

'She is in Pakistan.'

'Where in Pakistan?' said Grace.

'She is staying with my family.'

'Where?'

'Look, what is this all about. All you keep telling me is that you have concerns about her. What concerns?'

'That she might have come to some harm.'

'My daughter has not come to any harm. She is with my family.'

Hunter looked from the man to his wife. Something was not right between them but he did not want to damage the enquiry at this early stage. 'Mr Hassan, we're not here to cause you and your wife any anguish, it's just that a close friend of hers has not seen her for a while and has not been able to get hold of her and therefore reported it to us because they thought it was unusual,' he lied. 'Now, if you can just give us a little more information as to where she is, so that we can contact her, it would be a great help.'

After a short delay, Mr Hassan answered. 'You won't be able to get hold of her, it's a small village in the mountains. My family do not have a phone. It is not like it is here in England. They are quite poor. They have to walk miles to the nearest town.'

'What about your daughter, did she not take her mobile?'

After a hesitation, he replied, 'It will not work in the mountains.'

'When did she go to Pakistan?' interrupted Grace. 'And where did she go from?'

'I can't remember the exact date. It was about two months ago. She flew to Lahore from London. I can't remember if it was Gatwick or Heathrow.'

Grace scribbled some notes in her notebook. With a warm fake smile, she said, 'Thank you for that. That's a big help.'

'Mr Hassan, just one final thing before we leave you in peace,' Hunter said. 'It's just a procedural thing, but in all cases where someone reports something like this to us, we have to check physically for ourselves that they haven't come to any harm in their own home. You do understand, don't you? We would be heavily criticised by our bosses if we didn't do that check.'

There was an uneasy silence for the best part of twenty seconds. Mr Hassan glanced down, seemed to be checking his hands, then shot a glance at his wife before turning his attention to Hunter. 'I don't suppose we have any choice.'

'It's not a matter of choice, it would just help us with our enquiries. We'd be able to report back to our bosses that we're okay with everything.' Hunter dished out his own fake smile.

Mr Hassan spoke to his wife in their language, to which she responded with a loud huff and made an exaggerated gesture of throwing part of her sari back over her shoulder before turning and making for the back of the shop.

'My wife is not happy with this interference. We are very private people. We have not done anything wrong.'

'We're not accusing you of anything, it's just a formality we have to go through,' Hunter replied. 'If you can just show us Samia's room, then we'll leave you.'

Mr Hassan locked up the shop, turned the sign to 'closed' and pointed them through to the rear.

The entranceway at the back led them into a small, dimly lit stairway. It was cooler back here. Beyond, Hunter could see a large breeze-blocked room full of boxed goods, obviously the store room.

Bare wooden stairs led up to a door marked private and beyond it they found themselves in a lavishly carpeted hallway. There were five doors off the hall. A couple were open and Hunter could make out the lounge and what appeared to be a kitchen area. He guessed the other three rooms were the bathroom and two bedrooms.

'This is Samia's old room,' said Mr Hassan, pushing open one of the closed doors.

Hunter and Grace followed him inside. The room looked more like a guest room than someone's bedroom. It was devoid of any personal effects. There had been pictures or photographs hung up at one time, judging by the marks on the wall. The bed had a duvet draped over it, but the duvet cover and bottom sheet had been removed and were neatly folded and lay across the pillows. It looked like it had not been slept in for some time. Against one wall was a bare chest of drawers and next to the window on the back wall was a wardrobe.

Hunter slipped past Mr Hassan and moved towards it. 'Do you mind?' he asked, but didn't wait for an answer.

He looked inside. The wardrobe was empty, except for a few wire coat hangers dangling from a metal rail. Next, he checked the chest of drawers, tugging open the bottom drawer first. Moving up, Hunter slid out the next three drawers, asking background questions of Mr Hassan as he went along — how long had he and his wife owned the business? How long had they been resident in this country? Which region of Pakistan did they come from? What was the name of the village where the family lived and the place and date of Samia's birth? He tried to make the questions sound unimportant, making a mental note of the answers to keep the man at ease.

Pushing all four empty drawers back into place, Hunter straightened and did another scan of the room, gaining a mental picture for his next visit, which he knew would not be too long away. This room is soulless, he thought. Things were definitely not right, but they couldn't move too fast under the circumstances. He had to be patient — make the enquiries first and cover all angles.

'Did your daughter take all her belongings with her? Did she not leave anything behind?'

'My daughter has gone to join my family back in Pakistan. If you want to know, she has gone to marry my cousin out there and make a new life for herself.'

While Hunter had been checking out the bedroom with Mr Hassan, Grace had slipped away. He found her in the lounge with Mrs Hassan. She was trying to talk to Samia's mother but the woman was having none of it, repeating 'No speak English.'

This would be a good time to withdraw and plan the next steps.

'Well, Mr Hassan, thank you for your time. You have been most helpful. You have put our minds at ease I'm sure this can be sorted out now.'

'I hope it can, officer, I hope it can,' the shopkeeper responded.

Hunter and Grace sat in the CID car. He had started the engine but not yet set off, just sat running his hands around the steering wheel, staring out through the windscreen, not focused on anything in particular.

'Are you thinking what I'm thinking?' he asked.

'You bet I am. It is Samia we've found in the lake, isn't it?'

Hunter nodded in agreement. 'Having just done that search and watching Mr Hassan and his wife while you were talking, I'm convinced that they're either responsible for or involved in her death. We've got some digging to do to match our hunch.'

The Major Investigation Team regrouped at 2 p.m., the meeting called by DS Michael Robshaw who had sat with the HOLMES team as updates came in. Information had come in thick and fast and for the first time since the investigation had started, he could see a clear picture emerging as to where the enquiry was heading.

The timeline sequence on the incident board had been brought up to date, with the addition of new photographs. Only ten minutes earlier, DC Isobel Stevens, the HOLMES manager, had added information ready for the meeting.

Michael Robshaw took a look at the board and slipped off his glasses. 'Okay, guys. Firstly, well done everyone, you've made some significant inroads this morning. As a result of your feedback from the tasks you were given, we now believe we know who our victim is.' He folded his spectacles and popped then into his shirt pocket. 'Hunter, you and Grace have been to see Samia Hassan's parents. Would you tell the team what you have learned?'

Hunter scooted out his chair beneath his desk and faced the squad. 'As you know, Samia's parents, Mohammed and Jilani Hassan, are the owners of a convenience store in Hoyland. They have lived there for the past 15 years and have been resident in this country for 24 years.' He glanced at his scribbled notes. 'Samia was born here 21 years ago, on the 25th of July, 1984.'

As accurately as he could, Hunter recounted the morning's visit to the Hassans, only occasionally reading from his notes.

'I managed to tease out of him that the place where he says Samia has gone. It is a very small village set in the foot of the mountains, twenty miles from a town called Sul Banda. It's in the North East of Punjab, at least a day's journey from Lahore. He says the cousin she has married is also called Mohammed. He was edgy but I think that was because of us. I'm pretty sure he hasn't seen yesterday's news bulletins. If he had, he would have been far more guarded. However, from now on, there is no doubt he will be, especially when he sees this week's local newspaper.'

'You did a cursory search as well?' asked Robshaw.

'Yeah, without making it too obvious.' Hunter recounted what he had done. 'There is nothing left in that flat to indicate Samia ever lived there. All her personal effects have gone and there are no photos of her anywhere. Grace managed to check out the lounge as I was looking over Samia's room and there were no pictures of her there either. It's like she never existed.'

Robshaw thanked him, taking back the briefing. He turned to Detective Sergeant Mark Gamble, supervisor of Syndicate Two. 'Mark, will you input your team's info?'

Gamble made his way to the incident board. Three new photos had been added, shots of Samia Hassan with a group of girls of similar age. They were smiling, happy images and from the background lighting and red-eye effect it looked as if they had been taken either in a pub or nightclub. The pictures of Samia bore a striking likeness to the facial reconstruction done by Frankie Oliver.

This just has to be our lady from the lake, Hunter thought.

'My team were given the job of tracking down the girls named by Dr Chambers during her time at Sheffield University. We have so far caught up with four of her closest friends. They all describe her as a very bubbly, intelligent girl. Two of the girls shared rooms with her for several months, prior to her moving in with the doc. She discussed much of her relationship with all of them at some point and there is no doubt she had formed quite a good relationship with Dr Chambers.

'Her friends said everything changed when Samia told her parents about that relationship. Mr and Mrs Hassan completely disapproved, and one of the girls recalled that one Friday afternoon, both her mother and father turned up at the flat they were sharing and had a stand-up row with Samia and tried to get her to come home, which she refused to do. She saw Mr Hassan smack Samia across the face. After that visit Samia was in floods of tears. She said her parents were threatening to disown her because she had brought shame on the family.'

Gamble leaned against the panel. 'All of them mentioned the attack on Dr Chambers by two Asian men. It happened one Friday night, just as they had all come out of a wine bar near the university. The girls confirm it was unprovoked. The guys appeared from nowhere in their car, jumped out and attacked him. One of the men tried to drag Samia into their car. They describe it as an old battered white Corsa.

'Anyway, the girls bravely went to Samia's aid and managed to attract a crowd, so the guys backed off and drove away. The police were called but Samia persuaded the doc not to make an official report and said she would sort it out. She later told the girls the two men were her cousins. They confirm the damage to the doctor's flat as well, and they have confirmed that the e-fits which the doc has done are very good likenesses of the two men.'

Gamble tapped the three new photos on the board. 'These pictures are from Samia's Facebook page. They were posted after she had finished uni. She kept in touch with all four girls and occasionally phoned them. They all say she was down, that her parents were continually pestering her to marry a cousin who lived back in Pakistan and that she didn't want to. The last contact anyone had with her was on the 29th of July. They have tried phoning her but it goes straight through to voicemail. We have the number to see if the "techies" can put a trace on it. We've also posted messages on her Facebook page but that's not been updated since the 29th either.'

Robshaw puffed out his chest, took out his spectacles, wiped them with a handkerchief and put them on. 'Thanks everyone, the case has moved on with some real momentum today and I think we all know where it is going. I have no doubt that we are dealing with an honour killing here. I'm sure you have drawn the same conclusion. Because of the sensitivity and the repercussions it could have, I want a sealed lid on this. No one discusses anything outside this room. Everything we get from here on we follow up with the utmost discretion, just on the off-chance that we might have got this completely wrong. I want no backlash.'

Robshaw turned to the incident board and the list of actions he had written. Looking back to the room, he said, 'Okay everyone, these are the tasks and there are quite a few. The majority are phone calls and will involve diplomacy and patience from you guys. For some of these enquiries you will have to go through the British Embassy in Pakistan and Interpol, okay?'

He checked the first bullet point he had written. 'First on the list, we will need to check if she was ever on any flight out of this country into Lahore. We will also have to check with Border Control here and in Pakistan, and we need to check the Passport Agency to see if Samia was ever issued with a passport. And now we have Samia's details I want another check done of local dentists here and in Sheffield, to see if we can come up with an identical match to our body. I also want triangulation done of her phone — see if we can pinpoint where her last call was made from. Finally —' he tapped the two e-fit images on the incident panel — 'I want a check of the intelligence system and I want these faxed to surrounding forces. We need to find out who these two are. My guess is these are the guys our witness Kerri-Ann Bairstow saw dumping the body off the jetty.' He put his hands on his hips, taking in a deep breath. 'When we have got all those answers

— and only when — we go and pay an official visit to the Hassans.'

Hunter pulled his sons' sports bags from the boot of his car as Jonathan and Daniel bolted from the back seat and into the house. As he slammed down the tailgate, he saw they had left the car doors wide open and was about to call them back when Beth shouted from inside the house, 'Dirty boots off now,' and 'Jonathan, where have I told you to put them?'

He smiled and shut the doors himself. *Typical lads.*

Hunter had managed to leave work shortly after four and he was glad. It meant he could take the boys to their football coaching session. He enjoyed it, especially the final twenty minutes when the session ended with a 'dads against lads' kick-about. It reminded him of the days when he'd played regularly for a Sunday pub team in his 20s. The last time he had been able to play with any regularity was two years ago — weekly five-a-side games while he was in the Drug Squad.

He walked indoors to find Beth at the bottom of the stairs bawling up to emptiness, 'Put your smelly clothes in the wash basket the pair of you and then get in the shower. I'll be up in ten minutes to dry you off. And no putting on SpongeBob SquarePants until you've done that!'

Hunter closed the front door with his heel. As it slammed shut Beth spun round and glared. He held up his son's sports bags. 'What?' he said, trying to suppress a smirk. 'I've got my hands full.'

'You're as bad as they are. How am I supposed to get them to treat the house with respect if you won't take any notice?'

He put on his best scolded-boy look and leaned in to plant a kiss on her cheek.

She held him off with her hand, breaking into a smile. 'You stink as well. You can have a shower before you come anywhere near me. Here, give me the bags. I'll sort them out, and for your sins you sort out the boys.'

She relieved him of the sports bags and he gave her bottom an affectionate tap before sprinting up the stairs.

'You're not too big to feel the back of my hand yourself, Hunter Kerr!' Beth shouted as he arrived at the first of the boy's bedrooms, bundling up Jonathan's discarded football kit and confining it to the wash basket.

Fifteen minutes later, clean and refreshed and dressed in jogging bottoms and T-shirt, Hunter skipped into the large dining-kitchen, a rear extension of their three-bedroom semi.

Beth was taking a hot dish from the oven. He slid behind her, wrapped his hands around her waist and nuzzled the nape of her neck.

'Smells good.'

'Home-made lasagne.'

'Hmm, yummy. Fancy a kir?'

'Oh, I'd love one Hunter. I've had a pig of a day. A man had a heart attack in the waiting room this morning. We managed to get his heart beating again, thank goodness, but by the time the ambulance came we were an hour behind with patients. And you can imagine that some of them were in a state themselves after witnessing it. I've been in catch-up mode all day.'

'And I think my day's been tough!'

Hunter took a bottle of wine from the fridge and two glasses from the cupboard, then placed a small amount of Frais des Bois liqueur into the glasses and added chilled Muscadet. He took a sip and savoured the crisp, cold fruitiness of the French aperitif.

He handed a glass to Beth before sliding into a chair at the farmhouse table that took centre-stage in their kitchen. Hunter ran his palm over the oak surface and remembered when they had bought the table. They'd spotted it in an antique shop when they'd spent a week in the Yorkshire Dales a few years ago. It was old and battered and only three of the chairs matched but they'd fallen in love with it and bought it on the spur of the moment. It was an ideal gift to one another and suited the shabby-chic appearance of the rest of the kitchen perfectly.

'I've left the boys in Jonathan's room. I said they could play on their Xbox until tea was ready,' he said. 'I called in at Mum and Dad's with the boys on the way back.'

'Oh yes, what did they have to say?'

'Mum was in on her own. I asked her where Dad was and she said he'd had to go back up to Scotland for a funeral.'

'Oh, that's sad. Anyone we know?'

'She mentioned a name, Archie something, but it didn't ring any bells.'

Beth stopped what she was doing and turned around. 'This is going somewhere, isn't it, Hunter? Come on, spit it out. I can read you like a book.'

'It was just the way she said it. She said it was an old friend of his — she couldn't remember his full name. I asked a few questions but I could tell she just wanted me to shut up.'

'Well, you've given your dad a hard time just recently.'

'And rightly so, after what went off. I saw him arguing with someone and he denied it. What am I supposed to do when he won't say anything? I know he's hiding something but I don't know what. Now this sudden disappearance up to Scotland — he's not been back there for years and years. In fact, come to think about it I can't ever remember him going back up there.'

'You're too suspicious, Hunter, do you know that? It could be a genuine funeral for all you know. Think about it, all your dad's pals from his past will be getting on in years now.'

'I can't help but feel that if I hadn't called in to see them it wouldn't have been mentioned.'

'I know what you're saying, Hunter, but there's nothing you can do about it, is there? He'll tell you when he's good and ready. Just give him some space.'

'There's something not right,' he muttered. 'I'm going to get to the bottom of this if it's the last thing I do.'

'Cop!' Billy almost upended his fish supper onto his lap as he fought frantically to pull his baseball cap down over his eyes.

'Where?' said Rab, sliding lower into the driver's seat.

'There!' growled Billy, pointing over the dashboard. He pulled the peak of his cap lower and, satisfied that he had hidden enough of his face, lifted his head and peered through the windscreen, watching the dark-haired man in the short grey overcoat leaning against the driver's door of a dark blue Vauxhall twenty yards up the road. The man was scanning the street and he shot a fleeting glance in their direction.

Rab went for the key in the ignition but Billy snapped a gloved hand around his wrist.

'No, just wait! I don't think he's spotted us.'

'How do you know he's a cop?'

'I saw him a couple of weeks ago at the bail hostel, talking to the supervisor.' He leaned forward to get a clearer view. 'I wonder what he's doing in this neck of the woods? Let's just wait a moment and see what he's up to. If he clocks us then we piss off.'

Billy leaned back in his seat and returned to his supper. He loaded a couple of chips into his mouth, his eyes not straying from the plain-clothes cop. Five minutes later a slim, dishevelled man, appeared from a side street opposite where the cop was waiting. He stood, looking around.

'Well, just look who it is.' Billy's eyelids screwed into hardened slits as the man strolled across the road and struck up a conversation with the detective. 'I wonder if we're on their agenda by any chance?'

The shabbily dressed man accepted a cigarette from the detective. Billy reached beneath his seat, grabbed hold of the wheel brace and began to slide it out. 'Once they've finished their cosy chat, you and I are going to have a wee word with our pal. I don't like it when people go behind my back.'

DAY SEVENTEEN

'What's the address again?' Hunter asked, pulling the car into the kerb. He had been driving around back streets, searching for their destination, for the past five minutes.

Grace handed across the note she'd written back in the office. They were following up yesterday afternoon's telephone call from Zita. She had got back to Hunter with the address of the Asian Women's Refuge and had fixed up a meeting with the owner.

They'd found the street easily enough — off the Wicker in Sheffield — but all the buildings looked the same, three-storey Victorian red-brick houses with dusty windows and soot encrusted frontages. At first glance, it looked like most of them were empty or used as storage for the small shops or last remnants of businesses which still operated in this run-down area, but given the absence of a number, and because the secret address would have no signage to advertise itself, finding it was proving extremely difficult.

'Give the woman a ring, will you, Grace? Tell her where we're parked and ask her to come out and make herself known, otherwise we'll be here all day.'

Grace reached into her handbag, took out her mobile and tapped in the telephone number from the note. Within seconds it was answered. Less than thirty seconds later, Grace ended the call and slipped the phone back into her bag.

'She'll be down in a minute. She's been watching us drive up and down from her office somewhere up above us, but because we're in an unmarked car she didn't come down.'

Hunter turned off the engine and, as he was parked on double-yellow lines, placed the 'police visiting' card on the dashboard.

A sharp rap on the front nearside door startled them. Hunter turned to see a middle-aged Asian woman crouched down looking in. She was smiling but half of her face was covered by a white cotton veil.

They got out of the car and introduced themselves to Nahida Perveen. She greeted them with an energetic shake of the hand.

She was dressed in a long, white cotton dress, embroidered with a gold neckline. Hunter could see she was tall and slender, though he still couldn't make out her features because of the veil.

'Sorry I didn't come down and make myself known. We have to be very careful here as you can guess. I forgot to ask Zita what you looked like and some of the husbands and fathers of the women who are staying here will do anything to find this place.' Her voice was perfect BBC English — not a hint of an accent.

The building she showed them into had an old but solid door badly in need of paint. The entranceway was gloomy, but Hunter could pick out detailed Victorian tiles covering the lower half of the hallway and the floor that told him this had once been a fine residence.

They followed Nahida up a stone stairway to the first floor where the lighting was better.

'We have ten ladies with us at present but I don't think any will make an appearance. They've gone through such a lot and have come here for safety until we can help them turn their lives around. They knew you were coming but you still won't see any of them. Some of them don't trust the police, unfortunately.' She led them to the top of the stairs, only occasionally looking back as she spoke.

Unlocking another solid-looking door, Nahida guided them along a corridor and through a door at the back of the building. It led to a sitting room, big and brightly lit, with a high ornate plaster ceiling, again in need of a fresh lick of paint. It was furnished with four sofas and three armchairs, draped with throws, though none of the fabrics matched. They were arranged around two low wooden coffee tables. The carpet was thin, stained and threadbare. The place had been furnished on a tight budget.

Nahida sat on one of the chairs and pointed to one of the sofas. Crossing one leg over the other and leaning back, the veil fell away and that was when Hunter saw her badly scarred face. A clump of pink leathery flesh marred the left side of her head.

'You're probably wondering how I got this scar?' she said.

Hunter concentrated on her warm brown eyes. He felt embarrassed. He had taken too long looking at her face and could feel his cheeks flush.

'Don't be embarrassed.' Nahida smiled. 'I've lived with this for almost twenty years. That's what made me set up this place.' She pulled back her cotton veil a fraction, enough for Hunter to see the full extent of her injuries. The scar wound its way from the side of her left eye, over her ear and down towards her jaw. A portion of her hair was missing. In its place was a lumpy piece of scarred flesh.

'My boyfriend did this with drain cleaning fluid — a powerful acid.' She re-covered her face. 'It ended my career. I was a TV news journalist working in London — an in-front-of-camera reporter.' She gave them an awkward smile. 'I'll not bog you down with the details because I know you're here on

147

other matters, but it's why I set up this place. The man who did this was chosen for me to marry. He came from my parents' village in Pakistan, was from a family who had been very good friends with them. My father and his father had been business partners before my parents came to live here.

'I'm British born and although I've been brought up with my parents' values, I quickly discovered that his values and culture were far stricter. I knew it wasn't going to work within weeks of meeting him. Firstly, he wanted me to pack in my job. He started to accuse me of flirting with my colleagues. After nine months, I told him I had taken enough and wouldn't be going through with the marriage.

'I left him one night when he was at work and went to stay with a friend. He started pestering me with phone calls, threatening me, so I changed my number. Then he'd turn up at work and security had to intervene. Anyway, one night we were celebrating a colleague's birthday in a bar and he turned up. He started accusing me of having an affair and then threw the cleaning fluid in my face. Fortunately, some quick thinking by my friends prevented me from serious injury — they poured drink all over me and used water from behind the bar, but it still left me with this.' She smoothed a finger over the scar. 'The police arrested him but he was given bail and fled back to Pakistan to his family. He's still on the run out there.' She shrugged. 'I continued my career as a journalist but it was all desk work. My editors didn't say as much but I realised my career in front of the camera was over and so I persuaded the company to make me redundant and I used the money to come up here where no one knew me, and to set up this place so that I could help protect other Asian women from what happened to me.'

'And have you been able to help many?' asked Grace.

'Hundreds over the years. Word of mouth and contacts through solicitors have made this a very popular place for women to turn their lives around.'

'And from what you've told Zita, I gather that you believe the women we've found in the lake contacted you for help, had made arrangements to come here but never turned up. And that you haven't been able to get hold of her since?' Hunter said.

'That's right. I've tried her mobile several times since our meeting and it went to voicemail. In fact, I rang it as late as yesterday and now it appears to be dead. Not only that, but I saw the reconstructed face on the news the other night and it looks remarkably like the girl who came to me for help. She told me her name was Samia.'

Hunter and Grace glanced at one another. Grace opened her folder and slid out an A4 colour copy of the facial reconstruction. She also took out pictures from Samia's Facebook page and slipped them across the coffee table.

'Is this the girl you met?' asked Grace.

Nahida lined up the photographs and picked up one which showed Samia holding a drink to camera. She scrutinised it for a few seconds before setting it back on the table. She tapped the photograph. 'This is definitely the Samia I met and spoke with.'

'When did she come here?'

'Oh, she never came here at all. She originally left a message on our answer machine and left her mobile number. It would have been a good six months or so ago now. I arranged to meet up with her at a coffee place at Meadowhall. It's a place I always use. It's public and it's busy. I also need to suss out the people I'm meeting with before they find out where we are. You wouldn't believe the tricks the husbands and parents pull to track down the girls who flee here. I have had people posing as police officers, social workers, solicitors — you name it, I've had to deal with it.' Nahida leaned forward, hands clasped. 'I suppose my job is a little bit like yours. When I meet up with the people who request my help, I have to sort out who is genuine and who is not.'

Hunter knew where she was coming from. He nodded.

'Can you remember what she said to you?' said Grace.

'Not word for word but I can give you the gist of our conversation.' She settled back. 'She wanted to get away from her parents but needed somewhere to hide while she sorted out somewhere permanent. She said her parents were putting pressure on her to go to Pakistan to marry a cousin out there and that she didn't want to. I told her I could help her out with that.

'Samia said she had been constantly watched since she finished university, her parents wanted to know virtually her every move. She felt she was being followed and mentioned two cousins. At our first meeting, she also gave me details of other problems she had encountered because of a relationship with a young doctor.

'At the end of that meeting I gave her a number of options, which included talking to the police as well as meeting me again. She felt she couldn't go to the police because she didn't want to get any of her family into trouble and felt it would just make things worse. She really just wanted to get away.'

'Did you meet again?'

'We did, but that didn't go to plan. She contacted me a couple of times beforehand and told me she couldn't get away without anyone knowing. Then right out of the blue, about six weeks ago, Samia rang me. She was on a train coming to Meadowhall and asked if I could meet her again at the coffee place just by Marks and Spencer. She was in a bit of a state when I finally got there. She was agitated, looking around. She made me nervous even though I've been involved in so many of these cases. I was really glad that there were a lot of people around.

'She'd managed to sneak out of the flat while her father was at the warehouse and she'd brought some things for me to store for her until she could get everything together and leave. She was in one hell of a state and I suggested she should come with me there and then. I said I could arrange with the police to pick up her other bits she needed later, but she didn't want anyone else to be involved. Especially not the police. I didn't want to leave her to do all that but she said everything would be okay, she was confident she could finish getting together the last of her things. She said she'd contact me and arrange to be picked up in a couple of days.'

'Can you remember when that was exactly?'

'It will be in my diary.'

Nahida got up and left the room. A few minutes later, she returned carrying a red knapsack and a large diary. She set the knapsack down on the coffee table, covering the photographs of Samia, then sat back in the chair, flicking open the book. Her roving finger drifted over several pages, checking each one before moving onto the next. After a couple of minutes she stabbed at a page. 'It was Monday the 28th of July,' she announced, looking across at Hunter and Grace. 'She was already at the coffee shop waiting for me.'

Hunter caught Grace's eye. Her friends had last reported speaking with Samia the day after — the 29th of July. Since that day on no one had heard from her.

Nahida closed her diary. 'From what I remember it was about half ten in the morning. As I said, she was really agitated.

She was convinced someone was following her. I said I could call security or the police if she wanted and I would bring her here, but she said it was only a feeling she had, that she hadn't seen anyone. Also, she wanted to pick up some final things before she left home permanently.' She leaned forward and tapped the red knapsack. 'This is what she asked me to keep safe for when she got here.'

Hunter pulled the bag towards him. 'Have you had a look inside?' he asked, unzipping the top.

Nahida shook her head.

The section he had opened contained items of clothing and he lifted out each piece in turn, laying them down across the coffee table. He counted out two pairs of jeans, four T-shirts, a hooded sweat top, several items of underwear and a pair of trainers.

He ran his hand around the inside lining, empty. He then switched his attention to the side pockets, where he found make-up and a few items of jewellery — a mix of expensive gold items, a bracelet, two necklaces and a pair of gold loop earrings, together with inexpensive costume jewellery, which consisted of various bead bracelets.

Finally, he zipped open the front and couldn't hide his surprise. With forefinger and thumb he removed the item and carefully placed it on the laid-out garments. It was a British passport. He opened up the back section for Grace and Nahida to see.

The personal details and photograph left them in no doubt that it belonged to Samia Hassan.

DAY EIGHTEEN

Jock Kerr poured himself a generous shot of Lagavulin.

Just a wee dram after a hard day in the gym.

He reclined in his captain's chair and propped his feet on the desk. Swilling the golden liquid around the crystal tumbler he cradled it against his upper chest, allowing the peaty aroma to tease his nostrils. In dream-like state, his gaze roamed around the room, surveying the many framed photos and promotional posters adorning the walls; memories of his past boxing career. Then the dream switched to nightmare as the vision of how it all finished tumbled into his thoughts.

Just when he'd been on the cusp of greatness, with a Commonwealth medal to his name, his prospects were ended prematurely with a single punch, thrown after the bell, which sliced open an irreparable deep wound above his right eye. At the tender age of 20 his career was over. That one punch had ended everything and landed him where he was now — in one hell of a mess.

Deep down, he knew some of it had been his own fault — if only he had known at the time what he was getting into.

Foresight is a wonderful thing.

Back then, he had been a young, naïve man with a living to make and his fists were the only tools of his trade. He'd even used that phrase to the two detectives who interviewed him three days ago in his native Scotland.

Detective Chief Inspector Dawn Leggate and Detective Sergeant John Reed had picked up Jock from Motherwell railway station and driven him to a quiet hotel where they'd questioned him in the empty bar. They said they'd chosen it because they did not want anyone to know he was back in Scotland. At first, they hadn't asked him about the three detectives who had been murdered, but whether he thought he had been followed on his journey. And they had driven a long, circuitous route to the hotel. Jock had watched the Detective Sergeant constantly checking his mirrors, satisfying himself that they did not have a tail.

That was when he had told them about the shaven-headed man in Staithes and the subsequent hit and run on the moors.

The DCI said it confirmed their worst fears.

They had talked for well over two hours, piecing everything together between them. Jock had been able to add much of the background to their investigation, and although initially he sensed the two detectives were suspicious of what he told them — he recognised the signs from his son — once they had double-checked his story with information on their briefing notes, they had ended the interview by thanking him for his help, which had significantly moved on their enquiry.

Before they dropped him back at the railway station, they had advised him about his personal safety and the DCI had given him her direct mobile number.

Time and time again during the past two days Jock had run through everything they had talked about — checking that he hadn't left anything out. He knew deep down he hadn't — it had been locked away in his memory for so long. He shivered, staring back at the framed photographs. He'd done his best to bury the past but it had caught up with him.

What a bloody mess.

Jock swilled the single malt around the glass and drained it in one gulp. For a second, he considered pouring another but he checked himself. He had to keep a clear head. It was time for home.

He wiped the tumbler with a paper tissue and placed it back on his desk. Then he returned his whisky to the bottom drawer before turning off the lights and locking his office

He made his way through his gym, returning a couple of misplaced dumbbell weights to their respective spots on the rack, before taking a last look back — like he always did — and turning off the last of the lights.

Outside, the temperature had dropped. Jock shivered and zipped up his training top. The car park was empty save for his rented Toyota; the insurance company was still assessing the damage to his car.

He was about to step away when he noticed a padded envelope at his feet. Puzzled, he surveyed the car park again — this time with a critical eye. It was quiet.

He bent to pick up the small brown package. There was nothing written on it. He turned it over to see that someone had scribbled 'JOCKS GYM' in thick black lettering. The handwriting was poor.

He felt the envelope — there was something lumpy inside — then pulled open the seal and peered in.

Jock recoiled in horror and dropped the package, causing the contents to roll out. He gasped as his stomach leapt to his throat. Three severed fingers lay in front of him.

DAY TWENTY

Hunter leaned back in his seat, stretched his arms and folded them behind his head, interlacing his fingers. Physically he felt drained, yet mentally he was energised. Since he and Grace had met with Nahida Perveen, the investigation had clicked up a gear.

Samia's passport had been the catalyst. Fingerprints found on it matched those from the body.

He mulled over what they had uncovered in the past few days. The team had tracked down a dental practice near to the university in Sheffield where Samia had been a patient. Records held there matched the x-rays from her post mortem. They now had official confirmation — the body recovered from Barnwell Lake was Samia Hassan.

Phone calls to UK Border and Immigration Control and the British Embassy in Lahore confirmed no air ticket had been purchased in Samia Hassan's name. There was no record of her passing through Immigration Control in the UK, or of her arriving at Allama Iqbal International Airport in Lahore.

Locally, they had tracked down and interviewed several more of Samia's friends and acquaintances, found through her Facebook page. The interviews had reinforced many facts they already knew; the attack on Dr Chambers, the burglary and damage to the flat, and Samia's fear of a forced marriage, and they had also determined that no one had spoken with her since the 29th of July. Presently, they were tracking down the police officers who had turned out to those incidents, in the hope that one of them might have recorded the names of Samia's cousins. It was a long shot.

Civilian Investigator Barry Newstead had been assigned to Meadowhall to liaise with the police and security team there and view CCTV footage. Nahida had provided times, dates and the exact place where she had met Samia and Barry had been given the job of locating the footage to check if anything could be of help.

There had been a meeting with Duncan Wroe from Scenes of Crime and his counterpart from the Forensic Science team, and Task Force had been booked for that Sunday to execute a warrant at the Hassans' shop and residence.

Things were coming to a head, thought Hunter, as he viewed the work in progress on the incident board. Long lists of actions and names had now been added to the timeline. In big red capitals 'MOHAMMED HASSAN, JILANI HASSAN and SAMIA'S COUSINS?' had been ringed as main suspects.

Everything was taking shape.

'Who's the redhead with the gaffer?' asked Tony Bullars, entering the office.

His appearance brought Hunter back to the present. He unlocked his fingers and came out of his stretch. 'Redhead?'

'Yeah, good looking, late thirties. I've just come past the office and they seem to be thick as thieves. The door was open and she sounded Scottish.' Tony stopped and gave a wry smile, then said, 'It's murder!' in the style of TV detective *Taggart*. He laughed and dropped a bundle of papers in front of Hunter. 'That's the operational order and the warrant for this weekend's raid at the Hassans. The magistrate asked a few questions but nothing I couldn't handle. I just flashed my bestest smile at her and she signed it up.'

Hunter smirked. Tony had been a ladies' man for as long as he'd known him. He was tall and slim, with blue grey eyes, chiselled features, gelled and styled light brown hair and was always immaculately dressed. He was 28, still single and a charmer. In fact, Hunter couldn't recall seeing him with the same girl more than twice, and they were always stunners. He glanced at the warrant and then back at Tony. 'Bully, don't give me half a story. What do you mean good looking redhead, Scottish accent, in with the gaffer?'

Tony shrugged. 'I smell cop — and senior cop at that.' He tapped his nose and turned away. 'Get you a cuppa?' he shouted, making for the office kettle.

Hunter's head was suddenly elsewhere. Hadn't the gaffer told him the offenders arrested in the car that ran his parents off the road were from one of the sink estates outside Glasgow? Since then, he'd managed to track down the officer in the case from North Yorkshire, only to be told he'd handed over the paperwork to a female DCI up in Stirling. After several phone calls he had finally found out who the Detective Chief Inspector was and he had left four messages for her, none of which had been returned. There had to be a reason why she hadn't phoned him back.

Well, there's only one way to find out.

He picked up the signed magistrate's warrant for the Hassans. It was a good excuse to get a foot in the door.

The Detective Superintendent's door was ajar. Hunter slowed his pace and strained his ears, hoping to pick up some of the conversation. A woman's voice drifted out. Definitely Scottish, though he couldn't make out what she was saying. He paused at the door for a second and then knocked.

'Come in.'

Hunter stepped inside Michael Robshaw's office. The redhead was in one of the comfy armchairs, looking relaxed. She glanced up and flashed a smile. He remembered what Tony Bullars had said. She certainly was attractive and looked to be in her late 30s, wearing a well-tailored dark blue trouser suit over a white cotton blouse. A visitor's badge was clipped to her jacket pocket but he couldn't make out the name. A folder lay open across her lap. He tried to get a glimpse but she snapped it shut as if she knew what he was doing.

He flashed a false smile, greeted her with a nod and turned to his boss. 'Got the Op order and warrant for the Hassans this Sunday, boss.' He held out the documents.

'Okay, Hunter.' Robshaw took the paperwork from him and dropped it onto his jotter. 'I gather no problems with it?'

Hunter shook his head.

'Smashing. Everything in place as well?'

Hunter nodded.

'Right, thanks for that. Tell everyone briefing's at 7.30 on Sunday.'

It felt like Hunter was being dismissed. He turned to the redhead. 'I couldn't help but notice your Scottish accent. My dad's from Glasgow.' That was a good opener.

'Oh yes? I'm from Stirling.'

'This is DCI Leggate,' interjected Robshaw.

'Not DCI Dawn Leggate?'

'Yes,' she said, sounding surprised.

'I've been trying to track you down for the past few days. I was told by North Yorkshire Police that you'd taken over the enquiry into my parents' hit and run. Apparently, you've arrested two for it.'

'Oh yes — yes, of course. You're Hunter Kerr?'

She sounded hesitant.

'Have they been charged?'

'Has your father not said anything to you?'

'No, I wasn't sure if he knew or not. It's been like getting blood from a stone just lately.'

'Well, things have been discussed with him. He knows where we are in our enquiry.'

'Can you tell me then?'

'Well — er.' She seemed flustered. 'You should know better than that. Confidentiality, DS Kerr.'

'But this is different. I'm a cop.'

'So, you should be even more aware then. I'm afraid I can't tell you anything. It's an ongoing investigation. I suggest you speak with your father.'

'Sorry to interrupt, Hunter, but I have a few things to discuss with DCI Leggate,' Robshaw interposed. 'If you could excuse us.'

Hunter knew that his probing had been brought to an end.

'And if you could close the door behind you, Hunter? Thank you,' added Robshaw.

Hunter sank into his armchair and rested his eyes. He felt drained, had a thumping head and the TV was interfering with his thoughts; everything was spinning around so fast that he couldn't make sense of any of it. From the muddle of his mind, the sound of Beth coming down the stairs dragged him back to the present. He snapped open his eyes as she entered the lounge.

'You look tired,' she said, dropping down on the sofa with a big sigh. 'Boys were lively tonight.'

'Sorry, Beth, I should have taken them up and given you a break.' He tried to focus on the TV programme but it was washing over him.

Beth pushed herself up. 'What's the matter, Hunter? You've been at odds with yourself since you got home. Something at work?'

He shook his head. 'It's my dad again.' He told her about the brief meeting with DCI Leggate. 'I called in at Mum's on the way home but they weren't in. I've rung their mobiles and Dad's gym but there was no answer.'

'Look, Hunter, do you think you might be reading into this more than you should?'

He pursed his lips. 'I thought that myself, but it was the way both the superintendent and the DCI reacted when I tried to probe about Mum and Dad's incident. She gave me all the confidentiality crap. You know cops don't do that with other cops.'

'She might just be a stickler for procedure, Hunter. She's from another force. She doesn't know you from Adam.'

'No. There was something in the way she answered me. She was bullshitting.'

'Well, you can't do anything about it, can you? You're going to have to wait until your dad tells you himself.'

Hunter closed his eyes again.

I'm going to get to the bottom of this if it kills me.

DAY TWENTY-TWO

By 7.30 a.m. the incident room was overcrowded with Murder Squad detectives, Task Force Search Team members, Scenes of Crime officers and Forensic specialists, squeezing into any space they could find. It was standing room only.

A large-scale street map and a blown-up aerial photo of Hassan's store, together with a hand-drawn layout of the property — both the store and flat — dominated one of the white boards at the front of the room.

Hunter led the briefing; he was orchestrating the raid. He handed around photocopies of the operational plan setting out the purpose of that morning's sortie and then quickly got into his preamble. He summarised the investigation to date and then outlined everyone's tasks.

Although the team had the Hassans as TIEs (Trace, Interview, Eliminate), they had not been able to identify the attack site where Samia had been killed. That was the crux of the day's task and the purpose of the warrant and he deliberated over his final words. He wanted no stone left unturned.

Shortly after 8 a.m., as the Police and Forensic teams were heading out of the station's yard, daylight had just broken through a heavy grey sky. The day ahead looked promising.

Hunter and Grace were leading the convoy and in less than 15 minutes they were hitting the outskirts of Hoyland. Hunter eased off a fraction but took the turning into the road at the side of the convenience store quicker than normal and had to brake sharply to avoid hitting a parked car. He mumbled an apology to Grace as the car rocked to a halt.

He was wired. A highly-charged tingling sensation surged through him. He was always like this on raids: a memory from the Drug Squad days flashed through his thoughts and just as quickly disappeared as he studied Hassans' convenience store.

In less than twenty seconds they had the premises surrounded. Hunter glanced at his watch: 8.20 on a Sunday morning and the shop was already open.

He and Grace entered first, Hunter holding out the warrant, while Task Force, Scenes of Crime and Forensics disembarked, sealing off the area and sorting out their equipment.

Mohammed Hassan was serving a customer with a morning paper. His jaw dropped as they entered but within seconds he had composed himself and his face hardened.

'What is the meaning of this?'

'We have a warrant to search these premises, Mr Hassan.' Hunter thrust the rolled-up document in his face. Simultaneously, he threw the customer an 'I want you to disappear now' look and followed up by using his head to indicate the door. The customer took the hint and left quickly.

'What for? I have done nothing wrong.'

'When we came the other day making enquiries about your daughter, do you remember me asking you a series of questions as to her whereabouts? You told me she had flown to Pakistan.'

Hunter paused and studied Hassan's face. Tiny beads of sweat had appeared on his forehead.

'We now know she was never there, because as you will have realised by now from the local news broadcasts we have recently found her body. She has been murdered and I suspect your involvement in her killing.'

'No, no, you have got this all wrong. I haven't done anything to Samia.'

'Mr Hassan, I am arresting you on suspicion of your daughter's murder,' finished Hunter.

Ten minutes later, in handcuffs and protesting loudly, Mr and Mrs Hassan were helped into separate police cars as officers sealed off the front of the store with crime scene tape. The premises were secure and ready to be searched.

Hunter took out a forensic oversuit from the boot of his car and slipped it on. He watched everyone else kit themselves out as he picked up his clipboard from the back seat. He made a beeline for Duncan Wroe, the Scenes of Crime manager, and the Task Force Sergeant, wanting to double-check their tasks. Grace was corralling her team together. She had responsibility for the search of the rear store-room.

For the next three hours, Hunter repeatedly moved from one doorway to another, watching the Forensics Team photographing, swabbing walls and furniture, lifting carpets, selectively dropping various items into evidence bags, while Task Force overturned chairs, sofas and beds and rummaged through and behind units and cupboards. The work was slow and methodical but the exhibits were soon stacking up on the landing, ready to be removed for tests.

As Hunter was about to call time for lunchbreak, the first positive call went up.

'Got something, Sarge.' It came from one of the Task Force officers in the kitchen.

Hunter strode excitedly to the doorway and waited; he didn't want to contaminate the search grid. A slightly built, dark haired female greeted him with a broad grin. Her white forensic suit hung loosely in baggy folds.

'Is this what you're looking for on your list?' She offered him an A4 folded document. He slotted the clipboard under his arm and took it, casting his eyes over the DVLA V12 form. As he peeled over the front sheet, he couldn't help but smile. It was a registration document for a white Renault Kangoo van — on a 53 plate.

Hunter loosened his tie and undid his top button. He glanced at Tony Bullars. 'Right, let's see if we can wrap this up,' he said, opening the interview room door.

The two detectives strolled into an already warm and stuffy room and eased themselves down on seats opposite Mohammed Hassan and his solicitor. Mr Hassan was looking uncomfortable, a damp patch stained the front of his shirt.

Another hour of questioning and I'll have you soaking wet with sweat.

Hunter pushed his legs under the table and for effect dropped his paperwork and exhibits onto the table with a resounding slap. He slowly and deliberately unfastened his cuffs and rolled back his shirt-sleeves to reveal sinewy muscled forearms.

Tony Bullars flicked on the tape recorder.

'Mr Hassan, you understand why you have been arrested, don't you?' said Hunter. 'We have explained to you that your daughter's body has been recovered from Barnwell Lake and that she has been murdered.'

Hassan nodded.

His bearded, overweight solicitor began making notes.

'Mr Hassan. I would appreciate a verbal answer. The tape cannot pick up nods.'

'Yes, yes,' he stammered, licking his lips. 'But you have got it wrong. I haven't done anything bad to Samia. I haven't killed her.'

'We'll get around to that in a minute.' Hunter steepled his fingers and looked over them. He tried to lock onto

Mohammed's eyes but they were darting around, avoiding eye contact.

A classic sign of guilt. 'When I was at your place a week ago you told me Samia had flown to Pakistan to get married to a cousin of yours. Do you remember telling me that?'

'I can recall saying something like that but I think you misunderstood what I meant.'

'Why would I misunderstand you?'

'Because I might not have explained myself.'

'Would you like to explain yourself now?'

'What I should have said is that I guessed Samia had flown to Pakistan to marry my cousin. You see she packed up all her things a couple of months ago and told me she was going to Pakistan to marry my cousin.'

Hunter gave a wry smile. He pulled his fingers apart and pushed himself back. 'Well, that is very interesting, Mr Hassan — because we have statements from several people which clearly state that she did not want to go to Pakistan to marry any cousin. In fact, those witnesses have said you were forcing her to go there.'

'They are lying.'

'Why should six different people all say the same thing? That you were trying to force her to go to Pakistan, to force her into a marriage with someone she didn't know?'

'She probably told them one thing but really meant another. Samia was happy to marry my cousin.'

'If she was happy to marry your cousin, why should she pack some of her things together with a view to taking refuge from you?'

'That is a lie.'

'No, it is not, Mr Hassan. We have a statement to that effect and we also have the things she packed ready to leave. We also have a statement from someone who states you went to Sheffield while she was staying with friends and argued with her about going to Pakistan to be married, and when she told you she didn't want to go you slapped her across the face.'

'They are lying. We rowed because I found out she was living with someone. She was bringing dishonour upon herself.'

'Because she had a white boyfriend?'

Mohammed's face coloured up. 'No, no, you are trying to put words in my mouth. She was bringing dishonour upon herself because she was sleeping with him before she was married.'

Hunter wanted to probe further about the two men who had assaulted Chris Chambers and tried to drag Samia into their car, but the team had not yet been able to identify them. He didn't want to alert Mr Hassan to the fact that they were aware of this incident, for fear his two relatives would go to ground, or even disappear out of the country — if they hadn't already done so. Anyway, he still had something else he wanted to hit him with. 'I put it to you, Mr Hassan, because Samia had made her mind up not to enter into a forced marriage and to get away from you that you decided to do something about it?'

'No, no, that is not right.'

'That you were angry with your daughter. That by her refusal to agree to marry your cousin, you thought she was bringing dishonour to yourself and so you murdered her.'

'No. You are making me out to be a bad man.'

The solicitor stopped scribbling and gave a loud throaty cough. 'I think my client has fully answered all your questions relating to this terrible act against his daughter. If you press him any further, you will be in danger of intimidating him.'

'Oh, I wouldn't want to do that.' Hunter leaned forward, rested his elbows on the table and interlaced his fingers. He fixed Hassan with a glare. The man stiffened. 'Okay then, Mr Hassan, seeing as everyone is lying against you and your solicitor is unhappy with my line of questioning about you being involved in the brutal murder of your daughter…'

'Detective Sergeant Kerr, that is out of order,' interrupted the solicitor.

Hunter shrugged and gave the solicitor an innocent look. 'I apologise if you find my questioning offensive, but my job is to discover the truth and all your client has given me are answers which are evasive. I don't want to get into a cat fight here on such an important issue so I'll move on — okay?' He paused. 'Mr Hassan, this morning when we searched your flat...'

'You had no right to do that,' Hassan interrupted.

Hunter raised his clenched fists a fraction then dropped them back down with a thump.

Both Hassan and the solicitor jumped.

'Sorry about that,' Hunter said, unlocking his fingers. 'Now, where was I before I was so rudely interrupted? Oh yes, this morning when we searched your flat — with a warrant,' he added in an exaggerated tone, 'we found this at the back of one your kitchen drawers.' He slid out a clear plastic exhibit bag which contained the registration document for the white Renault Kangoo van. 'I am showing Mr Hassan exhibit RA One.' He slid the document into the centre of the table. 'This VR Twelve relates to a white Renault Kangoo van registered in 2003. Is this yours, Mr Hassan?'

Hassan blushed. A droplet of sweat ran down the side of his face.

'It was mine. I used the van for collecting stock from the warehouse.'

'Where is it now? It's not at your premises or parked nearby.'

Hassan looked up to the ceiling.

'Mr Hassan, can you give me an answer?'

'It, it,' he stammered, 'it has been stolen.'

'And when was it stolen?'

'I — I can't remember exactly,' he paused. 'I think it was taken a couple of months ago.'

'Did you report the theft to the police?'

'No.'

'And why didn't you report the theft of your vehicle, Mr Hassan?'

'Because I didn't think it was worth it.'

'You didn't think it was worth it?' Hunter returned dryly.

'Well, it wasn't worth that much.'

'Detective Sergeant Kerr,' interjected the solicitor again. He rested his pen on his notepad and stroked the line of his beard to its point. 'Is there some significance to this line of questioning, or are you on some fishing expedition?'

'No, I am not on some fishing expedition. There is something I am working towards.'

'And what would that be?'

'Mr Hassan — your client — has so far indicated that everyone is lying against him and also there is a big coincidence here that I am struggling with.'

'A coincidence?'

'Yes, a coincidence that your client owns a white 2003 plate Renault Kangoo van and a similar one was seen in suspicious circumstances at Barnwell Country Park, shortly after we think Samia's body was dumped in the lake.'

'You say *shortly* after you think Samia's body was dumped.' Hunter wished he had chosen his words more carefully. 'I gather by that comment you do not know for certain that was what exactly happened. These might be coincidences, Sergeant Kerr, I'll grant you that, but as you well know coincidences do not make a case. Now, unless you have any pertinent questions for my client, I suggest we finish things here. That is unless you have something more concrete?'

The solicitor had the upper hand and Hunter realised it was futile to carry on unless he wanted to reveal the information about the two men seen dumping Samia's body, men the team strongly felt were related to Hassan.

Hunter pushed himself back in his chair and pasted on a false smile. 'Mr Hassan, I am going to bring this interview to a close. We have a number of further enquiries to make, especially to track down your Renault van which has been so conveniently stolen. But I'm sure that when we will find it there will be some further questions for you.'

Hunter picked up his papers and the exhibit bag and scraped back his chair. He maintained his false smile as he nodded to Tony to turn off the recording machine and then he cast Mohammed Hassan a threatening look. 'In the words of the Canadian Mounted Police — we always get our man.' Before the solicitor had the chance to challenge, he turned and strode purposefully out of the interview room.

As he closed the door behind him, Hunter gripped the handle, squeezing the very life out of it. In the corridor, he turned to Tony. 'Fuck, fuck, bastarding fuck,' he muttered through gritted teeth.

Tony smirked. 'I gather by that outburst, Hunter, that one is a tad fractious and frustrated. You could always resort to torturing him for a confession.'

His colleague's words lightened Hunter's mood and he smiled. 'Now, now, Bully, you know that's not my style.' He winked and let go of the door handle. 'That smug solicitor may have won that battle but he hasn't won the fucking war.'

As Hunter walked into the incident room, half a dozen members of the murder squad, including Grace and Mike, turned expectantly in his direction. He raised his hands in surrender. 'Sorry guys — I failed. No cough, no job. It's back to the grindstone, I'm afraid.'

The detectives returned to their tasks as Hunter beckoned to Grace. Flopping down opposite her, he asked, 'You have any joy with Mrs Hassan?'

She shook her head.

Hunter's shoulders dropped and he sighed. 'What a bummer.' He picked at his nails as he recounted the interview to Grace. 'And I'm afraid SOCO can't help us either,' he added, 'I rang Duncan Wroe ten minutes ago and he says the Hassans' place is definitely not the attack site.'

'Me and Mike haven't made any progress either,' said Grace, picking up where Hunter had left off. 'We couldn't get any momentum going with Mrs Hassan. Every time we asked a probing question, she'd say she couldn't understand what we were saying. Going through an interpreter as well as a solicitor was bloody awful. I even tried the mother-daughter approach to empathise with her. You know, tell her what I'd do if it was my daughter and I thought my husband was responsible? But she just sat there, stony-faced. The woman is a real heartless bitch. I'll tell you what, though, I'll be ready for her next time.'

She tried to put on a brave face but Hunter saw through her veneer. He nodded. 'The one solid thing from this is it reinforces my belief that these two are guilty of some involvement in their daughter's death. Neither of them has shown any sorrow or remorse.' He leant forward. 'Unfortunately, a jury won't convict them for that. I hate to say this but we're going to have to release them on bail.' He pushed himself up from his desk. 'Come on, no time for dwelling on our misfortunes. We owe this to Samia if nothing else. We've still got to find the white van. If that was used to dump Samia's body — and my guess from Mohammed's reaction is that it was — then it should have some forensics.' Hunter headed towards the door. 'And we'll also seize their mobiles before they leave. With a bit of luck, they might give us the names of the faces from the e-fits.'

DAY TWENTY-FIVE

Marcus Hill had been a police officer for fifteen years and had developed a nose for sniffing out when something wasn't right. And as he watched the grey Ford Mondeo in the distance, circling ever so slowly around the recently cropped field, he had the feeling something was wrong.

Firstly, because the farmer who owned this field had a red Nissan Navarro and he'd only ever seen the farmer's tractor going around in that field. And secondly, there had been quite a few complaints over the years about fly-tipping in this area. Thirdly, the lane above the field was where a couple of burned out stolen cars had been found in recent months.

Marcus had spotted the Ford Mondeo two minutes earlier. He was heading back to the station for his meal, having spent the past twenty minutes driving around the countryside section of his beat, where the roads were less congested and the scenery was better. It had been an unusually quiet afternoon and he was savouring the tranquil moments. These instances were few and far between, especially on the afternoon shift.

The car attracted his attention when it emerged from a copse of trees which he knew was the site of a ruined eighth-century chapel. He had an interest in local history, and he knew the place had protected status.

Marcus pulled his police car off the road, mounting the grass verge and settling next to a gap in the hedge where he hoped for a better view. The Mondeo had come to a stop, but such was the angle of its parking that he was unable to get a view of the number plate. He watched as the passenger door opened. A man dressed in a long, dark coat disembarked.

Leaning across the passenger seat, Marcus strained his eyes to get a clearer description but he was too far away. The dark clothed man made his way to the rear of the Mondeo, where he popped open the tailgate.

Marcus had seen enough. His suspicions aroused, he radioed in, telling the communications room operator what he could see and asking for backup. Then he pulled back onto the road and set off towards a track which led to where the Mondeo was.

The public bridle path he turned onto was rutted and undulated and lined by heavy hawthorn bushes, and it took him much longer than he had anticipated to find an opening into the field.

Marcus spotted the gap at the last moment. He pulled the steering wheel hard left, bounced up and over a tufted incline and dropped down onto the recently harvested field. The heavy landing knocked the wind out of him and he slammed on the brakes. The police car skidded to a halt. As he fought for breath, he scoured the fields to gather his bearings. The Mondeo was twenty yards away, though both front doors were open and the car was devoid of passengers. He had lost the element of surprise.

Marcus flung open his door and sprinted towards the car, giving an update over his personal radio while scouring the field to see if anyone was making a run for it.

There was no sign of life. He guessed they had dashed into the copse where the old chapel stood. Once his colleagues arrived Marcus knew that there would be nowhere for them to hide. They'd soon flush them out.

He stopped at the Mondeo, craning his neck inside just in case one of them was laying low in the seats. The car was empty. Then he walked to the rear where the tailgate was still up.

Now let's see what you were up to, shall we?

Curled up in the foetal position lay a man, and Marcus had seen enough corpses in his time to realise this man was dead.

The rustle of leaves from the coppice made Marcus jump. A stocky built man emerged through the bushes, a black woollen ski mask hiding his face. Marcus reached for his baton, simultaneously depressing the emergency button of his radio — a signal which overrode all other communications on that channel and let colleagues know that he was in danger.

Marcus never heard the footsteps behind him and never felt the blow to his head, though his ears registered the sharp crack as his skull fractured.

The last thing he saw before his vision pitched into darkness was the galaxy of stars that exploded inside his head.

DAY TWENTY-SIX

It took Hunter ages to find a parking spot. He had never seen the police station car park so full. And inside, the station was no better. The rear foyer and corridor were crammed with uniformed officers milling around. He didn't see any familiar faces.

As he reached the first-floor stairwell, he recognised one of the duty group sergeants, who was carrying a clipboard and seemed deep in thought.

'What's going on?'

The sergeant looked up. 'Oh, morning, Hunter. You mean the Task Force officers? Haven't you heard?'

'Heard what?'

'Marcus Hill was attacked last night. He's in a bad way.'

'Marcus!' Hunter knew him. A few years ago, he had joined Hunter's team as a CID aide, but had then passed his sergeant's exams and decided to go back into uniform where he would have the regularity of 'acting-up'. Hunter had chatted to him a couple of weeks ago when they'd bumped into each other in the canteen. Marcus had smiled as he shared the news that he'd just passed the last round of sergeant's boards and was waiting for a suitable vacancy.

'What happened?'

The sergeant elaborated. 'Fractured skull. And he suffered a bleed to the brain. They operated on him late last night and he's heavily sedated. We won't know anything else about his condition until later this morning.'

'Have you got who did it?'

The sergeant shook his head. 'He called in a grey Mondeo acting suspiciously in one of the fields opposite the Crown Inn at Barnburgh and called for backup. Then he went status-zero, but it took the first car a good ten minutes to get to him. By that time the Mondeo, and whoever had attacked him, had left. We've got everyone available out looking. Task Force are going out to do a thorough search of the area.'

Hunter patted the sergeant's shoulder. 'Okay, let me know how you go on, and keep me updated about Marcus.' He turned and climbed the stairs to the MIT room, his thoughts drifting.

As he shouldered through the doors, Hunter sensed the atmosphere in the office. It was a complete contrast to downstairs. This place was buzzing and it brought him back from his gloom.

He slipped off his jacket and left it on the back of his chair. Grace glanced at him as she put a mug of coffee down on her desk.

'Morning, Grace. Have you heard about Marcus?'

'Yeah, terrible, isn't it?'

Hunter nodded. He pointed to his colleagues who were at their desks, cradling their own hot drinks and chatting excitedly in small groups.

'Something going on that I should know about?'

'That's appeared this morning.'

Grace thumbed towards the incident boards at the front of the room. Beside them, stacked on a trolley, was a large flat screen TV on stand-by and a DVD player.

'I called in to speak to Isobel first thing and she said we were in for a treat this morning. There's been a breakthrough but she wouldn't tell me what.'

Before Hunter and Grace could discuss things further, they were interrupted by Michael Robshaw and Barry Newstead making a noisy entrance. Barry swaggered to the television, his face beaming as he switched on the monitor, while the SIO took up centre stage.

'Okay everyone, settle down. I'm guessing you've all heard a whisper that progress has been made in this case, especially after the disappointment of the interviews with the Hassans.' Robshaw turned to Hunter and Grace. 'And that's no reflection on you two by the way. We had nothing to go on.' He grinned. 'That was until yesterday afternoon.' He rubbed his hands together. 'When Barry discovered what you are all about to see. All yours, Barry.'

Barry smoothed a hand over his loosened tie. He took a deep breath and made a vain attempt to pull in his beer belly. 'As you know, I was given the task of visiting the security team at Meadowhall to see what, if any, CCTV footage they had of Samia Hassan and whether there was anything of significance which could take the investigation further. Well, thanks to the dates, times and precise location provided by Nahida Perveen, I was able to isolate the cameras which might have images of Samia. This is what I have found. The footage is disjointed because I have taken clips from hours of original CCTV film and cobbled them together.'

He stepped back from the TV and pressed the remote. A section of the huge shopping mall interior flickered onto the forty-eight-inch screen.

'Okay, this is where we first pick up Samia.' Barry pointed with the remote and homed in on a young, dark haired Asian woman strolling through the ground floor of Marks and Spencer's store and out through the entrance to the mall.

The murder squad was glued to the pictures playing out over the TV. Samia weaved her way between a throng of people seated in an open plan coffee lounge and took up a place at an empty table.

'At the bottom right, you'll see the time and date of the footage; the 14th of March — a good six months ago. I'll fast forward it a bit.' Barry zipped through to a point where another woman joined Samia and then pressed play. 'That's Nahida Perveen. I'll not go any further but I can tell you they have coffee and are obviously in conversation for about 25 minutes. Then Samia leaves and makes her way back into Marks and Sparks before heading off for the train.' Barry clicked the remote again. 'Okay, this is the second piece of footage. We jump forward to the 28th of July.'

Again, images played out of Samia walking through the ground floor of Marks and Spencer's to the coffee lounge. Samia sat at a table and Nahida joined her. Barry speeded up the footage, showing Samia handing over a red knapsack and then froze the picture. He turned to Hunter. 'I think this is the same knapsack where you found Samia's clothing and passport, is it not?'

Hunter nodded.

'Okay, there's not much conversation on this occasion.' Barry increased the speed of the footage for a few seconds then hit the play button. 'They're only together for ten minutes and as you can see they split up and leave.' Barry stopped the footage, looked away from the screen and scanned the room. He had the attention of every detective. 'Now, this next bit is very interesting,' he continued, clicking the remote back into play.

All eyes watched Samia travel the escalator to the first floor of Marks and Spencer's, stride through the aisles and leave through the exit doors. At one stage it looked as though she was heading for the ramp to the train station, but then changed direction towards the car park. She was continuously glancing behind her.

'At this stage, like you, I was wondering why she was looking around as much as she was, so I pulled up footage from other cameras and I found this.' Barry clicked the remote again, changing the image. The shots were back inside Marks and Spencer.

The picture zoomed in and a grainy image of an Asian male, mid to late 20s, dressed in white T-shirt and jeans, came into focus. He was dodging from one rack of clothing to another, acting suspiciously.

'As I pan the shot out, you can now see that this guy is following Samia and I'm guessing because of her reaction she has sussed this. Okay I'll play it out a bit more.'

The picture juddered for a split-second and then the drama was back on. Samia was picking up her pace, slipping between parked cars. In the background, visible but out of focus, the Asian man took something out of his pocket and put it to his ear.

'He's on his mobile.'

Samia took a final look in the direction of the Asian man before dashing into one of the stairwells which gave access to the ground floor car park.

'And finally this,' said Barry.

The image changed again to a low-lit underground car park. The view was wider and longer, taking in a considerable amount of the parking area, but the action being played out was unmistakable. Samia sprinted out of the stairwell like a chased rabbit, looking back over her shoulder. From out of nowhere, a blur at first to the right of the screen, another Asian man, taller and much stockier than the first, steamed into her like a rugby player, bowling her over onto the concrete floor. He was on top of her in a split-second, straddling her, one hand covering her mouth to prevent her crying out, the other pummelling her chest.

Seconds later, the man who had been initially following Samia emerged from the stairwell at pace, slipped on a wet patch at the bottom of the stairs, caught himself, re-balanced, and joined in the attack.

It was over in thirty seconds. Samia slumped under the onslaught. The stocky man pushed himself off her and sprinted away out of camera view, while the first Asian man stood over her looking around, but there was no one else in sight.

Less than a minute later a white van entered the picture and pulled directly in front of Samia's prostrate body, blocking the camera's view.

Barry glanced around the room. All eyes were fixed on the screen, the detectives unable to pull themselves away from the scenes unfolding before them. He turned back to the screen in time to see the two Asian men bundling Samia's limp figure towards the rear of the van. They slung her into the back like a rag doll. The doors slammed shut, both men jumped into the front and then the vehicle tore away.

'All that took less than three minutes,' Barry told them. 'The last footage I have is this.' It was a short snippet of the white van heading towards the exit of the ground floor car park, at the point before it entered the major road system around the Meadowhall Centre. Barry freeze-framed a close-up image and there were the faces of the two Asian men who had attacked and abducted Samia.

The eyes of the murder squad darted between the e-fit images on the incident board and the TV screen. There was no doubting they were an exact likeness. Just as important was the index number on the front number plate of the van — it was the same registration as the VR 12 vehicle document which had been recovered from the Hassans' home.

DAY TWENTY-EIGHT

Hunter's eyes were glued to the TV in the incident room. It was the third time he had watched the attack and abduction of Samia.

He shook his head as the violent images replayed — this time inside his brain. He cringed at the sheer brutality meted out to the young woman. Samia was so slight. She'd not resisted or put up a fight and yet those two men had beaten her mercilessly and tossed her into the back of the van like a sack of rubbish. He reflected on what the post mortem had revealed — the catalogue of injuries inflicted upon her and the violation she had suffered prior to her death.

What he'd like to do to those two bastards.

As he shook himself out of his reverie, he found himself trying to squeeze the life out of the plastic TV remote. He glanced around, red faced, hoping no one had noticed as he set it back down on the trolley.

Hunter strode back to his desk, dropped down onto his chair and began to immerse himself in the paperwork which had accumulated over the past couple of days. The majority of it was written off actions or reports as a result of his team's footwork and foraging. As he pored over their content, he summarised what they had learned to date.

The MIT teams had not eased up since Barry had discovered the CCTV footage; the investigation was now a manhunt. Blown-up footage of the two Asian men had been given to the Intelligence Unit, who had circulated it throughout South Yorkshire as well as to neighbouring police forces. On the back burner was a visit to the *Crimewatch* studios but they wanted to exhaust their own enquiries first. The pictures were so good that everyone was confident it wouldn't be long before they were caught.

Simultaneously, checks were being carried out at scrap dealers and car dismantlers for the white Renault van. It hadn't been found dumped or burnt out yet, and experience told them that if it wasn't still secreted away somewhere, these were the usual means of disposal.

Now they had the fixed time and date parameters for the attack and kidnapping, the technicians at force headquarters had been able to make a quick examination of the SIM card memory and mapping hardware inside Mohammed Hassan's seized mobile. The wizards had made a crucial breakthrough. From the downloaded data, they had discovered activity on his phone within minutes of his daughter's abduction and traced a name and phone number.

The name Ari was registered in his contact details and the same number had been dialled persistently over several days following Samia's kidnapping, with the last call recorded at 10:33 p.m. on Friday, the first of August. Since then there had been no activity to the number and the technicians were reporting the line was now dead — the phone switched off or more than likely dumped, especially since the raid at the Hassans'.

Kerri-Ann Bairstow had seen a white van driving away from the country park on either a Friday or Saturday. Hunter was sure that was when they had dumped Samia's body into the lake, which meant she had been held captive for almost five days.

The hairs at the back of his neck prickled; the post mortem had shown she had been raped and butchered. He couldn't imagine what she must have gone through during that time.

Hunter continued picking over the reports. The mobile number Mohammed had contacted was a pay-as-you-go phone bought in Sheffield with cash and the details of the purchaser were false. Nevertheless, from discussions during briefings the murder squad were confident Ari was the man's real name.

Together with the photographs from the CCTV footage, Hunter knew this was as good as they were going to get.

'Hunter, didn't you hear what I said?'

Grace broke his concentration. He looked up from his paperwork and caught her glaring. She was holding up the handset, pointing at the receiver.

'Sorry, Grace, I was elsewhere.'

'Yeah, I could see,' she said. 'I just said they've found the white van.' Her voice was up several octaves. 'It's Communications on the phone. Uniform have found it at a car dismantler's in Rotherham. A low-loader's on its way to pick it up and SOCO are heading out there.'

Later that afternoon, Hunter drove into the force's forensic examination facility and swung into an empty parking space. Excitedly, he jumped out, not bothering to lock the car, and quickly made for the drying room. Grace hurried after him.

Duncan Wroe, in a blue forensic suit, was just climbing out of the rear of the white Renault.

It looked in remarkably good condition considering it had been languishing in a car dismantler's for several weeks, though it was missing its rear number plate.

Hunter shouted to Duncan, who turned and acknowledged them with a wave, a small fluorescent light in one hand and a bottle of blood reagent spray in the other. He sauntered over.

'Hi, Hunter, Grace. Wondered how long it would be before you got here.' He set the spray down on a table.

'We wanted to give you enough time to work your magic on it, Duncan,' Hunter said.

Duncan smiled and mussed his fingers through his already tousled hair. 'Too early for miracles just yet, I'm afraid, though I have made a start on it.' He picked up the Luminol spray. 'Come on, slip on some overshoes and I'll show you what I've got so far.'

He left Hunter and Grace to fit on latex shoe coverings, still talking as he walked away. Hunter hobbled after him, struggling to fit on one shoe protector while trying to concentrate on what the SOCO manager was saying.

'I've only done a preliminary examination, you understand. The van's been out in the open for months and will need at least a couple of days in the drying room before we can bottom it. However, I have made a start.' Duncan stopped by the open rear doors as Hunter and Grace caught up.

'Is it the right van?' said Hunter, pointing at the absence of the rear number plate.

'Absolutely. The engine and chassis number are a match. This is definitely the van belonging to Mr Hassan.'

'And what have you got so far?' asked Grace.

'Well, I have found traces of blood — just small amounts. I've given it the once-over with the Luminol and it shows up under the fluorescence. Whose it is at the moment I won't be able to say, but my guess is Samia's. Her throat was cut as I recall and despite the fact she was bundled up in the carpet, I think some will have seeped out. I'll swab it and send it to the lab.'

'Anything else?'

'The impossible I can do, miracles take a little longer, Hunter. Once it's thoroughly dried out I'll be checking for fibres and DNA. I've got the samples from the carpet she was wrapped up in, so I'll be able to examine them and see if there is a match. I'll certainly be able to confirm if this was the vehicle she was carried in.'

Hunter returned a thank you smile. 'All very technical for me, Duncan, but I have faith in you.'

'In layman's terms it's a bit like the fluorescent lights in a nightclub picking out white clothing.'

Hunter and Grace nodded, understanding.

'I'll also be checking for soil samples in the wheel arches and on the wheels and see if I can marry them to the samples I've taken from the car park at the country park. Lastly, we'll swab the cabin's interior and see if there is a DNA composite for the driver and passenger. With a bit of luck, in a day or two I should have all the answers.'

Hunter found Barry Newstead reaching across his desk as he entered the office. Grace was only a few strides behind.

'Caught you!' Hunter said. 'Snooping through the boss's things while he's away?'

'It would take a real detective to ever catch me doing that,' Barry said, looking over his shoulder. 'I thought you'd disappeared for the day. I'm just leaving you a note before I knock off.' He finished scribbling on an A5 pad, then tore off the top sheet and handed it to Hunter. 'A couple of things I wanted to leave for you before tomorrow morning's briefing.'

'What's that, Barry?'

'Firstly, we might have identified Samia's cousins — the two men from the Meadowhall CCTV footage. I've been chasing up the Intelligence Units throughout the Force and Sheffield think they have a positive ID on the pair. It looks as though they're known to Drug Squad, so I'm just waiting on final confirmation of that. It looks promising.'

'Great stuff. And the second thing?'

'Remember we set up a trace search of the part index number of the Volkswagen Golf that Kerri-Ann Bairstow gave us, belonging to one of her punters?'

Hunter pursed his lips. 'Yes?'

'Well, you're going to love this. Guess who it comes back to? You've already interviewed him.'

Hunter shook his head. 'Surprise me.'

'Mr Christopher Chambers. An address in Sheffield.'

Hunter's eyes widened and Grace looked surprised too.

'Told you you'd love it.'

Hunter snatched up the phone, punched in a number and waited for a response. His feet were tapping ten-to-the-dozen. After a brief conversation, he slammed the handset back onto its cradle and turned to Grace. 'Have you got anything pressing this evening?'

'Nothing that can't wait. I'll just make a quick call to Dave to sort out the girls and then I'm with you.'

Hunter patted Barry on the shoulder. 'Cheers for this. Now I've got some arse to kick.'

Hunter listened as soft footfalls padded towards him. He looked away from the car park for a few seconds to check his watch. He and Grace had been waiting in the entranceway to the hospital generator room for less than half an hour.

While they were waiting, the last light of dusk had faded. The car park security lighting had activated, giving everything a blue-white tinge.

Hunter saw the shadowy outline of the man a few yards away. He recognised him from their previous visit to the infirmary.

'Good evening, Dr Chambers,' Hunter greeted him, stepping out of the shadows. Grace slipped in beside him.

The doctor started, slapping a hand over his heart.

'Christ, you made me jump!' Chris Chambers gasped.

'Good.'

The doctor looked perplexed.

Hunter took a few determined steps forward, stopping inches from his face. 'Give me one good reason why I shouldn't haul you down to the station right now for perverting the course of justice!'

Even in the low light from the glow of the security lighting Hunter could see Chris Chambers had coloured up.

'I — I,' he spluttered.

'Why, after contacting us and giving us all that information about Samia's cousins assaulting you and threatening you, didn't you tell us that on the evening of Friday the first of August you recognised them leaving the country park in their white van?'

The doctor's head drooped.

'You could have saved us a lot of time — do you not realise that? Instead, you gave us a storyline half pointing us in their direction. Is it because you were with a prostitute that night?'

Chambers nodded. 'I'm close to finishing my time as a junior doctor. If the hospital finds out about this I'll not get a post. Believe me, I didn't want to obstruct your investigation. I thought if I gave you enough to lead you to Samia's cousins and help catch them, this wouldn't come out.'

'Well, it's backfired, hasn't it? We've wasted time tracking down the owner of a VW Golf for weeks as a potential witness and all this time it was you. I'd be very careful how I'd answer this next question. Did you see the two men dump Samia's body in the lake?'

The doctor shook his head vigorously. 'Christ, no! I didn't spot them until they'd cut us up in the car park. When I saw who was in the van I thought they were after me again, because of my past fling with Samia. I thought they'd followed me there and I was going to get another hiding. When they drove away, I couldn't fathom it out. Then when I saw it all on the news, I put two-and-two together and realised what I had seen.' He paused and dropped his gaze again. 'I'm sorry. If it hadn't been for the prostitute I would have told you all this.'

'You might be able to save some face here. Can you definitely say you recognise the two people in the white van as Samia's cousins who previously beat you up?'

Chambers nodded. 'Yes, it was definitely them.'

DAY THIRTY

'These are our targets,' announced Michael Robshaw, holding aloft a pair of A4 size colour photographs. They were head and shoulders mug shots of two Asian men holding custody reference boards — at some stage they had obviously been arrested and charged.

'Ari and Pervez Arshad. 29 and 27 years old, from the Attercliffe area. These were taken just over five months ago when they were charged with witness intimidation after an assault on a young man at a taxi rank. Three witnesses stated Ari and Pervez pushed in on a queue and when a 22-year-old man challenged them they set about him. They punched him to the ground and witnesses say Ari jumped on his head with both feet several times. That young man is now permanently brain damaged and the three witnesses who initially came forward have refused to give evidence in court after being visited by the pair.'

Robshaw turned and pressed the images onto the incident board, directly beneath the two earlier e-fits, joining the enlarged CCTV image of the two Asian men driving away from Meadowhall in the white Renault van.

Everyone could see the likeness.

Robshaw turned back to the room. 'These two are well known to the Sheffield police and also to Drug Squad. They have been strongly suspected of knocking out cocaine and heroin to clubbers for some time but subsequent raids have only found enough gear for possession charges. Ari has been arrested twice for assault and aggravated burglary when he went to collect drug debts owed to him, though once again victims and witnesses refused to give evidence in court.' Robshaw scanned the room. 'However, their luck has finally run out. We now have clear identification placing these two at Barnwell Lake on the night Samia's body was dumped. It's by Christopher Chambers, who was previously assaulted by the pair. And he is willing to testify in court.

'So not only do we have CCTV footage of these two abducting Samia, we can now place them on the night her body was dumped in the lake. What we don't have is their address. They no longer live at the flat where they were arrested five months ago. That has been let to another couple who were living there on the date of Samia's abduction. Detectives from Sheffield have paid this couple a visit and given the place the once over. There is no suggestion these two people have any links to our targets or to the Hassans and therefore our priority now is to identify where they are currently living and bring them in. Tasks today relate to their known associates with a view to tracking them down.'

Mike Sampson raised his arm. 'What about bringing Mohammed Hassan back in, now we've found Ari's number on his mobile?'

'Not yet. I don't want him to know how much we've got until we have Ari and his brother Pervez in custody.' Robshaw tapped the incident board. 'All our efforts now are focused on these two. Good hunting, everyone.'

Prompted by an early finish from work — they still hadn't discovered the Arshads' address — Hunter made a last-minute decision to detour on his way home and call into his dad's gym for a quick training session to unwind.

As he took his bag out of the boot, he casually looked around the car park. There were a good dozen cars — more than usual at this time of day. *Must be a few in.* He might be able to get in a bit of sparring for a change.

As he set down his bag to close the boot, out of the corner of one eye he spotted movement in one of the parked cars. A grey Mondeo, its engine revving, was parked at the end of the row. It looked out of place here; not the type of car he normally saw in the car park — most of the trainees who used his dad's gym were young men who drove old bangers, the best of them done up with body kits which shouted boy racer.

After everything that had happened recently, Hunter went on alert — something didn't feel right. And weren't they looking for a grey Mondeo in relation to the attack on PC Marcus Hill?

He slowly closed the boot and slipped down the side of his car to get a better look at the Mondeo, especially the driver and passenger. It looked as if the two men were concentrating on the entrance to the gym.

Crouching, he shifted for a better angle. The passenger was the nearest. He was a middle-aged man with long straggly, greying hair and a neatly trimmed beard. Hunter was too far away to get a look at his face. The driver, also middle-aged, had crew-cut sandy hair. His head was back against the headrest and although Hunter couldn't see his features, there was something familiar about him.

As Hunter took another step forward the passenger sat bolt upright. He'd been eyeballed.

The Mondeo roared into life, its front wheels whipping up gravel as it jolted forward, fish-tailing for a split second before straightening and shooting out of the exit onto the side-street.

He had just enough time to log the registration number in his head before it disappeared.

As the squeal of tyres faded into the distance, his hackles rose. It was the look the passenger had thrown him — a cold-blooded granite stare. It was an animal-like expression he had seen only a few times in his career — usually when someone wanted to kill him.

Those two meant business and he had disturbed them.

DAY THIRTY-ONE

Billy Wallace looked up for a break in the clouds as more drizzle floated from a murky sky. Around him, puddles were forming. He gave an involuntary shudder as droplets of rain ran down his neck and onto his back.

It had been raining on and off for most of the day — but that wasn't a bad thing, he'd told himself as he sloshed through the wet that afternoon. It had enabled him and Rab to do what they had needed to do and not draw suspicion as they had scoured the streets for their target's address.

He wiped drips of rain from his hair and stepped into the smoking shelter at the rear of The Station public house, his slate grey eyes never leaving the station ticket office and waiting room fifty yards away. He was listening for the next train, the connection train from Edinburgh.

He stroked the recently grown beard that covered his craggy features and hid most of the hideous scar which made him stand out, mulling over his decision. They'd needed some extra muscle to finish the job, and the only way he could arrange that was by calling in favours with old contacts. It had meant a flying visit to his hometown two days ago. He felt uncomfortable; he always liked to know who he was working with, needed that level of control and trust, but this time he had no choice. It had cost him a few grand, but it would be worth it.

'Get that down your neck.'

Rab Geddes made him jump. He was edgy.

He took the pint of lager from his partner in crime and stepped to one side so he could come into the dry.

Neither of them smoked. They were using the shelter in the hope of not attracting attention — two strangers with Scottish accents would stand out.

'Not arrived yet?' asked Rab, sweeping a hand over his newly grown hair.

It was a long time since Billy had seen Rab with hair. It was still sandy in colour but it was now thin and wispy and he realised why Rab had taken to shaving his head over the past ten years.

Nevertheless, it was necessary. They needed a change in appearance for a few more days.

'Nope. It's a couple of minutes late,' Billy replied, looking at his watch again. He glanced back to the station. The rain clouds were easing and the light was failing, another half an hour and darkness would cover them.

His thoughts drifted to their recce earlier in the day. After they had finally found the house, Billy had done a circuit of the surrounding streets. Instinct told him cops would be close by, on protection duty, and he'd been right. He'd spotted the unmarked police car on the second sweep and had to smile as he checked out the Peugeot. Even after all these years in prison, though the make and models had changed, the police radio in the centre console was still a dead giveaway.

He mentally noted its number and position; it would have to be taken care of so they could make their getaway after the job. The car was empty and he guessed the detectives would be in a house somewhere nearby keeping observation, though he didn't stay around to check. He and Rab had driven back to the railway station, finalising their plans, making sure that when they parked the Mondeo it was well away from view. Since they had been clocked by that nosy bastard at Jock's gym they had kept a low profile. *It's only for a few more hours.*

In the distance he heard the rumble of the train and it brought him back to the present.

'Come on, Rab, they're here,' he said, nudging his partner and swallowed the remains of his lager. He swiped the residue from his mouth with the back of a gloved hand, then wiped a handkerchief around the edge of the glass several times. *No room for error*, he told himself, holding it up to the light before leaving it on a bench.

As he stepped into the car park, he pulled up the collar of his coat.

'Got the masks?' He turned back to Rab who jogging to catch up.

Rab waved two black woollen ski masks.

The corners of Billy's mouth creased into a malevolent smile.

The late evening news was starting as Jock Kerr set his steaming mug of tea on the coffee table and flopped onto the sofa. He was about to shout through to Fiona, who was in the kitchen opening a fresh packet of shortbread, when the telephone rang. The handset lay on the coffee table and its display was glowing. He snorted and glanced at the clock on the mantelpiece, even though he knew the time. He snatched up the receiver.

'Hello?'

'Do you know who this is?' said the harsh voice. 'I always said I'd catch up with you and I have. Your day of reckoning is almost here.'

The line went dead.

Jock stiffened as continuous purring berated his ears. An image from the past flooded his mind. He recognised the voice and now his head was in turmoil. As he pushed himself up from his seat the lounge window exploded. Shards of glass flew everywhere and the closed blinds were torn from their fastenings, as a weighted lump appeared through the opening.

Jock froze. His eyes registered what lay before him but his brain was grappling with the vision; confusion, disbelief and fear were all manifesting at the same time. The head and bare shoulders of a man's lifeless body lay flopped over the windowsill, entangled in the wreckage of the blinds. He felt cold as he stared at the long, unkempt hair hanging from the bloodied head and became conscious of an awful gut-wrenching smell.

His wife's piercing screams jolted him into action — the instinct to survive taking over. Jock jumped up and made a dash for the hallway. Flinging open the front door, he ran out onto the path. It took a few seconds for his vision to adjust, but then he saw clearly — slumped half-inside, half outside the front window was a naked man. The paleness of the flesh told Jock he was dead.

Out of the corner of his eye, he caught movement at the top of his drive and turned. A tall silhouetted figure stood looking at him. Behind the shadow, against the kerb, a hatchback had its engine revving loudly. In the half-light he could make out at least a couple more people in the front and rear, all staring at him. The figure at the top of his drive was slowly pulling off a ski mask. Jock caught sight of a beard, and as the woollen mask was completely removed straggly, wavy hair dropped, framing the man's face.

A shiver ran down Jock's spine. Despite the greying beard and hair, he still recognised his nemesis. Billy Wallace's eyes were wide and staring, glistening with hate.

In the distance Jock could hear the faint wail of a siren; the police were on their way and a wave of relief washed over him.

There was a stand-off as Jock scrutinised Billy, who stood, motionless.

For a moment Billy remained, staring back at him. Then he lifted a hand and dragged a finger across his exposed throat — a slow slicing movement. He gave a menacing smile before turning and climbing into the front passenger seat of the car. His door was still open as the wheels squealed on the wet tarmac. It shot away from the kerb, tearing towards a side street.

Hunter sank into his armchair with a tumbler of single malt whisky. He swilled the amber liquid around, listening to the chink of ice against the cut glass, then savoured his first sip, enjoying the pleasant afterburn tickling the back of his throat, drifting down his gullet and into his stomach.

It had been another long day.

He took another small sip, this time holding it in his mouth. Momentarily, he closed his eyes as the oak-aged flavour caressed his taste buds. He swallowed.

Moments like this were rare these days.

He'd got home an hour ago, in time for Beth to make her girls' night appointment. He hadn't even taken off his jacket before she was kissing his cheek and telling him his salmon was in the microwave and there was salad in the fridge.

'I'm only around the corner at Julie's,' she shouted over her shoulder. 'You know where I am. See you about eleven.' She disappeared out of the door.

He'd only just managed to get Jonathan and Daniel settled down. As he'd ruffled their hair affectionately and kissed their foreheads before tucking the boys in, it had jolted his conscience. He wished he had more time for this.

Hunter picked up the remote from the coffee table and powered on the TV; he would try and lose himself for a couple of hours before Beth got home.

He took another glug of whisky and listened to the sounds of the house. The central heating pipes creaked upstairs beneath the floorboards. He sank into his armchair, feeling himself relax. He swilled the contents around again; the tumbler was almost empty.

One more, and that's it.

He enjoyed a drink at home but never more than a couple to unwind. Many of his colleagues used it as a crutch to ease away the tensions of the day, only to find themselves relying on it too much. For some cops, drinking was second nature and he'd seen the disastrous consequences. He was determined not to go down that route.

Twenty minutes later, as he set down his second empty glass, he felt his eyelids drooping. He was close to exhaustion.

Time to call it a day.

He couldn't stay awake much longer. Not even for Beth. Never mind, he knew she'd understand.

As he eased himself up, the phone rang.

It was his parents' names on the screen, and he slipped the receiver out of its stand and answered.

Before he had time to speak, his mum's voice screamed down the line. Her panicked cries rattled him to the core. He tried to interrupt, make sense of her high-pitched ramblings. Finally, unable to get a word in, he shouted, 'I'm on my way!' and ended the call.

He speed-dialled Beth's mobile — she was only two minutes away — and bolted upstairs to sling on jeans and a sweat top. By the time he came downstairs again, Beth was falling through the front door, her face flushed.

'Sorry about this,' he said, snatching up the car keys from the hallway table. 'Something's happened at Mum's. I'll ring you as soon as I find out what!'

Hunter raced at break-neck speed towards his parents' home. The tiredness of ten minutes earlier had gone and it was like he'd never touched a drink. He was alert and trying to make sense of the hysterical screams he'd heard on the phone.

Within twelve minutes of leaving home he was screeching into his parents' road — to be greeted by mayhem.

The street was awash with police officers, and emergency vehicles of all descriptions lined the road, their whirling strobes lighting the area like a disco. Blue and white crime scene tape was everywhere — sealing off the approach to his mum and dad's semi and keeping neighbours back.

His stomach turned. This was the scene of a major incident.

Hunter slewed his car into the kerb and leapt out, leaving the driver's door open as he sprinted towards the house. A young uniformed officer was about to head him off but moved aside when Hunter flashed his warrant card.

He slackened his pace as he neared the driveway — he had never seen so much activity. Uniformed cops, plain clothed detectives and Scenes of Crime officers were swarming around the front of the house. It seemed surreal. This was his old home, he had moved here when he was twelve years old and had spent his teenage years growing up in its warm and loving environment. And this was close to where he'd met Polly, who had lived three streets away and with whom he'd fallen madly in love as his first girlfriend. It was here where he had heard about her murder. Finally, it was where he had made his most life-changing decision — telling his parents he didn't want to go to university to study fine art, instead, he wanted to be a cop and catch his girlfriend's killer.

A lot of water had flowed under the bridge since then.

He tried to focus as he walked up the drive. Much of the activity was by the lounge window which had a gaping hole in it. Two forensic officers were draping a plastic sheet over something half-inside the window and as he got nearer Hunter realised it was the naked shape of a gaunt, lanky man. This is why his mum was in in such a state.

On the front lawn, the skeletal frame of a forensic tent was in the process of being erected by SOCO. He recognised Duncan Wroe.

Then he spotted his boss emerging from the front door. In the hallway, behind him, stood the red-headed Scottish DCI. He tried to recollect her name but his brain was mush.

'Hunter!' shouted Detective Superintendent Robshaw.

Hunter's pace had dropped to a fast walk. 'What the hell is going on? Who on earth's this?' he pointed at the body. 'Where are my mum and dad? Are they hurt?' He machine-gunned questions one after another.

Robshaw held up a hand as Dawn joined him.

Hunter pointed at her. 'Why's DCI Leggate here?' He'd remembered her name. 'What's she got to do with this?'

'Whoa! Just a minute Hunter, calm down. Both your parents are okay. Shook up, but neither of them are hurt. They're on their way to the Victim Interview Suite at Maltby police station. The FME is en route to check them over.'

'Who's that?' Hunter asked again, pointing at the naked corpse which had finally been covered up.

'Steady down, Hunter, and we'll tell you.'

Robshaw glanced sideways at the Scottish DCI.

She shrugged and took a deep breath, pushing her hands into her rainproof jacket. 'That's the body of a junkie.'

'A junkie?'

Dawn nodded. 'He was abducted two weeks ago near to where he lived in Glasgow.'

Hunter was dumbfounded. Everything was spinning round in his head.

'What's having the body of a druggie from Glasgow thrown through the front window of my mum and dad's home got to do with them?'

'It's all linked to an investigation I'm involved in,' Dawn said.

He looked from Dawn to Robshaw and pointed his finger at her like a weapon. 'I knew you were down here for something. What's this shit you're hiding from me?'

'That's enough, Hunter,' said Robshaw. 'Don't say something you'll regret later.' He took a step forward. 'DCI Leggate is here under my sanction, and she and her team have been trying to protect your father. As I have already told you, your mum and dad are safe and should be at Maltby police station by now. I want you to go there with DCI Leggate and when you get there, she and your dad will fill you in with everything you need to know.'

Given the time of night, the main roads were quiet, enabling Hunter to step on the accelerator as he headed towards Maltby Police Station.

Beside him sat Dawn Leggate.

'The junkie's name is Fraser Cullen. He was a snout for one of my DSs.'

Hunter watched her out of the corner of his eye. She never took her eyes away from the windscreen.

'It's a long story, but basically, me and my team have been investigating the murders of three retired detectives and just over two weeks ago Fraser contacted my DS with information about one of the murders. Fraser gave us the names of two men who had beaten to death a retired detective in Glasgow. Ten minutes after the meeting between Fraser and my DS, we got an anonymous phone call to the effect that someone had seen Fraser being bundled into a grey Ford Mondeo. We've been searching for him, the car, and the two men he named since that call.'

There was the grey Mondeo again. The same colour and make of car that was involved in the attack on one of Hunter's uniformed colleagues, and which he had disturbed in the car park of his dad's gym yesterday.

What the fuck is going on? 'I don't get it. What's the relevance of Fraser's — whatever his name is — dead body being thrown through my parents' front window? Are you saying my dad's involved in drugs?'

'Cullen. Fraser Cullen. And no, it's nothing to do with drugs. As I've said, it's a long story, and soon you'll be told everything. Let's just see if your mum and dad are all right first. That's the main priority. Then if your dad's in a fit state to talk he can tell you everything. I promised him he could be the one to tell you when the time came.'

Hunter's head was in a whirl and he was doing his best to focus on his driving. He gripped the steering wheel so tightly that a tingling sensation shot through his fingers and into his forearms. His brain was desperately trying to make sense of the muddle and as he glanced down at his hands, he felt nothing but frustration and vexation.

He spotted the road sign for Maltby police station — the journey had flown. He flicked down the indicator and turned off the main road.

Pulling into a visitor's bay, he killed the engine and took a deep breath.

Dawn Leggate grabbed Hunter's forearm.

He stared at her.

'I'm not trying to hide anything from you, DS Kerr, believe me. I made a promise to your father and I'm simply keeping it. In another ten minutes you'll know everything. Some of what you are going to hear is not going to sit comfortably so I'm warning you to be prepared.'

Hunter led the way into the station; he had been here before. They both flashed their warrant cards to the receptionist and she buzzed them through and directed them to where they needed to be.

The Victim Reception Suite was where rape victims and abused children normally came to be supported, examined and questioned. Hunter had used similar rooms at other stations when he was in CID.

Hunter pushed through the door into an overbearingly warm room furnished like someone's front lounge. His mum launched herself from the sofa and flung her arms around his neck.

Hunter felt her body convulse as she mumbled his name. It took him aback; he had never witnessed an outburst like this from his mum — she was such a strong character.

It deflated his anger and frustration, bringing him to his senses. He looked over to his dad who was slowly rising from one of the seats, his face a picture of shock.

Hunter gently eased his mum away. Her eyes were bloodshot.

DCI Leggate guided her back to the sofa and sat next to her.

Hunter dropped into a chair facing them.

Dawn flashed an awkward smile at Jock. 'I've not told your son anything yet, Jock, but now it's time for him to know. We agreed that if things ever came to this it would be the right thing to do, didn't we?'

Jock nodded forlornly.

Dawn turned her attention to Hunter. 'Before your father tells you his bit, I'll explain where I fit into all this. Just over three months ago two prisoners serving life for the murder of a 24-year-old woman and her four-year-old daughter were released from Barlinnie prison after spending 36 years behind bars. Those two prisoners are Billy Wallace and Rab Geddes. I didn't know either of them — way before my time — but I know them now. Billy had the nickname Braveheart in his younger days. He had a fearsome reputation and used to boast that William Wallace was his ancestor. I'm not sure that's true, and knowing what I now know about Billy Wallace I think it's an insult to a great Scottish hero.

'Billy comes from bad stock. His father, Gordon, did time for a couple of warehouse robberies and was involved in the black market during the 1950s in Glasgow. Throughout the 60s, Gordon built up a bit of a criminal empire and formed one of the leading gangster families in the suburbs, offering protection to pubs and clubs and at one stage he was peddling guns around to criminals.'

She leaned forward, clasping her hands. 'Gordon introduced his son into the fold when he was about 18. Billy was a real tough-nut who could handle himself and he quickly made a reputation for himself because of the extreme violence he used. Rab Geddes was a lifelong school friend and between them they began to run the Wallace family business. Billy started to push drugs — something unheard of in the gangs back then — and began to amass quite a fortune.

'Then things took a turn for the worse for Billy and his family. The police began to crack down. A few rogue cops who had been taking backhanders to turn the other cheek, or in some cases lose evidence, were investigated and dismissed and many gang members had their collars felt. Rival gangs started to turn against one another.

'The Procurator Fiscal and the CID from Shettlestone nick began looking at the Wallace gang round about 1970 and Gordon decided to call it a day, happy to live off the wealth he had amassed from his earlier criminal activities. His son Billy didn't, and one night back in 1971, when he went to collect a drug debt, things boiled over. He couldn't find the dealer who had ripped him off and so in a fit of temper he shot the guy's girlfriend and her four-year-old daughter before setting fire to the flat.

'Within days, snouts from opposing gangs had dropped Billy and Rab for it and detectives got a breakthrough with a witness who had been there on the night of the murders and who provided crucial evidence. The upshot was that they were both arrested and as a result of the evidence they were convicted and sent to prison for 36 years.

'You will have gathered by now that Billy is a bit of a psycho, and even in prison he continued his violence. He was responsible for at least one prisoner's murder and he was also involved in the stabbing of two others.' Dawn sat back and crossed one leg over the other. 'He vowed revenge against the team of detectives who'd arrested him and the main witness who had helped to convict him. And that's where I've come in. Several weeks ago, Billy and Rab disappeared off the radar when they did a bunk from a bail hostel. Shortly after, four people — three men and a woman — were brutally murdered. The man and woman were from my neck of the woods — Stirling, the other two men lived near Glasgow. The men are all retired detectives — the same detectives who were responsible for getting the convictions and putting Wallace and Geddes behind bars. My team from Stirling are involved in a joint investigation with Glasgow CID and we have enough evidence to link Billy and Rab to the murders.' She uncrossed her legs and hunched forward. 'Your dad recognised Billy Wallace this evening. The grey Mondeo he came in got away before we got there but we have circulated it. There are a lot of officers on the ground looking for them as I speak — but you'll have guessed that.'

The mention of the grey Mondeo flashed an alert inside Hunter's head. Now he remembered where he'd seen the driver before. The newly grown, thinning, sandy hair had tricked him. It was the shaven-headed man he'd seen arguing with his dad at Staithes. It was all fitting into place.

Dawn continued. 'Me and my team are down here for two reasons — one, to track down Wallace and Geddes, and two, and just as important, to protect the main witness from that trial back in 1972 — your father.' She looked across at Jock. 'I'll let you take over.'

Jock took a deep breath and glanced at his wife. Then, as he had done so many times recently, he avoided eye contact, instead staring down at his clasped hands.

'This is very difficult for me, son,' he began. 'I've not tried to hide this from you — I just didn't know how to tell you what you're about to hear, especially with the important job you have. I suppose naively I hoped it would never come to this. What do they say about the best laid plans?' Tears welled up in Jock's eyes. 'You know I've told you all about my younger days as a boxer and how my career ended and how me and your ma came down to Yorkshire where you were born and I set up the gym?'

Hunter nodded. He felt his stomach knot as his dad wiped the corner of an eye with the back of a hand.

'All that is true but I have never told you why, have I, son?' He looked at Hunter for the first time, took his wallet from his trousers, fished into it, extracted a folded piece of paper and held it out.

Hunter took the yellowed, Sellotaped news cutting, which he unfolded. The headline read: GLASGOW GANGSTERS SENTENCED FOR BRUTAL SLAYING OF MOTHER AND DAUGHTER. Below that was a smaller sub-heading: SUPERGRASS TURNS QUEEN'S EVIDENCE. Hunter started to read.

'That's what I've been trying to avoid all these years, you finding out the full facts. My name's not Jock Kerr — or rather my birth name wasn't that.'

Hunter felt like he'd been punched in the guts. His stomach turned. From the look on the faces of his mum and the DCI, he knew he had heard right. His head started to throb.

'I'm sorry, son, I know this has come as a bit of a shock but now you know. I've been living under an assumed name for years. I was forced to change it after the trial. I took on your grandfather's name from your mother's side, and the Procurator Fiscal and the detectives on the case helped me to relocate to Yorkshire.'

'So, you're the supergrass in the article?'

'No — no, nothing like that. That was just what the papers wrote. Let me tell you the full story before you judge me.'

'I think you'd better.'

'After I had to give up my boxing, I didn't know what to do, and Billy's dad — Gordon Wallace — came to me one night when I was in the club having a beer. He said he'd heard good things about me and maybe he could put some work my way. I was good with my fists so he offered me some door work looking after a couple of clubs. I knew Gordon as being dodgy but I genuinely didn't know the level of crime he was involved in. Then one day he turns up at the flat I had with your ma and says he wants me to keep an eye on his son, Billy. Some people were after Billy and he asked me to drive him around and watch his back. Said he'd pay me a hundred pounds a week. Well, I jumped at the chance, didn't I — where else could I earn that type of money? All he said to me was I wasn't to ask too many questions, just watch his son's back.

'Well, the first time I picked Billy up he introduced me to his pal Rab and asked me to drive them to this tenement because he had some business to sort out. I had no idea what he was up to until he and Rab came running back to the car and told me to get them out of there. There was blood everywhere. Billy said the woman in the flat had slashed him with a knife. Him and Rab were arguing over shooting a kid and Billy was flashing this shooter about. I was really scared, Hunter. I drove them to some wasteland and watched them bury the gun and then they told me to drop them off.

'I was physically sick when I got home. The next day, I saw on the news that they'd killed a woman and her four-year-old bairn. I told your ma what had happened and she told me to go to the police. I didn't at first but I called anonymously and gave them Billy's and Rab's names. I don't know how, but a couple of days later two detectives came to the flat and asked me about the murders. I told them everything and they told me to find somewhere else to live until the trial. I knew I wouldn't be safe, especially when I found out about the gangster connections and it came out about my links to Gordon Wallace, and so I agreed a deal with the police. I said I would give evidence if they gave me a fresh start — and they did. I stopped being Iain Campbell.' For a second Jock closed his eyes. 'Little did I realise what repercussions there would be. Do you realise now why I wanted to hold this back?'

'And that guy I saw you arguing with in Staithes?'

'Rab Geddes. It was sheer bad luck he recognised me, especially after all these years. Apparently, he was visiting an old girlfriend.'

For a few seconds, Hunter felt like a great weight was pushing down on him. He was trying to make sense of what he had been told. What kind of person was his dad, and just as important, who was he?

'This may seem a strange question, Dad. Is my name really Hunter Kerr?'

Jock looked shocked. 'Of course it is. Only I changed my name. It was done by deed poll. Your mum was already a Kerr so she reverted back to her maiden name. You were christened Hunter and your birth certificate says that.'

Hunter dropped his head into his hands and rubbed his face. He could feel a migraine coming on for the first time in ages. In another hour or so the pressure would be so great that he'd see flashing stars and be physically sick.

DAY THIRTY-THREE

Hunter adjusted the rear-view mirror, stared at his reflection and noted the dark rings under his eyes. He stroked his jaw-line — he was in need of a shave.

Overall, you look like shit, Hunter Kerr.

'You look crap,' said Grace.

It was like she'd heard the voice in his head. He glanced across at her in the passenger seat.

'I feel it. I've hardly slept the past couple of days.'

'Your dad?'

Hunter nodded. 'He and my mum are staying with us.'

'They'll catch this Billy Wallace and his mate soon and then you can all put it behind you. It sounds to me as though they've got them bang to rights and they'll be going back inside and die in prison.' Grace examined her fingernails. The pearlescent polish glinted in the sunlight.

'We won't be able to put it behind us, though, will we? It's always going to be there, isn't it?'

She fixed him with a glare. 'Oh, for goodness' sake, Hunter, stop feeling sorry for yourself. How will it affect you in the future? It's your dad this has happened to.'

'Grace, he's not the man I thought I knew. All these years he's lied to me.'

'Listen to me, Hunter. This is me talking to you, not only as a colleague but as a friend as well. Your father has not lied to you and never has done. Yes, he's held back the truth but that is not lying. And the way I see it he did it with all best intentions, especially with the job you've got. How could he have told his son — a cop — that he was involved with gangsters in his past? Think about it for a second — would you tell your sons?'

He held her stare. He had no response. He hadn't looked at it that way.

'And from what you've told me it seems to me he had little choice. He was only 20 at the time with all kinds of problems to deal with, especially how to make a living for him and your mother after his promising boxing career had ended. I'm sorry but I don't agree with you on this one. I feel for your dad. It must have been a living nightmare for him the last couple of months. Can't you imagine what must have been going on inside his head? He was trying to protect your mum and you from this. You need to take a long, hard look at yourself, Hunter. You've only got one set of parents. You know how much they've been there for you and how much you've got in common with your dad. He's your friend as well as your father. If you carry on like this, you'll be in danger of destroying your relationship. Anyway, what's Beth say about all this?'

Hunter hesitated. He'd had a similar hushed conversation with his wife. Finally, he said, 'Practically the same as you.' He felt a lump in his throat.

'Well, there you are then. Listen to her. I don't know what you men would do without us women. For god's sake, take him out for a beer and clear the air.'

Suddenly, their radios broke into the conversation.

He, Grace, and the majority of the MIT team had been on plot since 7 a.m., in unmarked cars at locations dotted around Parkhill Flats in Sheffield, lying in wait for Ari and Pervez Arshad.

Grace yanked across her seatbelt and Hunter started the car, straining to hear the report coming over the radio net.

213

The information he was listening to spirited his thoughts away from the problems of his dad and took him back to the previous afternoon, when Superintendent Robshaw had bounded into the office with the news that they had found out where Samia's killers were hiding. A Drug Squad informant had revealed the location — a flat which the team was now staking out. The pair had false passports and were making plans to leave the country in the next few days.

'They should be coming into view in the next minute or so,' Grace said, ear close to her radio.

Hunter was listening too. DS Mark Gamble and DC Paula Clarke were on foot and had Ari and Pervez in their sights. They gave the targets' descriptions and location.

Hunter parked on an elevated section of road overlooking the concrete monoliths, which he had read somewhere were now an icon of 60s architecture. Many of the blocks were in the throes of refurbishment and their frontages had been given a vibrant colour scheme of red, blue and yellow in an attempt to hide their drab greyness.

Within seconds, Hunter had the targets in sight.

The two Asians appeared to be in no hurry. They were sauntering across a grassy slope 150 metres below. The pair were dressed identically in dark hoodies and baggy jeans and the glint of gold in the bright mid-morning sunshine revealed that both wore a number of lengthy chains around their necks, dangling to mid chest. They were huddled together and appeared deep in conversation.

Hunter leaned forward as the pair made a surprise sharp movement. They stopped in mid-step and turned to look behind.

Something had spooked them, thought Hunter.

A split second later the brothers were off and running, with DS Mark Gamble scrambling after them. His voice was screaming over the airwaves, letting everyone know that the foot surveillance had been compromised.

Hunter kept watch on the fleeing figures, checking where they were heading before he made a move. Gripping the handbrake, he squeezed the accelerator and felt the engine surge. He was ready for the chase.

The pair dropped from view, disappearing into a line of trees at the edge of the estate. They were making for the road.

Mark Gamble was doing his best to keep the commentary going, his voice trailing off now and again as he tried to make ground. Within seconds his excited tone was alerting the team.

'They're getting into a new-shaped silver Astra!'

Hunter craned his neck, scouring the road system beyond the line of trees. He heard the Vauxhall before he saw it as tyre rubber screeched on the tarmac. Then it sped into his sightline, heading away from the estate and towards the suburbs of Halfway. Hunter locked the steering wheel sharply and pulled away from the kerb. Whipping through the gears quickly he soon made the junction and he guessed he would be a fraction in front of the speeding Astra. He could hear over the radio that two other cars were in hot pursuit but trailing.

Hunter slung his car at an angle to stop the Vauxhall turning into the road. He tightened his hold on the steering wheel and braced himself.

Ten seconds later the Astra gunned into view, rocking out of a right-hand bend and veering towards them.

Hunter gritted his teeth and in one swift movement spun the steering wheel sharply, hitting the accelerator and the brake almost simultaneously. His car jumped forward into the carriageway, giving the impression he was going to deliberately ram them.

The action had the desired effect. There was a long screech as the Astra tyres crabbed across the road. It slewed sideways, the nearside wheels smashing into the opposite kerb.

Hunter could see Ari, the driver, fighting with the wheel, trying to straighten up as the car bounced back into the road. His actions were in vain. It bucked and scythed violently, whipping into a screaming 180-degree turn before smashing its back end against a street lamp.

Hunter threw open his door, released his seatbelt and leapt out of the car.

Ari was as quick, kicking open his door so that it smacked Hunter's legs and spun him sideways, giving Ari the few seconds break he needed. He was out of the blocks like a sprinter on a running track.

Hunter winced at the pain to his right thigh but then adrenaline kicked in and he set off in pursuit.

Ari had gained ten yards. Hunter could make out the word SEMTEX in large white letters across the back of his black designer hooded top and thought how much he'd like to demolish him once he got hold of him.

Within moments his chest was pumping in rhythm with his arms and legs. His lungs clawed for air as he put in an extra burst. In less than fifty yards Hunter was in grabbing distance and he lashed out with a swift kick. It connected, crashing one leg into the other, sending Ari sprawling into a heap. Hunter was on top of him and wrestling an arm up his back before he had any time to react.

He screamed as Hunter yanked his shoulder joint against the socket.

'You're breaking my fucking arm!'

'Think yourself lucky it's not your fucking neck,' Hunter snarled. 'You're nicked!'

As he turned to drag his prisoner back, he saw the chaos behind him. Uniform and CID cars were everywhere and Grace was trying to snap handcuffs on the wrists of a dishevelled Pervez. He was being restrained by Tony Bullars, who had been the lead car in the chase.

As Hunter neared, jamming Ari's arm up his back, forcing him to walk on his tip-toes, he could see Pervez was doubled up, struggling with Tony Bullars, trying to rub his face and moaning loudly.

'What's the matter with him?' he asked, releasing his prisoner to Mike Sampson who was waiting with cuffs.

Pervez raised his head. Tears were streaming down his face and he was having difficulty opening his eyes.

'That fucking bitch has CSed me,' he moaned.

'Stop rubbing your eyes, you'll only make it worse,' Grace said with a smirk, slipping the CS gas canister back into her jacket pocket. She turned to Hunter. 'I thought he was going to attack me so I gassed him.'

'Fucking liar, I said I was coming quietly.'

Hunter kept a straight face. 'I don't know, Grace, what have I said to you about police brutality and that temper of yours?' He opened the back door of his car and shoved Ari onto the rear seat. 'I wouldn't dream of doing anything like that. I don't know, I can't take you anywhere.'

He turned to see her rolling her eyes and shaking her head in mock despair and he shot her a wink.

'Well done, everyone,' he said, slamming the rear door shut. 'Let's wrap this up and get these two back for questioning.'

Hunter picked up a Pakistani passport, flicked through the inside pages and added a few more notes to his pre-interview record. He set it back down on the pile of evidence laid out across his and Grace's desks.

Upon their return to Barnwell with their prisoners, the team had emptied the contents of Ari and Pervez's Vauxhall Astra. In the boot they found clothing in three holdalls, together with two single airline tickets to Allama Iqbal International Airport and two Pakistan National passports bearing Ari and Pervez's photographs, but under other names.

The Drug Squad informant had been spot-on about the brothers making ready to flee the country, thought Hunter as he looked across to where Grace was still logging the evidence.

The incident room was empty. Mark Gamble and Paula Clarke had shot out to Hassan's convenience store. They were going to arrest Mohammed and Jilani, now the Arshads were in custody, while Andy France and Alex Mills were in Sheffield, trying to find an address for the brothers. They had refused to divulge where they lived when they were booked into custody and nothing in their possessions had offered a clue. However, they had recovered the brothers' mobile phones, which were now with the technical experts in the hope that they could locate the last spot where a signal was emitted. It was a long shot.

'Ready?' Hunter asked. He and Grace were to interview Ari, while Tony Bullars and Mike Sampson had the job of questioning his brother Pervez. They were already in one of the other interview rooms.

Grace nodded.

Hunter pushed back his chair and gathered his notes. He took a final lingering look at the incident board, confirming and double-checking in his head that he had it all lodged, ready for when he needed to dig in to his memory banks. He nodded. He was prepared.

'Okay, Grace, let's put this job to bed.'

Ari Arshad looked cocky despite the painful pink graze to his right cheek, caused when Hunter tripped him prior to arrest. He had bleated to the Custody Officer about assault when he was booked in. He leant back on the rear legs of his chair; arms folded defensively.

The duty solicitor was next to him, making notes in his legal pad. As the two detectives walked into the room, Hunter saw the solicitor check his watch and make a note of the time.

Hunter slapped his paperwork on the table, making the solicitor jump and scowl at him over his spectacles. Hunter cracked a false apologetic smile. 'Sorry about that.' He took a seat opposite, nodding to Grace and she started the tape-recording machine.

Hunter went through the customary preamble to an interview, flicking open his folder even though he knew he wouldn't need to refer to it.

'For the tape, can I confirm you are Ari Arshad?'

The prisoner exchanged a look with his solicitor, who shrugged his shoulders and nodded.

Ari rocked slightly on the back legs of his chair. 'That's right, I am the one and only Ari Arshad,' he said.

'And not Habib-ur-Begum, as it says in the Pakistan National Passport we found in your car?'

'No comment.'

'Why were you in possession of a false passport and a one-way airline ticket to Pakistan?'

'No comment.'

'Okay, if that's the tack you wish to take, Ari, I'll ask you a less incriminating question. Just for the record, what relation are you to Mohammed Hassan?'

Ari glanced at his solicitor again, who gestured with raised eyebrows that it was okay to answer.

'Mohammed is my uncle.'

'And so Samia Hassan, his daughter, is your cousin?' Hunter removed a photo of Samia from beneath his papers. It was a blown up shot from the Meadowhall CCTV footage. 'For the tape, I am showing the defendant a colour photograph of Samia Hassan. Is this the Samia we are talking about?'

Ari nodded. 'Yes.'

'When was the last time you saw Samia?'

Ari bunched his shoulders. 'Can't remember.'

'Rough guess. Couple of weeks, couple of months?'

'Couple of months, I guess.'

'Where was that?'

'At my uncle's place.'

'What address is that?' Hunter was hoping for a slip up. They still did not know the attack site.

'His shop in Hoyland.'

'You have already been told the reason for your arrest this morning, haven't you?'

'Yes, but that's shit. I haven't murdered Samia. You've got the wrong man, Mr Smart Detective.'

Hunter rolled with the sarcastic retort. 'I'm guessing you've seen the TV news and the newspaper headlines about Samia's murder?'

'Yeah.'

'When did you first become aware of her disappearance?'

'Can't remember.'

'Who told you about it?'

'My uncle, I think.'

'Can you remember when that was?'

'Nope.'

Hunter needed to move things forward. He replaced the photograph in his folder and took out another. It was of the white Renault van recovered from the Rotherham car dismantlers. 'Ari, slight change of questioning now. Do you recognise this van?'

Hunter clocked Ari's reaction. He dropped his chair back on to its four legs but didn't respond.

'I'll ask the question again. Do you recognise this white Renault van?'

Ari coughed. 'I think so.'

'You think so?'

'My uncle owned a similar van.'

'This is the van owned by your uncle, Mohammed Hassan — I can confirm that from its index number. Have you ever driven this van?' From Duncan Wroe's SOCO report, Hunter knew Ari's fingerprints and DNA were all over the van and that he had been seen in the Country Park by Dr Christopher Chambers.

There were a couple of seconds silence then Ari replied softly, 'Yeah, I used to do deliveries for him.'

'When was the last time you drove or were in this van?'

There was a delayed response again. 'Can't remember.'

'Let me help you remember. Have you ever been to Meadowhall in the van?'

Now there was a clear reaction. Ari locked his arms tighter and his face hardened.

Hunter waited for twenty seconds but there was no reply. 'I'll ask again. Have you ever driven to or been in this vehicle at Meadowhall shopping centre?'

Ari turned to his solicitor as if seeking help with an answer. His solicitor picked up on the look. 'DS Kerr, is this line of questioning going anywhere?'

Hunter opened up a CD case, took out a DVD and slid it across to Grace, who slotted it into a small TV/DVD player set in the corner of the room. The screen flashed from dark grey to blue.

Hunter turned to the solicitor. 'There is some significance to this line of questioning which your client obviously finds uncomfortable answering. Could it be he has something to hide?'

'DS Kerr, that is out of order.'

Hunter fixed Ari with a determined stare. 'Mr Arshad, my question relating to your use of your uncle's white van at Meadowhall has in my view hit a raw nerve. I am therefore going to show you some CCTV footage which may help jog your memory.'

He nodded to Grace, who hit the play button on the TV. Over the next five minutes the horrific attack on Samia by Ari and Pervez in the underground car park at Meadowhall played out across the screen. The entire time Hunter studied his prisoner's face. He put on a front as he watched the damning evidence but from the continued movement in the young man's Adam's apple, Hunter knew he had him rattled.

Grace stopped the footage.

'Do you want me to play that again or are you happy for me to ask you questions in relation to what you've just seen on the TV?'

Complete silence.

'You have just watched an attack upon Samia Hassan in the underground car park at Meadowhall shopping centre which was carried out by two men on the 28th of July this year. Do you recognise the two men you have seen carry out that attack?'

Ari's eyes widened. He glared back in defiance.

'Mr Arshad, I would appreciate an answer. From what you have just been shown, do you agree that the one of the people who beat Samia Hassan until she was unconscious was yourself?'

Ari unfolded his arms and slammed them onto the table. 'No comment. No fucking comment.'

The solicitor reached across and tapped Ari Arshad's arm. 'DS Kerr, I would like ten minutes with my client,' he announced.

The ten minutes went beyond twenty minutes. Hunter leaned against the wall outside the interview room, his eyes on the gap at the bottom of the door. He knew that inside the room there was some serious client solicitor storyline being hammered out. A smile played on his lips; they had Ari on the rack.

Just as he was checking his watch again the door opened and the solicitor stuck his head around it. 'My client is ready to answer your questions.'

Hunter and Grace started with fresh tapes. Grace switched on the recording machine and Hunter reminded Ari of his rights. 'Okay, before we had a break you were shown CCTV footage of an attack upon Samia Hassan by two men. Was one of those men you?'

'Yeah, but I didn't kill Samia.'

'And who was the other person who carried out the attack with you?'

'You know who it is. It's Pervez, my brother.'

'Why did you attack Samia?'

'We were forced to do it.'

'Forced?'

'Yeah, you don't know what my uncle Mohammed is like. He's a violent man, we're scared of him. He told us to do it.'

This didn't ring true, especially given the criminal records of the pair, but Hunter encouraged Ari to continue.

'Mohammed used to ring me lots, telling me Samia was dishonouring the family. He told me she was sleeping with a man outside of marriage and wanted us to warn her and get her to come home. Then a few months ago he came to see me and Pervez and said we had to do something about Samia. She was refusing to marry a cousin of ours after agreeing to the marriage and he wanted us to make her go to Pakistan. I told him we couldn't do that but he threatened me and Pervez. He is a very violent man. That day at Meadowhall, me and Pervez were making deliveries for our uncle and he phoned me up shouting and swearing. He said Samia was at Meadowhall threatening to run away and he told us to go and get her and bring her back. I know on that footage it looks worse than it was.'

'Looks worse than it was,' interrupted Hunter. 'You beat her unconscious and threw her in the back of the van like a rag doll.'

Ari shrugged. 'We didn't mean to beat her like we did, we just got carried away.'

'So, what happened after you left the car park?'

'Mohammed met us on an industrial site near Rotherham and took her out of the van and drove her away. We didn't kill her. The last time I saw her was when we helped put her in the back of Mohammed's car.'

Hunter hadn't expected this response. He had damning evidence to refute what had just been said. His spirits lifted.

'You say you took Samia out of the van and put her in her father's car?'

'Yeah.'

'Was she conscious or unconscious?'

'Conscious. She was struggling.'

'Then why did you get need to get rid of the van. To dispose of it at the car dismantlers like you did?'

Ari lowered his head for a few seconds before looking up again. 'Because Mohammed told us to. If he tells you something, you obey.'

'Did you do this straight away?'

'No, we hid the van in a garage for a few days then took it there.'

'Did anyone else use it?'

'No, we hid it.'

'Ari, I've let you go on a bit but that's because I wanted to give you enough rope to hang yourself. What you have just told us is complete bullshit. And how do I know that? Well, firstly, how do you account for fibres being found in the rear of the van? Fibres which match the rug in which Samia's body was found? Before you try and dig your way out of that one, I also want to introduce some other evidence as well. Do you remember a few years ago when Samia was at university and she had a relationship with a young man who was training to be a doctor?'

Ari looked up to the ceiling.

'A young man who you and your brother assaulted because of their relationship?'

Ari's eyes lowered. 'No complaint was ever made about that.'

'No, it wasn't, but we know you and your brother paid him a visit another time when he was working at Barnwell Infirmary and you warned him off and also damaged his car. And the bad news for you is that he just happened to be driving his car at Barnwell Lake on Friday, the first of August, the night you and your brother dumped Samia's body in the lake, and he recognised you driving your uncle's white van.'

From Ari's expression, Hunter knew he had him. The man closed his eyes for a few seconds then snapped them open. 'I've told you what happened, now I'm saying fuck all else.'

Hunter tried a few more probing questions which Ari batted off with 'no comment'. He'd lost the impetus of the interview and decided to sum things up, draw it to a close, and return Ari to his cell.

Hunter and Grace waited in the custody suite. Tony Bullars and Mike Sampson had not fared any better with Pervez, who had also made no comment to the majority of the questions. Once he was shown the CCTV footage of the attack on Samia, he refused to talk to the detectives except to demand to be locked up back in his cell.

They still had to interview Mohammed and his wife Jilani. At least Ari's evidence had implicated Samia's father and would provide a wedge, though Hunter doubted the truth of that, especially as they knew Samia had been violently raped prior to being murdered. That just didn't feel like something a father would do. They had made inroads that afternoon but were still no nearer to getting a clear-cut confession.

As they returned to the incident room for debriefing, Hunter knew the priority was to find the attack site. It would provide them with so many answers and much needed evidence to swing the enquiry.

DAY THIRTY-FOUR

Hunter pulled another bacon sandwich from the pile that Angie, the cleaner, and Grace had made. He'd heard them chatting and laughing in the small kitchen next to the incident room and wondered what they had found so amusing. He guessed they were gossiping about someone in the station.

Most of the team were in, hugging mugs of tea or coffee, munching on the surprise breakfast and chatting as they waited for the morning briefing.

This enquiry had just turned the corner, despite the lack of confessions to Samia's murder. The implication from Ari that his uncle Mohammed was responsible for his daughter's final days and hours was the starter for the day, and with a bit of luck it might just be the lever for obtaining the proper story.

Grace walked in with another plateful of sandwiches. 'That's it, all the bacon's gone now,' she said, plonking the plate down between hers and Hunter's desks.

'What muck have you two raked up on someone then? You were going at it hammer and tongs back there.'

Grace flopped into her seat and leaned across. 'You will never guess what I've just found out from Angie,' she said in a hushed voice.

'Go on, enlighten me.'

'The boss is only having a thing with that DCI from Scotland.'

'You are joking?'

'Nah, nah. One of her friends is waitressing at the Stables restaurant. The pair have been in there most evenings.'

Hunter shook his head in amazement and grinned. 'Well, the crafty bugger.'

Grace smiled, settling back in her chair.

Hunter took another bite of his sandwich. The mention of DCI Dawn Leggate caused him to drift away for a few moments. His parents were still staying with them. He'd wanted so much to sit down and sort things out with his dad but he hadn't had the chance because of the investigation. He had talked about it to Beth, who said his dad was moping round the house like a caged animal and wasn't eating properly. Hunter's mum had taken Beth to one side and told her his dad was desperate for some time with Hunter to explain everything.

The sooner we put this enquiry to bed, the sooner I can get things sorted with him.

'You lot owe me a gallon of beer,' announced Barry Newstead, as he strode into the room, breaking Hunter's daydream. 'You are going to really thank me for this.' He waved a CD aloft and headed for the TV, switched it on, inserted the disc into the player and grabbed the remote. 'I spent most of yesterday afternoon with the neighbourhood team for the Parkhill Flats. Did you know most of it is covered by CCTV?'

The screen fluttered into life.

'There are 20-odd cameras fitted around the outside of the place, plus they have lift cameras at each floor inside the flats. I searched various time frames between the 28th of July, when we know Samia was abducted from Meadowhall, right through to the first of August when we believe her body was dumped in the lake and I found this little lot.'

Barry grinned widely. He loved to take centre-stage. He fired the remote at the DVD player like he was shooting a gun. A grainy image fluttered onto the screen.

'This was captured at 9.36 p.m. on the first of August. This camera is looking down on a grassed area in front of one of the buildings.'

Suddenly, in the right-hand corner of the screen, two men in dark hooded tops stumbled into view, struggling with a rolled-up bundle. Barry zoomed in on the hazy images.

One of the men had his back to the camera and was bent over, dragging what appeared to be a large rolled up rug along the ground.

Although their hoods were up, hiding the men's faces, Hunter could clearly make out the white lettering on the back of one of the designer hooded tops. The word SEMTEX was visible. He felt a surge of excitement.

The team watched in silence. The play continued with the two men disappearing off camera with their bundle.

'I also found this footage,' said Barry.

Another image flashed onto the screen. The pan of the camera was a lot wider and covered a larger portion of the complex. Into view came a section of road below a grassy knoll. Along the bottom of the screen was a line of parked cars.

'This is one of the slip roads just below the flats.'

From the top of the screen, the camera picked up two fuzzy images, silhouettes at first, but their movement was evident and they were obviously the same two characters, from their clothing. And they were struggling with the rolled-up carpet. The one at the back slipped and his end of the carpet slumped to the ground.

The person humped it back up towards his midriff and then the pair continued waddling down the slope with their bundle until they reached the road.

Barry zoomed in on the footage again. It was grainy but the images could be made out, though not well enough for facial recognition.

The pair pulled the rug towards a white van parked in a row of vehicles. The one wearing the SEMTEX designer top opened its rear doors and the pair loaded in the bundle. Both jumped into the front of the van and it pulled away and drove out of camera view.

Barry freeze-framed the shot. In the top left-hand corner was the time and date sequence 9.52 p.m., 01:08:08.

It all fitted. The time to travel from Sheffield to Barnwell Lake was approximately 40 minutes. It meant that their witness, the sex worker, Kerri-Ann Bairstow had been spot-on with the timings of her sightings of the two men and the white van at the Country Park.

'And for my encore,' Barry added with a flourish. He restarted the DVD player. 'This was captured in the entranceway of one of the internal lifts.'

The image which flickered onto the screen showed a floor area with a section of lift doors at the top quarter of the screen. From the angle of the shot, this was captured by a camera at ceiling height.

Suddenly the person in the SEMTEX designer hoody came into view. He was bent double, dragging the rolled-up carpet. Quickly following, lumping the other end of the rug, came another hooded figure. The clarity of these images was excellent and sections of pattern on the carpet were a perfect match to those of the rug in which Samia's body had been found. Hunter had no doubt he was watching the first stages of her being taken away from the place where she had just been raped and butchered.

The pair stopped by the lift doors, dropping both ends of the carpet and the one in the designer hoody straightened, easing out his back with his hands. As he pressed for the lift, he flicked back his hood and stretched his neck. There was no mistaking that face — it was Ari Arshad.

Hunter wanted to punch the air.

'That lift is on the fifth floor. Now all you've got to do is some old-fashioned door-knocking and you should have your attack site.'

Hunter studied Barry. A pneumatic drill couldn't remove that contented smirk on his face. He was so pleased for him and so glad he had brought him onto the team.

'Ever thought about being a detective, Barry?' said Hunter, straight-faced, leaping out of his seat.

Barry scrutinised him for a second then said, 'Detective Sergeant Kerr, if I didn't know you better, I would say you're jealous because an old hand has beaten you to the end-game.'

They grinned at each other.

'One up to you, Barry,' said Hunter, wetting a finger and striking it in the air. 'Well done, you old fart.'

As he switched off the TV, Barry said, 'I'll take that as a compliment, shall I? By the way I will accept payment with several pints of John Smith's amber nectar.'

'Let me have a go at Jilani,' Grace said to Hunter.

At briefing, Superintendent Robshaw had decided that now they had the CCTV evidence damning Ari there was no rush to re-interview him — the team should focus on Samia's parents because no one had spoken with them since their arrest the previous afternoon.

He had allocated that task to Hunter and Grace, sending the remainder of the team across to Sheffield to find Ari and Pervez's place, now Barry had narrowed down the flat location and floor level.

Hunter looked up from his notes.

'Let me try the empathy approach — mother and daughter thing again. It might work this time. I can guess she's been subservient to Mohammed for years and even afraid of him, but I can't believe deep down that she is involved in all this. My gut instinct is she's keeping silent because she's more afraid of her husband than she is of us.'

Hunter stroked his chin. 'Okay, let's go for it.' He clicked the top back on his pen and slid the folder of evidence across the desk. 'She's all yours.'

Jilani looked haggard. Her dark hair was unkempt, her red and gold sari was crumpled and black streaks stained her cheeks from crying.

Grace could see the woman had suffered a sleepless night and guessed she was feeling jaded and vulnerable. It all stacked in her favour.

An interpreter and her solicitor were present.

Hunter started the tape recording machine.

'Jilani, I want to make things easy for you. Yesterday we interviewed your nephews Ari and Pervez and one of them has admitted to being involved in the abduction of your daughter Samia.' Grace concentrated on Jilani's face, looking for reactions as the interpreter repeated her opening lines in Urdu.

'He has also implicated your husband Mohammed in this, saying your husband forced them to carry out the abduction under threat of violence.' Grace deliberately held back Dr Chambers's evidence.

There was a flicker in the woman's eyes and she gave a quick shake of her head.

'Mrs Hassan, I don't want to prolong this agony for you, because what happened to your daughter was horrendous. But we have a duty to investigate this thoroughly and if we find you are involved in her murder then you will suffer the consequences. Do you understand what I am saying?'

Jilani nodded before the interpreter finished and Grace realised the woman had a better understanding of English than she had initially made out. That was good. It would be easier for her to look for the signs in her facial expressions and body language.

'I'm going to show you some film footage now that was captured by CCTV cameras about two months ago at Meadowhall. I must warn you, it is disturbing, but I want you to concentrate on it.'

Hunter got up, switched on the small TV, and started the DVD rolling with the same footage they had shown to Ari Arshad the previous day.

As it played Grace kept her eyes on Jilani. Five minutes had gone by when the woman dropped her head onto her chest and started to weep. As the tape came to an end, Grace said, 'I'm sorry you had to sit through that, Mrs Hassan, but I needed to show you just how your daughter started her suffering. I also have to tell you that we now believe she was held for five days before she was killed and during that time she was violently raped.'

The woman's anguish increased to a sob.

'I can tell you that we now have enough evidence to take this to court and prosecute for murder. Ari has implicated your husband in your daughter's murder and your prolonged silence in all this is not going to help you. If you continue to refuse to talk then we will suspect you are involved and you will also go to court.'

Jilani looked up at Grace. Black kohl eyeliner ran down her cheeks.

'Mrs Hassan, I am a mother of two daughters and if I thought my husband had been involved in their deaths I would move heaven and earth to see him punished. As a mother yourself, I do not believe for one second you would want anything different. Am I right?'

With glazed eyes, Jilani nodded. Then she began to speak in Urdu. After about twenty seconds, she stopped. 'I never realised they had done that to my Samia,' she delivered in broken but understandable English.

Grace took hold of Jilani's hands, giving her a sympathetic look. 'Mrs Hassan, do you want to tell us what you know?'

Jilani hung her head and dropped her gaze. 'I never wanted Samia harmed. I went along with my husband and told her I would disown her after what she had done with that young doctor. She knew our values and she went against them but I never wished any harm against her. It was Mohammed — he wouldn't let it go. He arranged for her to marry a cousin of his back in Pakistan. He said it would be the best thing for her but she flung it back in his face. Then he discovered she was planning to run away and he got very angry.'

'What did he do?'

'I knew he was arranging things with Ari but I didn't know what he intended. I know Ari and Pervez are not good people — that they have been in trouble, but I do not know what for. I pleaded with Mohammed to let things be, just disown her, but he wanted to punish her for bringing dishonour to him.' She broke into a fresh sobbing fit.

Grace let Jilani's hands go, fished a tissue from her jacket and handed it over.

Jilani dried her eyes. The kohl smudged further.

'Please go on, Mrs Hassan.'

'I never knew it was going to go this far. Mohammed told me Ari and Pervez were going to force her to go to Pakistan and everything would be sorted. When you came to the shop and I heard you say you were investigating her murder I was shocked. It was only then that I realised what Mohammed had done to Samia. Believe me, I did not know this. What you have shown me on the TV, the thing that has happened to Samia — it is evil.'

'Are you willing to give a statement?'

Jilani wiped her eyes again. Then she nodded.

For evidential purposes the first statement was written in English followed by a second in Urdu, by the interpreter. The evidence against Ari and Pervez Arshad and also Mohammed Hassan was damning and Hunter couldn't wait for that evening's briefing. He was eager to get back into the incident room to find out if the flat had been found.

Hunter followed Grace out into the custody suite corridor and closed the interview room door. He could hear Jilani Hassan sobbing. He turned to Grace with sparkling eyes and gave her a 'you did it' look, then planted a kiss on her forehead. 'You little beaut,' he said, before strolling back to the incident room.

Hunter and Grace rode the clanking lift to the fifth floor; they were looking for flat 508.

An hour earlier they had returned to an empty incident room and learned from Isabel Stevens that the whole team were over in Sheffield — the Arshads' flat had been found and they were doing house-to-house enquiries. They decided they wanted to be in on the action. Scooping up a set of car keys, Hunter told Grace that Pervez and Mohammed could sweat in the cells a little longer.

They lodged the statements made by Jilani Hassan with Isobel and quickly drove to the Parkhill Flats complex.

The instant the metal doors screeched open, Hunter was greeted by a strong smell of pine disinfectant and he could hear activity somewhere out along the corridor.

As he stepped out of the lift, he recognised the location from the CCTV footage Barry had shown them. He looked to the ceiling, at the small black dome housing the CCTV camera, and wondered how the pair could have been so stupid. He pointed it out to Grace and then made his way to number 508.

Blue and white police crime scene tape was draped across the dim corridor and a uniformed officer barred their way. Hunter ducked under the tape, flashing his warrant card.

The door to flat 508 was ajar and he rapped loudly before gently pushing it open. The hallway was in shadow, but they could see light from the gap of a door at the end and hear activity behind it. He and Grace walked towards the light and Hunter pushed open the second door. It was the lounge and Duncan Wroe was on his haunches, carrying out a careful examination of the carpet. Two other SOCO Officers were in the room, spraying and swabbing a wall. A bare bulb in the centre of the ceiling gave the only illumination. Close draped curtains covered one wall and were thick enough to keep out most of the daylight.

The room was sparsely furnished with a flimsy two-seater sofa and a single armchair of cheap quality, and yet fastened at chest height on a wall above the fireplace was a huge flat screen TV.

'They've obviously got their priorities right,' Hunter said wryly, pointing at the TV.

Duncan looked over his shoulder. 'I wondered how long it would be before you two arrived,' he said and returned to his task.

'You know us, Duncan, can't keep our noses out. Anyway, I thought you'd have finished with the scene by now. Are you holding out for overtime?'

'Very funny, Hunter. Very funny.'

'On a serious note, Duncan, is this the place where Samia was killed?'

'Oh, this is it all right.' Duncan slowly eased himself up. His knees cracked. 'I'm getting too old for this, roll on my pension.' He sauntered to the far wall where the two SOCOs were working. 'Attempts have been made to clean down the walls but we're already picking up blood spatter patterns low down, close to the skirting. By the looks of this lot I would say this is from a cut — a slashing effect. Didn't she have her throat cut if I remember rightly?'

Grace nodded.

'And there is also a pooling effect soaked into the carpet down to the floorboards.' Duncan lifted an edge of cheap nylon carpet to reveal a dark stain ingrained in the light wood flooring beneath. 'She'd obviously lost a substantial amount of blood.' He returned to the centre of the room. 'Finally, I have this for you. Switch off the light behind you.'

Hunter reached behind him and pitched the room into semi darkness. Just a little daylight poked between the gaps in the heavy drapes.

'Remember when I showed you how fibres could be lit up by a light source when I examined the white Renault?'

Hunter and Grace nodded.

'As you know, fragments of fibres are transferred when they come into contact with another surface. I mentioned different fibres can give off different wavelengths which can be picked up by fluorescent lights. I already told you that we had the wavelengths of the fibres from the Asian rug because of its unique make-up.'

Hunter acknowledged again with a nod.

'Well, this is what I've found.'

Duncan switched on a low voltage, hand-held fluorescent light and began scanning the carpet. As if by magic a line of bright blue fibres became distinguishable from the remainder of the room carpet. As he swept the area, an oblong outline began to appear over the surface. 'What would you say if I told you the perimeter of this is the exact same size as the rug Samia's body was found in? In other words, the rug once fitted in this exact spot.'

'You're a genius, Duncan.'

'Science actually, Hunter, but I will accept that accolade.' Duncan turned off the lamp, plunging them back into semi-darkness.

Hunter switched the room light back on.

'Another four or five hours and I'll have this room telling me what exactly went on — but at least for now I've given you something which will help to hold them in custody.'

Hunter and Grace thanked him and made their way back to the car.

It was just after four p.m. when they got back to Barnwell. Other members of MIT were still out on enquiries and expected back within the hour. They had gathered enough statements and material evidence to place Ari and Pervez in flat 508.

Armed with this information, Hunter and Grace headed to the custody suite to re-interview Pervez.

He was waiting with his solicitor in the sticky, warm interview room. He didn't have his brother's cockiness, but fixed them with a penetrating glare.

As Hunter and Grace sat down, Pervez folded his arms defensively and gave a smug grin.

Hunter loved a challenge.

Grace switched on the tape recorder and turned around to switch on the TV/DVD player.

'Mr Arshad, during your last interview you chose to make no comment and that is your prerogative. However, it is only fair to tell you that, since that last interview, things have moved on considerably. We have interviewed your brother Ari and I have to tell you that he has implicated you in the abduction of Samia. We have a statement from a witness placing you at the scene where Samia's body was dumped and I must also tell you that Jilani Hassan, Samia's mother and your aunt, has also made a statement implicating you and Ari.'

Suddenly his eyes were restless. He searched out his solicitor who had his head down making legal notes, then looked back across the table. 'You're bullshitting.'

'Mr Arshad, would I be telling you this in the presence of your solicitor, and on tape, if it wasn't true?'

Pervez rolled his eyes to the ceiling, unfolded his arms and wiped the palms of his hands down the thighs of his trousers.

'I know you have been shown CCTV evidence of you following Samia in Meadowhall and your involvement in her attack down in the car park and you chose not to respond when that evidence was presented. Now I want to show you some more footage we have recently acquired.'

Grace switched on the DVD player and started to play the latest footage compiled by Barry.

Hunter kept his eyes glued on Pervez, watching the sweat trickle down his face as he viewed. Hearing Grace switch off the machine he leant across the table, locking together his fingers. 'We have now found the flat shared by you and Ari. As we speak, forensics are going through the place with a fine-toothed comb. We already know this was where you held Samia where she was killed, and you've seen from that CCTV footage that we now have you on camera taking her body to dump in the lake. You have every right not to say anything, but I hope your brother will be as loyal when he sees this.'

Hunter watched Pervez's face change. He was rigid with fear.

'Ari raped and killed Samia,' Pervez said. 'I thought we were only going to kidnap Samia and force her to go to Pakistan. That's what Ari told me. He said Uncle Mohammed wanted to teach his daughter a lesson because she had brought shame on the family and we were to take her to our place and hold her there.'

'Is that what happened after you put her in the back of the van at Meadowhall?'

Pervez nodded feverishly. 'Yes, yes. We took her back to our flat and Ari tied her up in the bedroom. He phoned Uncle Mohammed and told him we had her and asked what he wanted to do with her.'

'What did your uncle say?'

'I don't know. Ari was always the one who talked to Uncle Mohammed, though he came to the flat the next day and started hitting Samia, swearing at her and saying she had brought dishonour to him and she didn't deserve to live.'

'Is that when she was killed?'

'No, no, he busted her mouth and nose and I cleaned her up with a towel from the bathroom. She was still alive. She begged me to let her go and then Ari came into the bedroom and dragged me away. Uncle Mohammed left and I could hear him and Ari talking in the hallway.'

'What were they saying?'

'I don't know — I couldn't hear. They were whispering together.'

'What happened next?'

Pervez's eyes moistened. He dabbed at them with the back of his hand. 'Nothing that night, but the next day Ari told me to go out and get some food for us. I went to the local Spar and when I came back Samia was dead. Ari had killed her.' Tears welled up in the corner of his eyes. 'That's the truth. I swear on the Prophet Mohammed.'

'When you say she was dead. Describe what you saw.'

'There was blood everywhere. Up the walls and a huge puddle around her head. She was lying on the carpet in the lounge near the armchair. When I left her, she was tied up in the bedroom. When I got back, he was pacing up and down and he had that knife-thing in his hand. He'd cut her throat with it.'

'Was she still tied up?'

'Her hands were behind her back but he'd untied her feet.' Pervez gulped and looked down at the table. 'She wasn't wearing her jeans or her knickers. I knew what he'd done.'

'When you say she was dead, did you check at all to see if she was still alive?'

'I looked at her but you could tell. There was a big pool of blood. Her eyes were wide open. She wasn't breathing.'

'What did you do?'

'I panicked. I couldn't believe he'd done that. We argued and I asked him why. He said Uncle Mohammed wanted him to do it. I didn't know whether to believe him or not.'

'What happened then?'

'Ari said we had to get rid of the body. He wrapped Samia in the carpet, wiped the knife-thing and put it in with her and then he asked me to help bind her up. After that he rang Uncle Mohammed.'

'Did Ari tell your uncle what he had done?'

'He told him she was dead. But I don't know what my uncle was saying. I couldn't hear that part of the conversation.'

'Is that when you brought Samia across to Barnwell and dumped her in the lake?'

'No, we kept her body in the flat a couple of days. We put the rug in the bath so no more blood seeped out. Ari said Uncle Mohammed was going to ring him and tell him where to take the body. Then that Friday evening Ari took a call from Uncle Mohammed and said he had found a place to hide Samia where no one would find her. That's when we drove to the lake and dumped her.' His voice started to quiver. 'That is the truth. I didn't kill Samia. It was Ari. My Uncle Mohammed told him to do it.'

It was after 6 p.m. when Hunter and Grace finally returned to the incident room, having completed another interview with Mohammed Hassan. He had been more stubborn than his nephews, had refused to accept their testimonies and the evidence presented and continually bleated that everyone was lying about him — including his wife. However, as they had walked him back to his cell, they had witnessed the first cracks. As Hunter slammed the reinforced door, he'd taken a final glance through the hatch. Mohammed had looked up from the bench with glazed eyes, before dropping his head to his chest.

With a satisfied smile, Hunter had slid the metal hatch shut with a resounding clang.

Feeling energised, despite the long day, he bounced into the MIT office. It was full, the Office Manager, Detective Inspector Gerald Scaife, and the SIO, Detective Superintendent Michael Robshaw, were among the team waiting.

Hunter could sense them searching his face. He guessed Grace would be experiencing the same good feeling. He surveyed the room before grinning widely.

'Result. Pervez has coughed. And he's given us enough to send down his brother and Mohammed.'

The cheer was deafening.

Jock Kerr slowly scanned the four walls of his son's and daughter-in-law's lounge. Though he had the place to himself he felt anxious and agitated. It was like being in prison.

This is doing my head in. I've had enough.

He picked up the car keys from the coffee table and left the house, jumped into the hire car provided by his insurance company and fired up the engine. Before pulling off the drive he phoned DS John Reed on his mobile.

'I'm coming down to the gym. I'm sorry but I can't take any more of this. I can't keep hiding away.' He listened to the detective's response, before replying. 'Look, there are four of you nearby. If Billy and Rab turn up then you'll nick them, won't you?' He hung up before the sergeant could object.

Jock kept watch in his rearview mirror more than usual but spotted nothing untoward and was feeling quite relaxed by the time he reached his gym.

The entrance doors were locked and he checked his watch. The boxing coach who had been looking after things in his absence must have gone home early. Jock unlocked the doors and let himself in.

The place was fairly tidy with only a few weights out of place. He took a long, lingering look around. The pristine whitewashed walls gave the gymnasium a clean and bright if not clinical appearance. A full-size boxing ring took up half of the floor space, with one side for weight training and another for bag work. This place was his pride and joy. It had taken him a long time to build it up. Most of his life was in this place.

I'm buggered if I'm going to lose all this because of those two evil shites!

Hunter swilled the remaining dregs of his pint around the bottom of the glass as if it was the finest whiskey and swallowed. He said, 'That never touched the sides.' Nudging Barry next to him, he added, 'Fancy another? I owe you one.'

Barry drained the remainder of his pint in one mouthful and wiped the froth from his dark, bushy moustache with the back of his hand before answering, 'I'll not refuse a free pint.'

Hunter weaved his way through the squad to the bar. They had congregated into small groups, as was usual at these celebratory gatherings. A couple of his colleagues gave him a congratulatory tap on the shoulder as he squeezed by.

Plonking the empty glasses down on the bar, Hunter took a look around at the faces of his workmates. He recalled the first words instilled into him on that first day in CID, after Barry Newstead had taken him out and got him rolling drunk. 'The spirit and bonding of a team is created in the pub,' Barry had said. 'Putting a frustrating, complicated and exhausting enquiry to bed with a celebratory drink is what gels everyone together.' How true that had proved over the years.

As he waited to be served, Hunter mused over the hurried briefing given by Superintendent Robshaw less than a half hour ago. The SIO had made energetic scribbled notes on the incident board, creating cohesive actions for tomorrow.

He and Grace had been given the job of charging Ari, Pervez and Mohammed with murder and the task of putting together the remand file for court, while the remainder of the MIT were to tie up all the loose ends, logging evidence and collecting statements to make everything stick.

The hard work wasn't yet over; their aim was to stack the evidence so much in the prosecution's favour that a guilty plea was inevitable.

Hunter was just trying to grab the attention of one of the bar staff when he felt his mobile vibrate in his trouser pocket. He dragged it out and took a look at the incoming caller. The word 'gym' flashed onto the screen. It had to be his dad. He took the call.

For a second all he could hear was heavy breathing then his dad's voice came on the line. He sounded frantic.

'Hunter, get down here quick,' he heard his dad say. 'It's Billy and Rab — they've just turned up.'

Then the phone call ended.

DS John Reed and his partner DC Craig McDonald stared out of the large plate glass window into the car park below. They had been in the first-floor office of the empty warehouse since 7 a.m. that day. It was their fourth stint in the observation post and they were weary.

John Reed was thankful for the sunshine beaming in through the large window. There was no heating in the building and it was all they had for warmth. He'd be glad when they had Billy Wallace and Rab Geddes so he could get back home. He hadn't seen his family for the best part of a week and the motel room he was sharing with his colleague was not exactly luxurious. To make matters worse, his working relationship with Dawn Leggate was compromised because of her dalliances with the local Detective Superintendent. Reed had dropped in on her last night and he had been there. She looked embarrassed as she explained they were just discussing the joint operation. All in all, he wasn't pleased with how things were progressing.

The hiss of the radio crackling into life broke his thoughts. Jock had just left his son's house and was alone.

John Reed huffed in frustration. He had only just got off the phone with Jock, trying to persuade him not to come to the gym. He made an entry in the log and set the video camera rolling.

Ten minutes later, Jock's car cruised into the car park below and the camera captured him making his way into his gym.

The screeching of tyres two minutes later startled John Reed. He saw the green Range Rover sway to one side as it swept into the car park, slewing into a skid before rocking to a halt. The passenger door flew open and he was mesmerised for a second as a stocky built man wearing a ski mask leapt out. Reed was on his radio in a second, shouting for backup. Grabbing the sleeve of his partner, he bolted towards the stairwell leading down to the car park.

Billy Wallace watched the Range Rover tear into the car park and slide to a standstill. Opposite the entrance, he pressed himself against the trunk of one of the trees lining the road, the shade from the canopy of leaves masking his features. Rab was close by. As one of the masked men leapt from the passenger side his slate grey eyes became watchful. He was ready and waiting.

It soon paid off. He saw the two detectives tumble out through the doors of a derelict warehouse and onto the car park.

He gave the signal and the masked man jumped back into the car. Before he had time to close the door, the back wheels were chewing up gravel as it sped away.

Billy smiled to himself. It was all going to plan.

The two officers weren't far behind. Sprinting across the car park DC McDonald aimed the key fob at a dark blue Vauxhall Vectra, triggering the locks as John Reed shouted an update into his radio and leapt into the front passenger seat.

Less than thirty seconds later, the unmarked car's engine was being gunned as it tore off in hot pursuit.

Jock saw Billy Wallace stroll into the gym. He was still wearing that signature Crombie of his.

After all these years and he still dresses like he's the 'big I am'.

Billy looked menacing as he stepped further into the room. His pupils were so dilated that his eyes appeared almost black. It was a look Jock had seen in those eyes before — the look of cold death.

Suddenly everything seemed to fast-forward. Billy made a quick jabbing movement with right arm and Jock saw the glint of a long blade emerge from the end of his sleeve. A tremor raced through him. Then he realised he was still clutching one of the free weights and it gave him a strange reassurance. He tightened his grip around the barbell.

'Don't be stupid, Billy. If you do anything to me you're going to go away for a very long time. You'll probably die in prison,'

Jock said, doing his best to sound calm. 'You can walk away from this right now and no one will be any the wiser.'

'I've done 36 fucking years already because of you. It will be worth it,' Billy growled, edging closer.

Jock was mesmerised by Billy's cold-blooded stare as he stepped closer.

Jock took up a defensive stance, lodging the barbell against his hip and balling his other hand into a solid fist. Two combatants locked in a fight to the death.

Billy catapulted forward, whipping his right arm across.

The knife slashed across Jock's forearm before he had time to react and he staggered back, clattering against the metal racks. The blood spread through the sleeve of his sweat top, though surprisingly he felt no pain. It bought back memories of his boxing days — he'd not recognised pain back then, either.

Billy pulled back the knife again, preparing for another attack. Every sinew in Jock's body tightened, stretched as tight as a bow as he felt an immense power surge through him. He dropped back on one leg and exploded forward, swinging the barbell up in an arc. It smacked Billy's jaw and his eyes went blank. Jock had seen that look many times during his boxing bouts. He followed up with a left hook, smacking the side of Billy's head. The knife clattered to the floor and Billy's legs buckled. Just before he sank, Jock caught him with the swinging barbell again, a dull thwack to the back of his head.

Jock dropped on top of him, took a handful of hair and yanked back Billy's head. He slipped an arm to the front of his neck, slotted his windpipe into the crook and began to squeeze.

Hunter grabbed Barry Newstead within seconds of the line going dead. 'My dad's in trouble,' he called, bolting for the side door of the pub.

A rush surged through Hunter as he jumped into his car and fired it up. Slamming into first and stamping the accelerator, he revved his Audi's 1.9 litre engine and tore out of the pub car park towards the gym.

Beside him, Barry was making an emergency call on his mobile.

Less than ten minutes later they sped into the gym car park, skidding to a halt.

Hunter flew from the car, leaving the engine running and propelled himself through the doors into the gym, with Barry only seconds behind.

Rab Geddes was waiting in the corridor, legs astride, smacking a baseball bat into his palm.

Hunter stopped a few yards from him. 'Where's Billy Wallace?' he yelled.

'You're too late!' Rab said with a sneer.

For a few seconds there was a stand-off. Hunter eyed the baseball bat bouncing in Rab's hands. Then anger took over. He flew at him, aiming for his face, mauling with clawing hands, gouging at his eyes like a rugby player in a ruck. The force spiralled Rab sideways smashing him into the wall. Hunter heard the breath explode from his lungs and felt the warm breath on his cheek, and in a white heat of berserk fury he pulled, punched and pummelled.

Barry jumped into the fray, forcing in his bulk. Within seconds Rab was pinned against the wall, the baseball bat clattering to the floor as he tried to protect himself.

Hunter fell away, gasping for breath and drenched in sweat. He doubled-up, retching, as Barry slammed in a couple more punches to the ribs before Rab collapsed into a heap.

'My dad,' Hunter gasped.

'You go and help him,' Barry said. 'This guy's going nowhere.'

Hunter turned on his heels, hitting the swing doors into the main training area with his shoulder. He readjusted his balance and scanned the room. His dad was by the weight rack, draped across a prostrate figure who he immediately realised was Billy. At first Hunter wondered what was happening, then the reality hit home. His dad was strangling Billy. He sprinted across, snapping his arms around his dad in an effort to drag him off but he had Billy locked tight.

'Dad! Dad!' he screamed. 'He's had enough, let him go. You're going to kill him.' He hooked his fingers into a gap and prised at Jock's wrists. 'Dad, I said let him go — NOW!'

Hunter saw the shout had registered. He prised at his dad's hands again and this time they yielded. Billy's head smacked the wooden floor.

Hunter pulled his dad to his feet, pushed him away and went to Billy's aid. He checked his airway, manoeuvred him into the recovery position and checked him again. He stared at Billy's chest and prayed.

Suddenly a spluttering cough burst from Billy's mouth.

'Thank god for that!' Hunter turned to face his dad, who was ashen-faced. 'Christ, Dad — you could have killed him.'

Jock stared at the blood pouring from the wound on his forearm, clamped a hand around it and started to shake.

From the entrance to the gym, Hunter watched Billy and Rab being loaded into the back of an ambulance. They had a catalogue of bumps and bruises between them, and Billy had a deep wound to the back of his head, but neither was seriously hurt. A couple of minutes later they were off to hospital with an armed police escort

DCI Dawn Leggate appeared with two members of her team. The man in the ski mask and the other hired help had been detained and were en route to the custody suite. The pair were known back in Scotland as petty crooks but since they hadn't done anything, except act as decoys, they had nothing to hold them, she added — although she'd make sure they had a night in the cells while checks were made to see if they were wanted elsewhere.

That was ten minutes ago. Now Hunter, Jock, Barry and Dawn were seated around Jock's desk. Jock had refused to go in the ambulance but one of the paramedics had put a bandage on the laceration and told him it required suturing and must be treated before the day was out.

Jock had promised he would. Now he sat in his chair, nursing his arm.

In a couple of weeks' time Hunter knew his dad would be showing off the scar, just like the one above his right eye, saying, 'Scars are the medals of heroes'. Hunter wished he had a pound for every time he'd heard his dad say it. Hunter shook his head and smiled to himself. At least there was no lasting damage.

Dawn needed to question them about what had happened. Hunter asked for a little time with his dad and for it to be carried out after he'd visited the hospital. He needed to check what his dad was going to say and prime him to use the words 'trying to restrain' in his defence.

Dawn agreed. Hunter could tell by her face that she knew what had really happened and he revised his earlier opinions of her. He gave an appreciative smile.

Suddenly Jock announced, 'I could do with a stiff drink.' He opened the bottom drawer of his desk and pulled out a bottle of single malt. Then he shuffled together four mugs and poured a generous amount into each. 'They say it's good for shock,' he added, handing Hunter, Barry and Dawn a mug each. 'Sláinte! Doon the hatch,' he toasted, chinking each mug.

Hunter glanced at his dad. The colour had returned to his face.

You and I need to sit down and talk.

DAY THIRTY-FIVE

Hunter flopped back on the small sofa in his conservatory. He had inserted a Michael Bublé CD into his Bose system and closed his eyes, allowing 'Summer Wind' to sweep into his mind. His head was thumping. The Detective Superintendent had given the team a lie in, allowing them all to work an afternoon shift that day. There was still a fair bit of mopping up to do to close the investigation — Ari, Pervez and Mohammed were to be charged with Samia's murder, and a remand file had to be put together for court.

Disturbing images from the previous day flashed into Hunter's already aching head. Sometimes he wished he could turn off his brain. He shook his head and replaced them with more pleasant ones.

Beth and his mum had joined them at the gym, thankfully after the melee had ended, and as his dad had poured them all another 'wee dram' Beth had given him a quick check-up and saved him from going to the hospital by applying several Steri-strips to close the wound to his forearm, before re-bandaging and giving him a clean bill of health.

Then he, Barry and his dad had returned to the pub to rejoin the celebrations at the end of the Samia Hassan enquiry.

Everyone was keen to hear what had happened but Hunter gave a potted version of events and promised to fill them in the next day. He needed a few more beers to bring him back down from the adrenaline rush and wanted to be beside his dad, to let him see he was there for him. Barry had lightened the mood in their small group but the conversation between

Hunter and his dad had been stilted and shallow. Despite this, Hunter had a feeling the ice had been broken between them.

They had fallen through the doors at 1.30 a.m. that morning and now Hunter was suffering.

'Morning, son.'

His dad's voice brought him back. He rolled his eyes.

'Feeling delicate?'

'An understatement. Rough as a bear's arse springs to mind.'

Jock chuckled. 'Here, get that down you. I've just mashed.'

Hunter took the cup of strong tea, just how his dad drank it. 'Thanks.'

Jock sat down beside him and put his cup on the coffee table. 'Son, I need to apologise.'

'Don't, Dad.'

'No, I do, don't stop me. I know I should have told you about this but I thought I was doing the right thing. I now realise I was wrong keeping you in the dark.'

'Dad —' Hunter tried to interrupt.

'Let me finish, son. I'm not proud of what I got myself into and with foresight I would have gone nowhere near that crew, but at the time I was a 20-year-old man with a career in tatters. I thought I was making a fast buck and didn't know what I was getting myself into. Nevertheless, I think I made the right decision to protect your ma and I haven't made a bad job of bringing you up. You've turned out a son I'm very proud of and I hope when things settle down you'll feel the same way about me. Just remember this, Hunter — even though I changed my name, you are of the Kerr clan. Your mum's a Kerr and you have every right to wear that tartan.'

Jock picked up his cup and took a drink.

Their eyes met again.

Jock said, 'You know, one thing has come good of all this. For years I've had to stay away from my family for fear of putting them in danger. Going back up there to meet the DCI when I did made me realise just how much I've missed them. I've been in touch and already fixed up a meeting. What about you, Beth and the boys coming up with your ma and me and I'll introduce you to your family?'

EPILOGUE

Hunter took a couple of steps back from his easel, angling his head, slowly scanning sections of his latest oil painting — a seascape of Robin Hood's Bay. Every few seconds he halted his gaze to focus on a particular part of the scene, checking that he had resolved it before letting his artistic eye move on. Five minutes later, pleased with how he had managed to capture the stormy mood in the piece, he set his brushes down on his palette and wiped his hands with a rag.

Time for a cuppa.

Before making for the kitchen, he took another lingering look. It was a process he always went through before he put the canvas to one side. He would get it out again in a week's time and repeat his actions. From speaking with other artists, he knew he was not alone in going through this critique.

As he focused on the blustery, rain-leaden clouds, brushstrokes laid down in tones of purple, ultramarine blue and pink, it reminded him of a word he had heard his dad use — *dreich*. That summed the spirit of the painting perfectly, he thought.

Bringing that word to mind conjured up feelings from the recent turmoil within his life. For a few seconds, images rode a carousel inside his head.

He shook himself and they cleared. It would be a while before they left him permanently — if ever. The main thing was that he and his dad had reconciled their differences. And he had discovered new members of his family. He had travelled up to Scotland with his dad to support him during his visit to Glasgow High Court for the plea and directions hearing for Billy Wallace and Rab Geddes, charged with five counts of murder and the attempted murder of his dad.

That court visit had been shorter than expected. The pair had refused to come out of their prison cells for the hearing and refused to enter a plea and in their absence the judge had set a trial date for the second week in January the following year.

Hunter mentally diaried the date so that he could take time off to support his dad when he returned to give evidence.

He had seen DCI Dawn Leggate at the court and taken her to one side to check on the prosecution's case. This time she was far more amenable, telling him that the evidence against the pair was overwhelming. She was expecting them to enter a guilty plea at the last moment and added that the Procurator Fiscal was requesting an indeterminate life sentence for both men. The likelihood was they would die in prison.

After that, they had gone on to Bellshill — his dad's old home town — and he had been introduced to his dad's cousins. It had been a weekend of celebrations, resulting in very thick heads for both of them. Since then he had witnessed a change in his dad's demeanour and they had spent some very enjoyable sessions together, especially down at the gym.

The ringing telephone in the lounge broke his reverie. He heard Beth answer it.

'Hunter, it's for you,' she shouted, walking towards him, holding out the handset. 'It's work.'

He held up his hands to her, indicating they were smeared with oil paint.

She switched it to speaker phone.

'Hello,' he said.

'DS Kerr?'

He recognised the voice of one of the duty group inspectors. 'Speaking.'

'Sorry to disturb you at home. I know it's your long weekend off, but I've been asked to call you in. Some of my officers are at the scene of a derelict pub. A couple of builders there have found the remains of a body in the cellar.'

A NOTE TO THE READER

Dear Reader,

Cold Death came hot on the heels of my debut novel *Heart of the Demon*. I began penning it while pitching the first book around publishers and agents and I was caught on the hop by a very quick response from a publisher who offered me a two-book deal; for the best part of two months I worked well into the evening to bring it to fruition.

It would be fair to say that none of my books make for comfortable reading and are certainly not for the faint-hearted. They are based on my own, or my colleagues experiences and that is the case with *Cold Death*. This story came courtesy of two cases, one of which I was in charge of and the other I worked on the periphery of.

Samia Hassan's story was sparked by a call from a British born Asian lady of Bangladesh parents who'd had her flat trashed, and was being harassed by cousins of her father, simply because she was in a relationship with a young man she had met at college, that hadn't been chosen by her father. Myself and a colleague visited her parent's home to be confronted by an angry man who wanted nothing more to do with his daughter and whom had obliterated any existence of her from his home. It was a very sad situation for the young lady and my first experience of prejudice through culture. Unlike Samia in the story, this young lady did not come to any harm and progressed well through college to begin a career in nursing.

The character Billy Wallace came about following my attendance at the scene of a brutal attack on a woman by a man she was in a relationship with. The scene I visited was one of the bloodiest I have ever been to. The woman had been hacked at with a boning knife and machete. She'd been stabbed 37 times, had her throat cut and several fingers severed. She only survived thanks to the quick actions of a neighbour who was a nurse, and she was eventually able to give evidence against him in court and see him jailed for a minimum of 22 years. When we looked into the background of the man it was discovered he was someone who targeted women at various church groups by pretending to be a religious Christian man who had fallen on hard times. He was nothing of the sort. He was evil. Once he befriended them, he subjected them to sado-masochistic sex and brutal violence. He came to South Yorkshire following his release from prison after an 8-year sentence for a brutal attack upon a man who tried to protect one of his victims. The man was left with severe brain damage. Within weeks of being here he targeted his next victim, a vulnerable woman who went to a church support group having already suffered domestic violence. Whilst on remand for his latest attack, knowing he had severed three fingers from his victim's hand, he sent a packet of fish fingers to her with a note 'These are to replace the ones you're missing.'

The scenario where Billy launches the dead body through Hunter's parent's window was also based on a true event. It happened where I worked in Barnsley, during a turf war over drugs. One gang broke into the mortuary at Barnsley hospital, took a body from the cold storage and as a threat of what was to come launched it through the window of their rival drug leader who lived at home with his mother. Can you just imagine the fear she must have faced that evening?

You will realise by now that I write about what I know and what I have experienced over my 32 years of policing and I want to bring out my feelings through my character Hunter Kerr. I hope you will want to read more about what makes him tick.

I'd love to think that readers will embrace Hunter Kerr and his casework and one of the ways you can let me know that is by placing a review on **Amazon** or **Goodreads**. And, if you want to contact me, then please do so via **my website**.

Thank you for reading..

Michael Fowler

www.mjfowler.co.uk

Sapere Books is an exciting new publisher of brilliant fiction and popular history.

To find out more about our latest releases and our monthly bargain books visit our website:
saperebooks.com

Printed in Great Britain
by Amazon

78235353R00150